Breaking
STARS

J. STERLING

ISBN-13: 978-1494467524

ISBN-10: 1494467526

Please visit the author's website
www.j-sterling.com

Sometimes our lives feel like they no longer belong to us.

This story is for anyone who has ever felt like their life was not their own, for whatever reason or circumstance.

I hope you fight for yours.

Breaking STARS

The Cheating Scandal

PAIGE

WHEN A TEXT message pinged on my phone, I clicked on the link included without thinking. I didn't bother reading the contents of the text or the link description; knowing it was from my best friend, Quinn, was enough of a reason to absentmindedly click for me. Usually she sent me links to things she thought I should see that involved our friends, coworkers, or her boyfriend. This link, however, had nothing to do with any of her usual subjects, and when I realized that, my heart stopped.

The video appeared grainy at first as the cell phone camera adjusted to the strobe lighting in the club. My boyfriend, Colin, suddenly appeared in the frame, a smile plastered on his face as his eyes focused on someone or something not in the picture. He raised a hand, waving someone over toward him, his grin growing more mischievous.

My brain screamed at me to stop watching. Something inside begged me to look away, turn it off, throw my smart phone across the room, but I couldn't. It was obviously bad enough for Quinn to send to me, so I had to keep watching.

No matter how much it was going to hurt.

An overly busty blonde sauntered into view, showing more skin than clothes, dancing seductively as she made her way toward my boyfriend. He reached for her waist and pulled her onto his lap. She straddled him, her legs wrapping around his very private area in very plain sight.

Who does that?

The blonde's skirt rode up, revealing her bare ass, and Colin's hands were suddenly there, squeezing it, slapping it, lifting her skirt higher. As she leaned her head toward his face, I honestly thought for a second he'd come to his senses. Maybe he wouldn't kiss her. Maybe he'd toss her off his lap, tell her to go to hell, and rush out of the club, humiliated. Then again, that type of thing only happened in the books I read and the movies I starred in. Most guys weren't anywhere near as well-behaved as we women wanted them to be.

As if reading my mind, Colin fisted a handful of her hair, and I watched as he yanked her head back, causing the rest of her hair to spill provocatively behind her. His lips pressed against her neck as he licked his way up to her mouth. She laughed, and then he kissed her. It was a mess of tongues and body parts grinding, with hands roaming in places hands shouldn't be roaming in public.

I'd seen more than enough, so I stopped the video and tried to remind myself how to breathe, my heart pounding as if I were on a treadmill. If anything came after that spectacle—no pun intended—I didn't need to see it.

Pushing off from the couch, I walked to my window and glanced down toward the street, noticing the swarm of paparazzi already beginning to form.

They're quick.

This wasn't the first time claims of infidelity like this had been leveled against my pop-star boyfriend, Colin McGuire, but it was the first time pictures had accompanied the accusations. If a picture spoke a thousand words, this horrendous video and the photos that accompanied it screamed a million. Colin could never talk his way out of my seeing his tongue being buried in that woman's throat, seeing him grab her ass and grinding on her for all to see.

Falling back on the couch, I tried to unsee what I'd just watched. I couldn't believe Colin was so blatant and stupid. Most celebrities knew if they were going to cheat, they should do it where people couldn't watch them or take photos for proof. Apparently the VIP section of a club in London was not that place. Maybe he wanted to get caught? But why not just break up with me first?

Staring down at my cell phone, my eyes stinging from humiliation and the tears that now slid down my cheeks, I scanned the various tabloid headlines being sent to me nonstop via text message and e-mail from what seemed like every person I'd ever crossed paths with in my entire life. My breath caught in my throat and I nearly choked, unable to believe this was actually happening.

Colin Cheats on America's Sweetheart with Stripper!

Colin McGuire Caught in Cheating Scandal with not One, but Three Buxom Blondes!

Not the First Time Colin has Cheated on Paige – See the Proof Inside!

Paige, Embarrassed and Ashamed, Won't Be Seen in Public!

Heartbroken Paige in Hiding! Where Has She Gone?

I swiped at the moisture on my cheeks before looking around at the brightly decorated walls of my apartment. Since when had sitting in the living room of my own home been considered hiding? Although I had to admit—the thought of crawling into a hole somewhere secluded sounded more appealing with each minute that passed.

Any breakup sucked, but going through one when you were a celebrity was ten times worse. Imagine every single incident in your life magnified, scrutinized, and published all over the world, usually portrayed in the most unflattering light and rarely accurate. The more scandalous the subject matter, the more the story took off. Over time I'd learned that people didn't care if what was being reported was true or not; they simply enjoyed observing the chaos and carnage from the safety of their own mundane lives. For whatever reason, the public enjoyed watching celebrities suffer, and it reminded me just how out of touch with one another we truly were.

Ridding my head of those thoughts, I wondered how many times in the past Colin had cheated, and just how much of a fool I'd been. We'd dated for almost a year, and I thought we understood each other's lifestyle, never being too possessive or jealous, never questioning each other's actions. Both of us were in the entertainment industry, and while groupies tossed their dignity at him every night, I suppose I was naive enough to think he'd never take them up on their offers.

I suddenly had the urge to slap my own stupid face and freaking kill him. Right after I picked up the pieces of my shattered pride and aching heart.

Startling me, my phone vibrated against the coffee table. I watched as it danced, shaking all the tabletop items around it like they were in a bouncy house. It had been doing that almost nonstop since the news broke, and I let it.

I glanced down to see my manager's name, Corryn, flashing on the screen. I pressed IGNORE only to have the phone start vibrating again within seconds. My agent, Jayson, was apparently next in line on the check-on-Paige train. Pushing IGNORE again, I wondered when they'd all get the hint to leave me alone. My publicist had called five times already and I probably should have answered her call, but honestly, this was Colin's screw-up, not mine. If anyone should be talking to their publicist about saving face, it was him, not me.

My mother always warned me that people in this business were not as good-hearted as I tended to be. This industry was vicious and brutal, but it was also amazing, life-changing, and spectacular. I loved my job, and up until about thirty minutes ago, I thought I'd loved Colin too.

Mom also constantly reminded me that I was far too trusting, but I didn't know how to be any other way. Being a Southern California native who spent most of my years living a normal childhood helped keep me grounded. My parents had normal lives, had worked normal jobs, and I had never planned on becoming an actress.

Fighting the urge to call my mom, I picked up the phone to dial my best friend, Quinn, instead. When the phone suddenly vibrated in my hand I almost dropped it, but quickly answered when I noticed Quinn's name on the display.

"I was just going to call you," I breathed out.

"Liar," she scoffed, and I almost huffed out a laugh. *Almost*.

"I swear."

"Verdict?"

I knew exactly what she meant. "There's no way that video's faked."

"I thought the same thing," she said, agreeing way too quickly.

"The other pictures too. They don't look Photoshopped to you, do they?" There were also pictures taken of Colin with other women. Apparently the blonde had friends, and she didn't mind sharing.

She sighed before admitting, "No."

"Me either."

"I can't believe this shit," Quinn bit out. "No. Scratch that. Actually I can, and I'll kill his scrawny ass the next time I see him. Pack some clothes and get over here. You're staying with me tonight." She paused briefly, seeming to consider before asking, "Unless you want me to come there and stay with you? Is that what you want? I'll do whatever you want. I'll totally come to you. I'm an idiot—"

I forced my hazy brain to make a decision, then I cut her off. "No. Your place sounds perfect. I'd love to get away from here. It's already a madhouse outside. Thanks, Quinn."

"Of course. I love you. Drive safe."

Quinn and I had bonded instantly on the set of my first movie when I was fourteen. She was a pro, had been acting since she was a little kid, and I'd been so nervous that I felt sick to my stomach when I arrived that afternoon. She had shared her french fries with me, reminding me that eating something was better than eating nothing when you were nervous and had to work until who knew when. I decided right then and there that any girl who would share her fries with a stranger was a keeper.

Plus, she was incredibly kind to me, and I envied the way she spoke her mind, no matter who she was talking to. Quinn Johnson never seemed afraid of anyone or anything, and I wanted to be more like her.

When production on our film wrapped, I wasn't sure I'd ever see Quinn again, but to my surprise we became virtually inseparable. She was the one person in the world who really understood what I was going through. We shared experiences that other people couldn't begin to relate to, and I was so happy to have her in my corner.

Tossing some comfortable clothes into an overnight bag, I wandered into my bathroom and gathered up my necessities as my phone rang yet again from my bedroom. I should have turned it off hours ago, but it wasn't in my DNA to be rebellious and unreachable. The fact that I'd ignored most calls today was pretty out of character for me. Ever the obedient one, Paige Lockwood had always played by the rules.

I walked over to where my phone lay on my bed and checked the caller ID to see Colin's name flashing across the screen. My stomach instantly churned and my heart seized. Willing my numb fingers to move, I pressed IGNORE, half-tempted to throw the damn thing against the wall and watch it splinter into tiny pieces like my heart. Taking some calming breaths, I focused on each inhale and exaggerated exhale as he continued to call my phone, the calls finally stopping as my text message notification beeped.

IT'S NOT WHAT IT LOOKS LIKE.

And then beeped again.

YOU KNOW IT'S FAKE. THOSE GIRLS JUST WANT MONEY.

JUST TALK TO ME, BABY.

PLEASE.

Baby? Lord give me strength if another man ever calls me "baby" again.

I rolled my eyes at his texts and wondered if he'd ever told me the truth in the last ten months. Thankful he was in another country and couldn't show up here unannounced, I gathered what was left of my wits and my things, and headed out my front door. I made my way downstairs, knowing all too well what I'd be faced with once I was down there.

The dreaded paparazzi.

Thank God I'd had the foresight to choose a place in LA with a doorman, private parking, and twenty-four-hour concierge service. My parents suggested the concierge, and I'd been convinced that no such thing existed in Southern California. I'd never been happier than in this moment to be proven wrong by that simple fact. I loved the security and privacy that living here afforded me.

Lowering my sunglasses over my face, I stepped into the lobby and was immediately greeted by Sam, the concierge, his salt-and-pepper hair falling into his eyes. He quickly brushed the stray hairs away and walked with me toward the building's exit.

"Good afternoon, Miss Lockwood." His thick Latino accent filled the space between us and I marveled at how beautiful it sounded. I always did this around Sam, acted as if I were studying the very fabric of the language for a part or upcoming role. I never was, but he humored me anyway, talking purely for my enjoyment.

"The paparazzi are across the street. Right over there." He gestured in the direction of a small crowd and I nodded in response, offering a tight-lipped smile as he continued. "They tried to come in, but I threatened to call the cops and have them all arrested for trespassing."

"I really wish they'd pass some laws against this type of thing," I said with a sigh.

"I know, Miss Lockwood. It makes me very nervous when you drive off and they chase you. Very nervous." He nodded his head and looked up into the air as if offering a silent prayer.

I leaned toward him, placing my hand on his shoulder. "It makes me nervous too."

His body tensed. "I'll have the valet get your car," he said, his tone defeated. "Please tell me you're going to Miss Johnson's? Or home to your parents?"

Sam loved Quinn. Everyone loved her, but Sam especially enjoyed her take-no-shit attitude and told her so every time she came to visit. I constantly spotted the two of them discussing Quinn's latest shenanigans whenever she came around. She loved embellishing her stories for Sam, and he loved hearing her tales.

"I'm staying with Quinn for a few days. I don't want to bring this to my parents' house. They have to work, and my sister would be beyond annoyed if it interfered with her senior year. They don't need this on their doorstep."

"Miss Johnson will take care of you. I suppose Mr. Miller will be there as well?" he asked hopefully.

I nodded my head and chuckled at his overprotective nature. "Yes, Dad number two, both Quinn and Ryson will be there."

He pressed his lips together in a cautious smile and shrugged. "I just worry."

"I know, Sam. Thank you. I'll be fine. But hey," I said as a thought occurred to me. "Will you please remove Colin's name from my access list? I don't want him coming up unannounced anytime soon."

Sam's face reddened, telling me he'd heard the news. "Of course. Hopefully he knows better than to show up during my shift."

I smiled, and it felt good after all the tears I'd shed today. Offering Sam a quick squeeze, I said good-bye and headed toward my waiting BMW as the paparazzi jumped into action at the sight of me.

Thank God for Best Friends

PAIGE

I WEAVED IN and out of traffic on the Pacific Coast Highway in Malibu, driving recklessly and way too fast. Glancing in my rearview mirror, I noted at least ten cars had followed me, all trying to maneuver as close as possible. No matter how I drove, I couldn't shake them. They'd been tailing me since we left my apartment on Wilshire Boulevard, and I was convinced they knew exactly where I was headed.

My anxiety level escalated as one car shot ahead, closing the space between us, the driver with a camera in one hand and gripping the steering wheel with the other. This was so dangerous, and I never understood why the police seemed to allow it. One of these days someone was going to get killed, and I silently prayed it wouldn't be me or anyone I loved. A quick turn off the main highway and into what Malibu considered a neighborhood with a view, I slowed my reckless pace and attempted to regain some self-control.

The chase cars screeched to a stop as I pulled up to Quinn's privacy gates. A group of men jumped out quickly to get to me before I could escape inside. I leaned out my window to quickly punch the pass code into the keypad, and breathed out in relief as the gates swung open before any of them could reach me.

My heart thumped as I maneuvered my car into the driveway and shut down the engine. As I stepped outside, the camera-wielding madmen lined up outside the iron gates of my best friend's house, shouting random questions at me as they shoved their equipment between the bars and snapped the shutters repeatedly.

"Paige, have you seen Colin?"

"Is it true?"

"We're sorry, honey. He's a jerk!"

"Has he cheated on you before?"

"How many times has it happened?"

"What about the woman in Vegas? Is it true she's pregnant with his baby?"

I paused for a millisecond at the pregnancy bit, but forced myself not to interact with them as I bit down on the inside of my cheek while I rushed to the front door. The paparazzi were rarely ever cruel to me, but then again I didn't normally give them anything to talk about. I stayed out of trouble, didn't get sloppy drunk in bars, and never put myself in a position where I might be photographed getting into—or out of—a car without wearing my underwear.

They called me America's Sweetheart for a reason, and to be honest, I liked being thought of that way. It suited me far better than something like America's Next Addict or Super-Slut. But I'd seen on more than one occasion how cruel and unforgiving the paparazzi could be, and the thought of being the target for their gossip terrified me.

Quinn sprinted through the front door, her blond hair swaying with her haste. She wrapped her arms around me and gave me a pained look as she bit down on her bottom lip.

"Don't do that. Please don't do that," I begged, squeezing my sunglass-covered eyes closed briefly before reopening them.

"Do what?" Her eyebrows pinched together.

"Don't look at me with pity like that. I'll break down right here on your front lawn if you look at me like that again," I warned.

She sucked in a quick breath. "Fine. I'll just project my feelings somewhere else." A sly grin spread across her lips before she narrowed her gaze and turned to face the firing squad of reporters. Quinn hooked her hands on her hips and her voice rose to a near shout as the shutter clicks and questions died down.

"Leave her the hell alone. Don't you have anything better to do? Give the girl a damn minute to deal with her life before you all do your best to make it worse for her. Why can't you focus on all the good things Paige does instead of trying to kick her while she's down? Go harass that asshole ex-boyfriend instead. He's the one that deserves this shit storm. Not Paige."

I tugged at her arm as my comfort level shrank to virtually nothing. "You don't have to do that," I whispered before she cut me off.

"Yes, I do. Screw them. They're vultures. They love to see any one of us in pain. Especially someone as good as you who never does anything wrong. It makes me sick and I can't stand it." She reached for my hand, pulling me into her house, then slammed the front door, shielding us from prying eyes.

"What would I do without you?" I breathed out.

Quinn grinned. "Be way too nice to everyone in your life, including all the assholes outside who don't care about you and only want to make money. You know, the usual." Then she grabbed my bag from my shoulder.

"I can carry my stuff," I started to complain, knowing it was futile. Quinn was hardheaded and strong-minded, two things I absolutely admired about her. They were also the two qualities I believed I lacked the most, which was why we probably bonded so quickly as teenagers. We balanced each other out. She was definitely the yin to my yang, and our opposite natures only made me love her more.

"So can I. Come on." She headed down her naturally lit hallway toward one of two guest rooms. Quinn had them professionally decorated in themes: the Jungle Room and the Goddess Quarters. I wasn't allowed to stay in the Jungle Room, even though I loved the rich greens and dark wood that dominated it. She always said, "The Jungle Room is for

15

boys, Paige, and you're not a boy."

The decor of my gender-appropriate room was gorgeous, however. Filled with rare and collectible Disneyland art, its classic symmetry and beauty was modeled after one of the suites at the theme park's hotel. A stunning four-poster bed was the focal point of the room, its heavy silver curtains tied off on all sides, revealing crisp white bedding and oversized pillows. Silver and blue accents swirled throughout the room and into the private bath, where Italian hand-crafted marble and a fairy-tale theme combined to create a heavenly escape. Whenever I stayed here, it was like being in a dream. Everything down to the knobs on the dresser had been carefully chosen for maximum effect.

Quinn tossed my bag onto the bed and then turned to face me. "Do you want to be alone, or are you hungry or anything?"

"If I wanted to be alone, I wouldn't be here," I responded with mock snarkiness, and she snarled back at me.

"Don't try to sass me. It doesn't work on you." Her upper lip curled as she shook her head, and I held back a grin.

"Where's Ryson?" I asked, assuming her live-in boyfriend had to be around here somewhere.

Her eyes lit up. "He's in the office on a conference call. The boy never stops working, I swear. He has so many things he wants to do, Paige. It's so hot."

Quinn always swooned as she talked about her boyfriend of the last four years. They met on the set of a movie where they each played the lead, and sparks instantly flew both on and off camera.

Ryson had a rough past, though, and Quinn had resisted dating him at first because of it. But he wore her down eventually after proving he was worthy and insisting that his reformed bad-boy ways were now all in fun. He liked to go out with the guys, get pissed drunk, and get into fights. That hadn't changed, and as far as I knew, Quinn never cared about those types of things. As long as he wasn't cheating on her, she not-so-secretly liked that bad-boy side of him.

"He wants to start directing, doesn't he?" I asked.

She waved her hand to shut me up. "Among other things. He's written a couple of movie scripts, and he has an idea for a reality show. I don't know how he has the time to do everything he does, but he's a maniac." She laughed. "Anyway, let's go grab some food and sit out back by the pool."

I sucked in a deep breath, wishing it would help the ache in my heart. "Sounds good."

We walked back down the hallway and into the kitchen where Quinn opened the door to her fridge. She grabbed a smorgasbord of food and slapped it all down onto a large tray.

"Okay, I grabbed us some ice cream, and I made brownies and chocolate chip cookie dough."

"You made brownies and cookies already?" I asked in disbelief.

"You know how I am in the kitchen!" she said, glaring at me.

Quinn couldn't cook at all, and I knew it quite well. "A disaster?"

She swatted my shoulder. "Fine! You know how I am with baking."

"A master," I said with a slight grin.

Quinn solved problems with junk food. If she couldn't bake it, she'd order it or buy it. She always said there wasn't an issue that couldn't be fixed with sweets and treats.

She shrugged. "I figured ice cream, cookie dough, and brownies were good breakup food."

I nodded instead of responding. My brain stuck on the word *breakup* and as if on cue, the video started replaying in my mind's eye.

Quinn placed a hand on my arm, pulling my focus back to her. "I'm sorry, Paige. I'm being insensitive. I don't mean to be so harsh with my words."

Shaking my head, I said, "No, you're not. It's the truth. I just…it's not that I can't believe we've broken up. I just can't believe the way it's happened."

"He's a loser. And a disgusting pig. He doesn't deserve you, obviously. But mostly, you don't deserve any of this."

"I'm too shocked, stunned, and numb to process that he's a complete waste of oxygen, but I'm sure I'll get there. Eventually."

"We'll get there together. I'll put all this together, and you get outside and get some vitamin D. Drinks are in the outdoor fridge," she instructed with a nod of her head, and I realized my staying inside was not up for discussion.

After grabbing a lemon water and a diet soda, I plopped down on one of her oversized lounge chairs next to the pool.

The sun immediately started soaking into my pores as I tipped my head back and sucked in a long cleansing breath. Closing my eyes, I silently thanked God for the eighty-degree warmth. It didn't seem right to feel so broken during such a beautiful day, as if my mood and the weather were a complete contradiction. I decided that if the sun had the ability to heal my broken heart, I wished it would hurry up and do it already.

Quinn maneuvered herself onto the chair next to mine and placed the tray of food between us on a small table. "Eat," she ordered, turning it in my direction so I could view the selection.

I grabbed some crackers and cheese, and made a show of nibbling at them. My appetite had disappeared somewhere between the time the news broke and Colin's pathetic attempts at reaching out to me.

"Has he tried to call you?"

I nodded, wishing we could avoid all things Colin, but knowing the reality of that would never happen. Sometimes I wished my life had a fast-forward button and I could skip ahead to the time when this was all in my past. But life didn't work that way.

"You didn't answer?"

I shrugged my shoulders and nodded my head again.

"You're my hero," she practically sang in response. "Remind me to take lessons from you if Ryson ever breaks my heart. I don't think I could stop myself from answering. That's some serious willpower."

I pushed up, folding my legs in a yoga pose as I turned to

face her. Searching for the right words, I said nothing as the tears started to fall.

Quinn noticed what was happening and jumped to my side immediately, then wrapped her arms around me. "He doesn't deserve your tears—" she started to say, but stopped. "But I know you're hurting. And I'm so sorry for that."

I sniffed. "Me too. I feel so stupid."

"*He* should feel stupid," she snapped.

I leaned my head against her shoulder. "He made me look stupid, Quinn. It's one thing when your boyfriend is cheating on you and all your friends know. I mean, that's embarrassing enough, but he made a fool of me in front of the whole damn world. It's mortifying on top of everything else I'm feeling."

"No." She leaned away from me and grabbed my shoulders to square them. "He made a fool of himself. He made himself look like a complete douche bag asshole. He didn't make *you* look like anything."

My pride longed to believe her. But it wouldn't. Or couldn't. I knew in my heart that no matter what Colin had done, or how badly it looked, he had included me in his actions. No one would ever think about his indiscretion without attaching my name to it. I didn't want to be associated with this, and I hated the way it made my stomach ache.

"He made me look like a fool, Quinn. People will look at me with pity in their eyes. With sadness. It's embarrassing. I'm mortified that I look like a stupid, weak, and pathetic girl who didn't know her pop-star boyfriend was cheating on her with silicone-injected strippers. I'm like a walking cliché."

"No, you're not." Quinn's voice was firm. "I know you don't believe this because right now you're hurting, but you're not a damn cliché, Paige. If anyone in this scenario is a cliché, it's him. Oh, you're a singer and you cheated on your perfect girlfriend with strippers?" She snorted. "How shocking. He's too stupid to even get creative about it."

"If he's so stupid, what does that make me?"

"Damn it, Paige! That's what I'm trying to get through that skull of yours. He is not you. His actions do not define you. They define him. HIM!" she shouted at me, her frustration rolling from her in waves. "They make statements about *his* character, not yours. How you handle yourself and how you react to all of this shit will speak volumes about you."

The glass door behind us slid open and Ryson called out across the yard as he walked toward us. "My two favorite ladies."

"I'm sorry," Quinn whispered. "I didn't mean to yell at you. I know you're hurting right now, but I just really hate him and I want to kick him in the balls for being such an asshole."

I sucked in a quick breath and then slowly released it. Quinn's theory was most likely right, but that didn't stop me from feeling like complete crap. No one could deny the fact that when one half of a relationship did something tabloid-worthy, the other half usually got dragged through the mud as well.

Ryson leaned down and planted a kiss on Quinn's mouth before giving me a hug and a kiss on the cheek. "How are you doing, babe?"

I tried to force a fake smile, but failed, so I shrugged my shoulders instead.

"I'll kick his ass. He better not come anywhere near me, Paige, I swear. I'll break his perfect little smug face." He smirked as he said it and my mood lightened. The idea of Ryson beating Colin to a pulp was definitely enticing.

"I appreciate the offer." I hesitated, knowing he most likely meant every single word he said and that I really shouldn't encourage him. "But he's not worth it."

"Let me know if you change your mind. It would be my pleasure to teach Colin a lesson." Ryson punched his left hand against his right palm. "Or twelve. Seriously. Just say the word."

"Oh Lord, Ryson. Stop. She's had enough for one day." Quinn kicked at him with her bare feet, and he grabbed one and started to tickle the bottom of it. She squirmed and screamed, begging him to stop.

"Say you love me," he teased, his fingers still prancing along her arch.

Quinn's lips pressed stubbornly together, and he only attacked her feet with more fervor than before.

I rolled my eyes behind my sunglasses and lay back against my chair, all too familiar with their antics.

"Say it, Quinn, or I'll never stop tickling you and you'll die."

"You're not the boss of me," she huffed out between fits of laughter.

"I beg to differ," Ryson said, moving his hands up her sides.

"You're so stubborn, Quinn AmberLynn Johnson! Just say it!" I shouted as I turned my gaze in their direction and fought back my laughter.

For as long as I could remember, Quinn and I made up fake middle names for each other and used them whenever we tried to get the other's attention. The more ridiculous the middle name, the more fun it was.

She bolted upright in an attempt to stop his fingers from moving and squealed to Ryson, "Okay, okay. I love you. Please stop." Then she turned to me and said incredulously, "AmberLynn? Really?"

I shrugged as Ryson planted a soft kiss on top of her nose and asked, "Was that really so difficult, AmberLynn?"

Quinn frowned. "Obviously."

"Obviously," he mimicked, and he wandered back inside just as my phone blared out the ringtone for Colin.

"Ooh, give me the phone!" Quinn practically shouted as she reached for me. "Please! Please let me talk to him!" She reached toward me, nearly falling off her chair as she grabbed at my phone.

"You're not talking to him. Stop acting crazy," I said, slapping her hands away as I pressed IGNORE and breathed out in relief.

"This isn't acting, honey," she drawled, waggling her eyebrows.

I almost laughed. I'd done a lot of that today. *Almost*

smiling. *Almost* laughing. *Almost* forgetting that my screwed-up love life was currently splashed across every tabloid and entertainment channel across the country. Squeezing my eyes closed, I couldn't stop a few new tears that forced their way out. I sniffed and wiped them with the back of my hand.

Quinn reached over and patted my shoulder. "Hey, don't cry. Are you okay?"

"I don't want to talk to him. And as angry as I am at him right now, I'm also hurt. Is that stupid?"

"He cheated on you, Paige. He took whatever trust you had for him and broke it. I think you're entitled to feel hurt."

"I do. My heart hurts. As much as I don't want it to because I feel so stupid about the whole thing, my heart is hurting. Every breath hurts," I reluctantly admitted before allowing myself to let the pain flow.

"Breakups suck."

"They do. Especially when you're in the public eye like we are. Then they're even suckier."

I leaned my head back against the lounge chair and let tears slide down my face as the sun continued to warm my body. The sound of water trickling in the gorgeous water feature tucked in the landscaping next to the pool soothed me, and the ocean waves crashing on the beach on the other side of the privacy wall helped me to relax.

I *had* trusted Colin. Truly and completely. It made me sick to think about how wrong I'd been and how naive. My phone blared out Colin's ringtone again, and I covered my eyes with a forearm and groaned.

Quinn reached for it before I could stop her. "What do you want, asshat?" She scowled into the receiver, and I couldn't help but stare at her as she spoke. "No." She paused. "I said no. Because she doesn't want to talk to you."

She rolled her eyes, and her hand opened and closed in my direction as she mimicked a mouth talking. "I swear to God, Colin, if you show up here I won't let you in. I'll feed you to the vultures outside just dying for a piece of meat. You'll be the meat and I'll help them devour you whole."

She shook her head as his voice blasted in her ear. "Are you joking? God, you're so pathetic. She doesn't want to hear your half-ass apology. Honestly, Colin, what could you possibly say to her that could fix what you've done? She saw the video. The whole damn world saw the video." She stayed quiet as she listened. "Exactly. There's nothing to say, so just leave her alone and let her get the hell over you. I already have." She pulled the phone away from her face and stuck her tongue out at it as she ended the call.

My mouth hung open. "Holy crap."

"Sorry, I couldn't help myself," she said as she placed my phone back on the table.

"Don't be sorry. That was sort of amazing," I admitted.

"Well, I am awesome."

"You kind of are."

"Kind of? Clearly this breakup has broken your awesomeness meter."

"You're so weird."

"I know. Hey, not to change the subject or anything, but

have you talked to your mom yet? I'm only asking because she sent me a text earlier."

Grateful for the subject change, I said, "Not yet. I should probably call her."

"You should. She'll make you feel better," Quinn said with a smile.

"She'll try." I pushed up from the chair to go inside. "I'll be right back."

Walking into the privacy of the goddess quarters, I dialed my mom's number and relaxed on the huge pile of pillows that surrounded me. My eyes focused on the rivets in the bed's canopy, and I stared at them while the phone rang in my ear.

"Hey, honey. How're you doing?"

My mom's voice instantly made me want to curl up into a ball and cry. There was just something ultra comforting about mothers and the way they allowed you to drop your guard with just one word.

I sniffed and wiped the tears off my face. "Hi, Mom."

"You okay, sweetheart? You need me to come over?"

I smiled, even though she couldn't see it. "No. I'm at Quinn's. I'm going to stay here for a few days."

"Okay." She sighed. "How are you holding up? Is there anything I can do for you?"

"I'll be okay. I just need to pretend Colin's dead and get on with my life," I said bravely, then started to cry.

"I could have your father break his kneecaps." She chuckled over the line. "Sorry, bad joke. But I'm so disappointed. I've had that young man over for dinner at our house. I cooked for him! Now I want to bash him over the head with something hard."

Wanting to laugh, but not quite there yet, I sniffed. "Get in line."

"I wish I had something better to say to you, honey. I'm just so sorry for what you're going through, and I wish I could take the pain away," she offered, her voice breaking.

"Thanks, Mom." I breathed in a couple of shaky breaths. "Let's talk about something else. What's going on with you? How's work? How's Dad? How's Stacey?"

"Everything's fine here. Work is the same. Never changes unless something goes on with you, then my phone starts ringing off the hook and I come home to people camped in our bushes and jumping out at me every time I pull in or out of the garage."

Guilt pinched at my heart. "I'm sorry."

"It's not your fault. Your dad almost ran one of them over. Claimed he didn't see them, but I think he did." She started laughing wickedly and it made me giggle. "And your sister's good. She just needs to decide which college she's going to attend in the fall so she can send them her acceptance and we can start planning."

"Do you think she'll leave California?"

"Honestly? I do. You know how she's always felt about New York. Ever since you took her there that one year, she's been obsessed with NYU. But I think she's trying to decide if she really wants to leave home or not."

I thought back to when I filmed a movie in New York

City when I was eighteen. Stacey was about to turn fourteen at the time, but I wanted her to experience some of the things I was, so I flew her out for a week during her spring break. Her face had lit up with wonder the second we entered the city. Neither one of us had ever seen anything like it in our lives: the tall buildings, the nightlife, the people. Just like the saying, New York was a city that never slept. No matter what time we were up or what we were doing, a hundred other people always surrounded us. It was exciting, and when we happened to walk past NYU one day, she'd proclaimed, "I'm going to go to college here," and I believed her.

"Yeah. It's a tough decision," I said, wondering what I would do if I were my sister.

"Call her when you have a chance. She's worried about you, but she never calls you because she doesn't want to bother you. She always thinks she bothers you."

"I know. It's because she calls right when I'm in the middle of filming, or at an interview or something," I said as the guilt squeezed me a little harder.

"You're always busy, Paige. Make time for her, please," my mom insisted.

"I will. I'm gonna go. I'll talk to you later, okay?"

"Okay. Be careful, sweetheart. We all worry about you. And I'm really sorry again about everything you're going through."

"Thanks. It will pass. It always does." Not that I'd been through anything like this before, but I'd been around long enough to know today's front-page news didn't last long before being replaced by someone else's front-page news. "'Bye, Mom," I said before hanging up.

Walking into the bathroom, I reached for a washcloth and splashed some water on my face to wipe away the tears that had left streak marks. Convinced it wouldn't be the last time today that tears fell from my eyes, I washed away any remaining makeup from my skin and rinsed out the cloth.

After digging in my bag for two ibuprofen, I swallowed them and downed a full glass of water before walking back outside. Moving toward the lounge chair, I positioned myself and sat back down.

"How's Mom?" Quinn chirped from her lounge chair without opening her eyes.

I sighed. "She's sad for me. And worried. And wants to come over."

"That's normal. Moms want to fix everything for us. Bless their hearts."

The wind whipped gently through my hair and I reached back, gathering it all in my hand before twisting it into a knot at the base of my head.

"Stacey's getting ready to choose which college she wants to attend," I said as my voice quivered.

"Oh no."

"Oh no, what?" I asked.

"I know that tone. You get it every time you talk about someone from your hometown going off to college." She rolled her eyes and glanced out toward the ocean.

"I know I do. I can't help it."

"I hate how much you want that life," Quinn said softly, her tone filled with sadness.

"It's crazy, right? That I'm jealous of my little sister when I'm one of the most sought-after actresses in the country."

Quinn shrugged her shoulders. "I don't know how crazy it is. As long as I've known you, you've always missed out on having those normal, boring moments. It doesn't surprise me that this whole college thing is springing back up."

"It's not boring," I complained.

"I beg to differ."

I laughed. "What do you even know about it? You've been an actress your entire life. You don't even know what you're missing," I reminded her with a sigh.

"Bingo." She placed a finger on her nose and pointed at me with her other hand. "And that's the problem."

Confused, I shaded my eyes with a hand and squinted at her. "Uh, what's the problem?"

"You were basically ripped out of school and shut off from all your friends. You know what you're missing because it was all taken away from you when you weren't ready."

I nodded because she was absolutely right. Sure, I loved acting, but looking back, I had no idea what I would be giving up. It all started for me when a scout approached me in the mall one day while I was shopping with a group of girlfriends. Completely typical, for sure, but that was how it happened. She handed me her business card and insisted I have my parents call her as soon as I got home. That led to a face-to-face meeting at her office in Beverly Hills, which led to my signing with her as my manager. Multiple acting classes followed, and a big-name talent agent signed me almost immediately. Apparently all of this was rather unheard of in this day and age, but they said I was a "natural" and that the camera loved me.

What had been normal for me quickly turned into anything but. My high school years were spent in makeshift classrooms on movie sets, and all my old friendships fell to the wayside. It wasn't intentional, and it wasn't even entirely my fault. My schedule was so busy it was hard to stay in contact with people, and all my old friends were doing their own thing as well. When we did talk, they were experiencing things I couldn't relate to anymore, and vice versa. We no longer had much in common, which made conversations difficult and uncomfortable. Eventually I stopped talking to almost everyone from my old school.

At the time, I never regretted all the things I missed out on. But looking back at it now that I was twenty-one, and with everything Stacey was getting to do, I wished that I *had* accepted Daniel Mack's invitation to prom. I could have never attended since I was on location filming a movie at the time, but I found myself longing for a sense of normalcy now more than ever.

I glanced over at Quinn. "I just don't see what the big deal is. Why can't I do what I want to do? I'm not saying I'm going to stay in college until I get a degree, but I'm not saying I won't either. I don't know, but I want to try. Why does everyone freak out when I mention it?"

Quinn lowered her sunglasses so she could eyeball me, and I narrowed my gaze to meet hers. "Because you're their cash cow, Paige. You know this. You stop giving them milk because you want to visit a new farm, they freak. I've told you this before, but I really hate your agent and your manager. They aren't good people. Why do you think Madison left? Jayson's an asshole."

"I know, but I've been with him since the beginning, so it's just easier."

"Easier to what? Compromise everything you want? Have absolutely zero say in your own life?"

"It's just easier to stay," I said sadly before slipping my sunglasses over my eyes to hide from her judgment.

"Paige Lockwood, the sweetest girl in Hollywood. Oh, if they only knew how true their headlines about you were." Quinn smiled as she took a swig of her lime-filled beer.

"What am I supposed to do then?"

She waved a dismissive hand in the air. "Leave them. Someone else would be happy to have you. Hell, sign with Madison. I'm sure she'd actually give a shit about you and your career. I've even thought about signing with her."

"Shut up," I said incredulously. "You have not."

Her eyebrows raised as she pursed her lips together. "I have so. I even talked to Walker the other day about it."

My interest was piqued. "What'd he say? Although he's completely biased, so you can't believe a word that comes out of his mouth."

Quinn rolled her eyes. "He is, but…" She hesitated for a

second. "He says that she's the greatest thing to happen to his on-screen career. They discuss everything he's offered and decide together if they think it's a good move or not. He says she's completely invested in what's best for his future and the things he wants to accomplish. And I know it's not just because she's dating him, it's because that's the kind of person she is."

I nodded. "That's true. Madison is a really good person and she has integrity. I always liked her."

"Just know that you have options, Paige. You always have options, okay?"

"Then why do I always feel so trapped?"

Quinn slipped her sunglasses over her eyes and leaned back in her chair. "Because you refuse to rattle that cage you're in. It's easier to stay behind the bars."

Her words struck more than just a nerve in me as I sucked in a quick breath and my chest tightened. The only question I had to ask myself now was: What was I going to do about it?

Meeting of the Minds
PAIGE

I SPENT THE next few days holed up with Quinn. The paparazzi refused to leave, and even though I felt incredibly guilty for bringing all this drama to Quinn and Ryson's front gate, they both insisted that they were used to it and couldn't care less. Plus, I think Ryson enjoyed having people to direct his pent-up anger at.

"You don't have to go," Quinn whined as I folded my clothes and placed them into my duffel bag.

"I can't stay here forever, Quinn. I need to go home and just…" I paused from packing to choose my words. "To just put all of this in the past. I can't do that if I keep avoiding it."

She tilted her head and blond strands fell across her eyes. "You're such a grown-up. One day I want to be just like you."

I swatted her shoulder. "Don't make fun of me."

"I'm not! I'm seriously not. You're just so damn well adjusted, it's almost nauseating."

"Thanks," I muttered, not quite sure if that was a compliment or not.

"No, really, Paige. I think it's because you weren't raised in this crazy environment your whole life. You're just more stable or something." She waved a frustrated hand in the air. "Geez, I don't know what the hell I'm trying to say."

"I love you," I said before launching into her arms and squeezing tight. "Thank you for saving me this week."

"I love you too." She pushed me away and leveled her gaze on mine. "That's what best friends are for. So are you really going to try to take a break and go to school?"

I nodded. "I think so. I have a meeting scheduled with Jayson at three, so we'll see what he says."

"Good luck."

"I'll need it," I admitted before slinging my duffel bag onto my shoulder.

"I know."

WALKING DOWN THE hallway toward my agent's door, I stopped myself from putting on a big smile for Madison as I remembered that she no longer worked there. Making a mental note to touch base with her and schedule a lunch, I exchanged pleasantries with Jayson's latest disaster of an assistant on my way into his oversized office.

"Paige, great. Sit down," Jayson directed me from behind his desk.

I did as I was told. Hazard of the job, right?

"Did you read the script? Pretty great, isn't it?" he asked without waiting for a response from me.

I hated when my agent and manager did that sort of thing. They were constantly asking me questions that they never let me answer. Both of them always expected me to agree, and I usually did, in part because I hated rocking the boat. Being agreeable kept everyone else happy.

Honestly, I loved acting. But there were times, like right now, when I really wanted a break. I longed to go to college the way my little sister was preparing to. My soul needed something normal back in my life. This world, no matter how much I adored being a part of it, was nowhere near normal.

I felt so out of touch with people my own age, the very people I should able to relate to the most. We basically had nothing in common anymore and it freaked me out. How could my fans take me seriously if I couldn't identify with what it was like to be like them on a typical day? It occurred to me in this moment that if I was surrounded by people my own age, I'd be the outcast, not them.

Thoughts weaved and bobbed inside my head as Jayson tapped his pen on top of his desk. "Hello, Paige? Did you hear me?" He frowned as I blinked twice before meeting his narrowed gaze. "I asked if you read the script?"

I sucked in a quick breath and decided to be brutally

honest for the first time since I started in this business. "I hated it," I admitted. The script was written beautifully, but the story was awful. The ridiculous message it conveyed was one of epic proportion. It was the same old unbelievable story, and I was tired of playing predictable, over-the-top, unchallenging roles.

"You hated it?" he sputtered as tiny balls of spit formed in the corners of his mouth.

"There was nothing special about it. I don't see what I'd bring to the role that any other actress couldn't." I shrugged and straightened my back, my sincerity giving me some much-needed courage.

"What's going on, Paige? Is this about Colin?" He cocked his head to the side, the look on his face not the least bit understanding. "Because everyone's on your side."

I waved my hand, cutting him off. "This has nothing to do with Colin," I said tersely. "This has to do with the fact that you keep presenting me with the same scripts over and over again no matter how many times I tell you that I need something different. I want to be challenged. I want to grow."

"But these parts scream your name, Paige. The public eats it up when you play these lovey-dovey roles. Especially now that you've been wronged by Colin. They'll flock to the theater to support you. This movie will make buckets of money for everyone involved," he insisted, practically foaming at the mouth.

"I don't care about the money."

Jayson narrowed his eyes at me. "And that's why you have

me. Because I sure as shit do."

"I think that's part of the problem," I muttered.

"Excuse me?"

"I think…" I paused before regaining my composure, then stared him right in the eye and said firmly, "I want to take a break."

Jayson's face screwed up so tightly I thought his bushy eyebrows might stick to each other. "You want to take a break from what?"

"From acting. I need some real-life experience to pull from. I'm ready to go to college. I've told you and Corryn that before. I'd like to do it now because I think it'll make me a better actor in the future."

Scrambling, I attempted to sell the point in a way he'd understand. If I spun it as helping me get roles in the future, maybe he'd see things my way.

He laughed. "What future?"

Then again, maybe not.

He quickly pressed a button on his phone as the ringing blared through the speaker and filled the space. "Jayson," Corryn's voice purred, and in that moment I realized that I was up against a wall. Bricks were being strategically put into place by my agent and manager as they worked in tandem against me. They held the keys to my prison cell, and we all knew it.

"Babe, I have Paige here with me, and she hated the script."

"Hated the script?" Corryn belted out. "Paige, darling, it's a brilliant part."

"It's really not," I tried to shout, but only a halfhearted mumble came out.

Jayson shifted in his chair and said snidely into the speakerphone, "She wants to go to college."

"Not this again."

Corryn's annoyed tone was the wake-up call I needed.

"Yes," I said loudly. "This again. And if you don't let me, I'm always going to want to go. I haven't stopped working since I turned fourteen!" I shouted before continuing my tirade. "You guys keep acting like I'm asking the world to stop spinning or something. I'm simply asking for a break. Just some time away so I can have some normal experiences and live a normal life. Why is that so hard?"

Jayson slammed his hand on top of his desk. "Because it's idiotic, Paige."

"No one in their right mind wants to go to college when they're the hottest actress on the planet," Corryn added. "You know how many other girls would kill to be in your shoes? Stop being ungrateful! You can be normal later."

I could be normal later?

"When, huh? Just tell me that! When will I get to go to college? When will I get to be normal? When I'm fifty?" I screamed, oddly embarrassed over the tears that had formed in my eyes.

I'd grown tired of them trying to placate me, constantly telling me that my chance for normal would come soon enough. But it never did. The next project was always waiting to start the second my current one ended.

Who becomes a spectator in their own life? Paige Lockwood, America's sweetheart, that's who. Surrounded by people who made every single decision for me, what I wanted never seemed to matter. Whenever I fought to have my voice heard, those around me always raised their voices louder to drown me out. I'd lost count of the number of times I'd been told that *they* knew what was best for me.

"You're making this film," Corryn demanded, and Jayson nodded furiously in agreement.

"I need a break!" I shouted back. "You never let me have a break." Dismayed at how my voice sounded defeated, as if I'd lost the fight already, I added, "Please."

"Do you have any idea how long people will want you in their movies, Paige? They won't want you forever," Jayson snapped, stomping his foot on the floor to emphasize his point. "If you leave now and try to come back in five years, there won't be a place for you. It doesn't work like that anymore. It might have twenty years ago, but you leave a hole in this industry and they'll find the next actress to fill it before you go to your first frat party. So, you *will* be doing this film and your so-called normal life can wait."

My life could wait?

My life had been waiting for the last seven years.

Instead of completely coming unglued on them, I laughed. Full-out belly laughed as I turned to walk out of Jayson's office. He shouted words at my retreating back I could barely make out over my own maniacal laughter.

Then I did something so out of character for me, I couldn't believe I was actually doing it. I flipped him the bird and bolted for the stairs before anyone could stop me. I'd come unhinged.

Running Away

PAIGE

MY INSIDES FELT like they were unraveling, every part of me untwisting and unfurling with abandon. Never in my life had I felt so out of control, so overwhelmed, so…*angry*.

I screamed into the emptiness of my car as tears of frustration spilled down my cheeks. Pressing the green CALL button on my steering wheel, I directed my car to "Dial Quinn."

The robotic voice announced she was calling Quinn's mobile, and I fought the urge to pull the car over and head toward Quinn's house. Shaking my head wildly, I dismissed that idea. This was something I needed to do on my own.

"Quinn." I sniffed and wiped my face with the back of my hand.

"Paige? What's wrong?" Her tone was cautious; she

obviously immediately knew that I didn't sound normal or okay.

"I just wanted you to know that I'm losing it," I said, practically hiccupping as my words came out on a choke mixed with sobs.

"Losing it? Losing what? What's going on?"

Another long sniff. "I got in a fight with Jayson and Corryn about my future."

"That's not surprising." She breathed out, and my speakers crackled with her exhale.

"They're trying to force me to do that stupid movie. I put my foot down, Quinn. I said no."

She let out a whoop of approval. "You said no? That's my girl!"

"I also flipped Jayson off on my way out the door," I said, then hiccupped.

"You flipped someone off and I missed it? Damn it, Paige, you can't do that sort of thing without me. If I didn't see it, it didn't happen."

I managed a choked laugh as I turned onto my street. "I'm pulling into my place. I'll call you back."

"Hey!" she shouted. "I'm proud of you."

I sniffed and sucked in a ragged breath before responding, "Thanks. I'll talk to you in a bit." Pressing the red button on my steering wheel to end the call, I pulled into the valet at my apartment.

Stepping into the lobby, I avoided eye contact with everyone I would normally talk to and headed straight toward the elevator doors. My thoughts raced, causing my head to feel like it was spinning off my shoulders. I should be able to decide whether or not I want to make a movie. It should be up to me what I want to do with my life. If I wanted to take a year off and visit the moon, I should be able to do just that. It was my prerogative.

But it's not. I'm owned.

By my agent, my manager, and my publicist. Directors, producers, and screenwriters who depend on me. The public. And the damned press.

Pressing my back against the elevator wall, I sank to the floor and rested my head on my knees. Squeezing my eyes closed, I let out a few sobs as tears spilled down my legs. When the elevator dinged and came to a jerky stop, I pushed myself up and stumbled down the hallway to my door.

Once inside the confines of my own space, anger replaced all other emotions. I started pacing the hardwood floors, tugging at my hair in frustration. This was ridiculous. All of this was beyond flipping ridiculous.

No one owns me. I'm a person, a soul, a being. I can't be enslaved to anyone else unless I allow it to happen. If everyone is the boss of me, it's only because I let them.

That was when I felt it. Something inside me snapped, and if my essence had the ability to make audible sounds, I would have heard the crack. The realization hit me like a runaway train.

I didn't have to be here.

I could leave.

Get the hell out of Dodge. And Los Angeles.

YES!

This was exactly what I needed!

A madness possessed me as I ran into my bedroom and searched for my oversized travel bag. I started stuffing clothes of all kinds inside it—pants, shorts, sundresses, T-shirts, dress tops—basically anything I could grab. I was laughing like a crazed lunatic as I found more things to toss inside—makeup, face wash, a fistful of bangles, necklaces, and earrings.

Adrenaline coursed through me, making my actions feel justified. I accepted the burst of energy as an indication that I was doing the right thing. It felt good to think of leaving, the very idea so freeing.

My head nodded to no one but my own thoughts as I entered my closet and eyed my shelves of shoes. I settled on five different pairs, all different types for different occasions. I stopped at the small painting between the rows of oak shelving and pulled it away from the wall. A small safe was tucked behind it, and I quickly spun the dial to the right and then to the left. When it clicked open, I reached for the envelope filled with cash that I kept inside, and counted out a few thousand dollars.

I wanted peace in my escape. And that meant no credit cards. My cards could be tracked, and they'd come get me and take me home before I even got away. I would pay in cash and use a fake name. And hopefully no one along the way would rat me out to the highest bidder. Knowing damn well I couldn't leave town without letting someone know, I dialed

Quinn again from my cell.

"So I was just calling to let you know that I'm all right, okay?"

"Okay," Quinn said warily, her tone slow and questioning.

"I'm going to get out of here for a while. I need to clear my head and think about what I want for once, and I can't do that while I'm surrounded by everyone who's trying to think for me." As I explained, all my thoughts made perfect sense as they spilled from my mouth.

"Where are you going?"

"I have no idea and I don't care. I need to get away before I completely break down and you all have to check me into a mental institution."

"Do you really think this is a good idea? It's not safe for you to travel alone. And I don't mean because you're a celebrity, but because you're a girl," she cautioned.

I clenched my teeth as I tried to ignore the practicality that Quinn was feeding me. I didn't want to hear any of that right now. I didn't want to think about anything that might stop me. For once in my life, I didn't want to plan every moment; I simply wanted to *feel* my way through it.

"I have pepper spray."

"Good. Don't be afraid to use it."

"I won't," I said, almost convincing myself.

"Do you want me to come with you?"

Waffling for a moment, I almost said yes. "No. This is something I need to do on my own."

"Are you flying?"

I laughed. "No way. They'll track my flight, show up there, and ruin my life."

"Dramatic much?" Quinn laughed. "But you're right. They will." She sucked in a breath. "Hey, do me a favor, though, before you go, okay? Just send everyone a quick e-mail letting them know you're out of town. If you don't give them some sort of heads-up, they'll put a freaking APB out on you. They'll have every town in America searching for you, Paige. You have to at least try to keep the peace, or they'll make it so you can't go anywhere without the world knowing."

My free hand balled into a fist as my nails dug into my palm. "You're right. Okay. I'll send an e-mail. And I'll call you when I get to wherever I'm going."

"Don't forget that they can track your cell too. I don't want you to fall off the grid completely, Paige, but if this is something you really need to do, then I support you."

"Thank you, Quinn. I don't know what I'd do without you."

"Just be safe, please. You're too damn naive and trusting. Try to be more like me on this trip, okay?"

I could hear the smile in her voice as she gave me advice, knowing full well I could never be as tough as she was. I hung up without even saying good-bye, then opened up an app on my phone and composed an e-mail to my manager, publicist, and agent, making sure I'd copied my family and Quinn.

I'm sending you this e-mail to let you know that I'm all right. I need to get out of town for a little while, so I've left. I'm not sure how long I'll be gone, but please don't come look for me. Please let me have this time to sort out my thoughts and find my footing. I need to be away from this town, this environment, and everyone in it until I can get my head right. Please understand.

I paused, feeling the desperation in my words, and knew I needed to end this e-mail with strength. Remembering that my agent, manager, and publicist worked for me—and not the other way around—I packed my closing punch.

If you come looking for me, you'll only make this worse and I'll stay away longer. Let me contact you when I'm ready, and not the other way around.

Before I could second-guess myself or change my mind, I clicked SEND. Nerves fluttered down my spine, but I pretended not to acknowledge them, not wanting to give them any power over me or my actions. Grabbing my packed bag and wad of cash, I headed out the door as quickly as I came in it. If I wasted any more time, they'd show up here and stop me before I could get out of the area code.

After jumping into my car, I drove onto the nearest freeway on-ramp I could find. I knew that this particular road would take me all the way to Florida if I let it. And at that point, I didn't care. Anywhere would be better than here.

Is It Hot Out Here?

PAIGE

I'D SPENT THE last few days driving through multiple states, only stopping for gas, food, the bathroom, or sleep. My sporty black BMW did little to help me keep a low profile, so I made sure to tuck my hair up into a baseball hat and wear sunglasses constantly.

So far I'd been able to avoid prying eyes, and no one I'd come across even spared me a second glance. Most people would never think to look for me in their town, not to mention the fact that the majority of people I'd run into probably couldn't care less about who I was. Consumed with only my own thoughts for company, I felt freer than I had in a long time, as if a weight had been lifted from my shoulders.

My thoughts drifted as I drove aimlessly down a near desolate highway, the sun sinking into the horizon somewhere in my rearview mirror. I had no idea if I was still in Texas or if I'd crossed over into Louisiana at some point, since the landscape was virtually unchanged. Lush green trees and tall grasses filled my view in every direction. Houses were few and far between, separated by acres of farmland.

I enjoyed taking in the scenery around me until *his* voice came over the radio and filled the empty space inside my car. Slamming the power button off on the stereo, I opted for the blissful sound of silence instead. I'd grown tired of listening to the same songs over and over again. Tired of hearing Colin's latest hit mock me from my own speakers.

Colin.

My heart ached in the rare moments I allowed myself to think of him and remember that we had shared some good times together. It wasn't all bad. Actually, it was rarely bad. The majority of our relationship had been happy and filled with understanding. At least, that was what I'd always thought it was.

No.

Colin made a fool out of me and continued to do so to better his public image, and I was determined to hate him for that. Or at least try.

But this wasn't even about him. Not entirely. Leaving Los Angeles was about so much more than just the public spectacle Colin created when the photos of his cheating hit every media outlet. And even though the public had taken my side, I still felt like a stupid girl. Like I should have known he was a complete cheating scumbag who lacked the ability to keep it in his pants.

But I didn't. Because I was too trusting. And so in a single moment, ten months of dating was flushed down the toilet and swept out to sea. Being this trusting made it hard for someone like me to stay in control of my own boat in the waters of Hollywood. Somewhere in all this fame and celebrity, I'd completely lost control of my life. I was no longer the captain of my own destiny.

My thoughts drifted to the hotel last night and my mistake at turning on the tiny television. Colin's face appeared on a sit-down interview on an entertainment show.

"Paige knows this is all a big misunderstanding," he'd claimed, and my stomach churned.

"The pictures and video look pretty damning, Colin," the interviewer had said.

Colin nodded. "They do. But you know everything can be faked these days. You know it and Paige knows it."

"So you've talked to her then?"

"Of course I've talked to her, Sandy. She's my girlfriend."

"Oh. I'm sorry, it's just that we were under the impression that Paige wasn't speaking to you, and that you two were definitely over. At least, that's what we'd heard from one of our sources."

"Can't believe everything you hear. You should know that by now."

"So the pictures were faked, the video was faked, and you and Paige are perfectly fine?"

Colin nodded and grinned. "I didn't do anything, Sandy. I

would never cheat on Paige. She's the best thing to ever happen to me."

"Then where is she and why isn't she speaking out? Our sources say she left town to get away from you."

I'd flipped the TV off at that point, my desire to shove it from the cabinet and onto the floor growing stronger with each lie that spilled from Colin's stupid lips. If I was on the fence about what a jerk he was before, I certainly wasn't after seeing that interview. Dating him had been a mistake to begin with. I knew that now.

After watching everything he'd said during that interview, I knew immediately the only reason he said everything he did was to better his public image. He'd been all but vilified since cheating on me, and he was in damage-control mode. Thankfully, I'd never had to spin lies like that for publicity purposes, but I'd seen it done many times. I knew the attempt to save face when I saw it. It sucked that he pulled me into it and I wasn't there to defend myself, which was why he probably did it in the first place. A hundred bucks said Colin knew I was off the grid.

When I made the mistake of using a computer in the hotel's business center, I caught sight of an online report that had the audacity to claim that this was all a publicity stunt coordinated by me since my newest movie was due out later this year. But I didn't give a damn about the publicity. This wasn't a stunt. My life wasn't a press release.

At least, it never used to be. I didn't even know what it was anymore.

Focusing my thoughts back on the road in front of me, I listened to the sound of each piece of stray gravel crunching and popping as I drove along the deserted highway. It soothed me in an odd sort of way. Searching the recesses of my mind, I couldn't remember the last time I'd been alone like this. The last seven years of my life had been scripted, scheduled, and planned out for me. At first it had all seemed so glamorous, my new life on movie sets around the world, the parties, the money, the lifestyle. But once all my friends from high school started going to college, I started craving what they had. Seeing their pictures on social media filled me with envy, and I longed to have one thing in my life be normal, or relatable to others my own age.

Lost in thought, a sudden hissing sound followed immediately by a hard jerking motion to the right pulled me into the present. I steadied the wheel and guided my now limping BMW to the side of the road. Ungluing myself from the black leather seat, I stepped out of the car as the sweltering humidity almost pushed me right back in.

Wherever I was, it sure was hot. Don't get me wrong, it was hot in Los Angeles, but it was a dry heat. This felt more like a blanket soaked in warm water and tossed across your shoulders. It wasn't comforting. And it wasn't refreshing.

Walking around my car, I noticed the shredded remains of what once was a fully functioning front tire. I crouched down, allowing my fingers to run along the rubbery edges, noting how eerie a tire looks when it was torn apart. The frayed pieces lay on the ground in different shapes and lengths, like a giant had ripped them in a fit of fury. Remembering I no longer had a spare, since I'd already used it and never replaced it, I plopped down with a defeated huff and allowed the hot summer sun to bake my uncovered arms. A light breeze blew past, and I was thankful as my hair moved with it, allowing my back and shoulders to breathe.

In my haste to leave town, I hadn't really thought this whole thing through. I simply wanted to get away. My entire thought process went something like this: (1) drive, (2) figure the rest out later.

So I wasn't that great at planning.

My thoughts were interrupted by the sound of a loud muffler coming my way. I pushed up from the ground, wiped at the back of my tan shorts, and walked back around the front of the car toward the driver's seat. A beat-up old green Chevy truck slowed to a stop behind my BMW.

Too late, I realized that my purse was sitting on the passenger seat with my pepper spray tucked safely inside. Not the best place for my only weapon right now. Shifting my weight from one foot to the other, I waited anxiously for the driver to emerge and for my survival instincts to tell me how to react.

The door creaked open and out hopped a freaking god in perfectly worn-in blue jeans and a fitted white shirt. The man was young, not much older than me, with a baseball cap pulled low, nearly covering his eyes. He had a muscular frame that wasn't overly done, but begged to be noticed.

Forget the pepper spray, I wanted to spray this guy with

love potion, or attraction potion, or come-here-and-put-your-lips-on-mine-forever potion.

Whoa.

Where did that come from?

"Afternoon, miss," he said in a sexy Southern drawl.

I found myself instantly attracted to the sound of his voice. Could you be attracted to something as simple as that? In an industry filled with fakes—fake accents, fake boobs, fake tans, fake hair color, fake personalities, fake everything—when something as genuine as this stood in front of me, I tended to take notice. There was nothing fake about this guy.

"Uh…uh," I stammered, which surprised me because I was never at a loss for words. "Afternoon."

As he cocked his head to the side and stared at me, it never occurred to me until that second that he might know who I was. Then he shook his head, as if to rid himself of the notion, and glanced back at my car.

"What seems to be the problem?"

"I got a flat."

He walked around the front of the car and stopped at the sight of the ruined tire, a frown twisting his perfect lips as he glanced back at me. "This needs to be replaced. Do you have the spare?"

I shook my head. "I don't. I already used it and never replaced it. Stupid, I know."

A slight grin appeared before disappearing just as quickly. "I'll get it towed for you to my shop."

"You have a shop?" I asked, assuming this guy couldn't be

more than a year older than me.

"It's my dad's. I'll tow it there, but I won't be able to get you the tire until tomorrow. Do you have someplace to stay or someone you can call?"

"I don't know anyone here," I admitted, feeling vulnerable and stupid. "Or even where I am exactly."

"I'll drop you off at the local bed and breakfast. It's the only one in town. And then I'll come back for your car."

"Um…" I paused as nervousness surged through my veins. "How do I know you're not a serial killer or something?"

He gave me a look that was part amusement, part irritation. "Do I look like a serial killer?"

Lord help me if this guy didn't look like a dang model, but there had been hot murderers before. Ted Bundy had used his good looks to lure women to their deaths.

"I don't know," I said slowly, "but how do I know you really own a shop? Do you have a business card?"

"Because serial killers don't carry business cards, right?" he said, mocking me as he fumbled around inside his truck. "I don't have any cards because I don't normally need them in this town, but here's the paperwork for some parts I just dropped off." He handed me the paper with the shop's name and number, and some signatures at the bottom.

"Just please don't murder me," I said seriously before walking around to the passenger side of his truck.

"I'll do my best," he said dryly.

"Do you think my car's safe out here?" I glanced back at

my pride and joy.

His Holy Hotness looked around at the desolate landscape surrounding us before pinning me with an annoyed glare. "Looks pretty dangerous out here. Better lock it up after you get your things."

I shook my head, feeling like an idiot. Reaching for my cell phone, I grabbed it and tucked it into my front pocket. Pulling my purse and duffel bag free from the front seat, I tossed my pepper spray in and gripped the handle of it tightly before locking the car doors and hopping into his truck where he waited.

"I'm Paige," I said as I offered my hand.

He stared at it like it might bite him, as if my hand might literally jump right off of my arm and eat his face. Which was something my lips sort of wanted to do. Then his gaze flicked up to mine before he put the truck into gear and pulled out onto the highway.

"I know who you are. What I don't know is why on earth you're all the way out here alone. Are you filming a movie or something?" He chewed on his bottom lip, and I fought off the urge to run my thumb across it.

I shook my head to clear the inappropriate thoughts and wondered who had taken over my body. "No, not filming. I just needed to get away."

"And you picked here? In the middle of nowhere to get away to?" His voice was thick with sarcasm and something else I couldn't quite place, but it certainly wasn't Southern hospitality.

Instantly I turned defensive, a side I rarely showed. "I didn't *pick* here. My car got a flat tire, remember?" This guy irked me no end, and I'd known him for all of two seconds. "So do you have a name, or do I get to make one up for you?"

He grunted. "Tatum."

"Like Channing?" I asked, dumbfounded.

"No," he snapped back. "Like Montgomery."

"Oh." I frowned, unsure which name was his first and which was his last.

As if reading my mind, he said gruffly, "It's Tatum Montgomery," his tone beyond annoyed at this point.

I fumbled to recover, and tried to play nice. "I've never met anyone with the first name Tatum before."

"Obviously."

Wondering why he seemed so angry at me, I asked, "Did I do something wrong? Maybe you didn't like my last movie or something?" I tried to lighten the mood by cracking a slight smile.

Keeping his focus intensely in front of him, he mumbled, "I don't watch chick flicks. And I'm named after my grandfather, not that it's any of your business."

I sucked in a breath. "You can just let me out here. Give me directions to the bed and breakfast and I'll walk there." I didn't care how good-looking this guy was, I refused to sit in a car with him any longer.

Tatum blew out a deep breath. "Look, I'm sorry, okay? I'm not the best at making small talk."

"Obviously," I said tartly, mimicking his earlier response,

and he smirked before straightening his face again. "I saw that."

"You saw nothing," he replied, but his tone had softened and I relaxed slightly.

We drove in silence through what I assumed was the town. I smiled to myself as we neared a bowling alley with an attached café. The last time I'd been bowling was with my family a few years ago on Christmas Eve. We spent part of the evening competing with each other for top score, but my dad won, just like he always did.

Tatum slowed his truck to a stop, and I looked around to see a grocery mart, the post office, a church, and not much else. A gas station and a mechanic's shop caught my eye across the street, and I assumed that was where Tatum's dad worked. It was quite possibly the smallest town I'd ever seen, but it was also maybe the most charming, each building filled with more character than what I was used to.

He picked up speed once the town was behind us and turned right onto another road. As we passed a small school, I asked, "Does everyone go to school in one place?"

He glanced at me, his eyes barely visible beneath the bill of the ball cap. "Yeah. It's three separate schools, but they're housed in the same place."

"I've never seen anything like this before."

"You mean you've never seen anything so small and boring?"

"No, that's not what I meant." I didn't know how to put my feelings into words, so I stayed silent, not wanting to upset him anymore.

Tatum pulled his beat-up truck to the right once more and turned onto a gravel road lined with green trees and land as far as the eye could see. His speed slowed until he stopped in front of the most charming ranch-style house I'd ever seen. Wooden rocking chairs lined the large porch on each side of the front door. The closest I'd ever seen to a house that looked like this was on a movie set.

There were no homes like this in LA, and I think the sight of it made me swoon. Out loud. Apparently I made a sound when the aged yellow house came into view, because Tatum shot a concerned glance my way.

"This is it. Miss Em rents out the converted barn in the back, and some of the rooms in the main home as well, if she needs to. I know for a fact that all the rooms are available right now," he added as he turned the truck off and opened the door. His cowboy boots hit the side of the truck with a bang before his feet landed in a pile of mud, sending a splash of the brown goo into the air.

I was definitely not dressed for walking around in mud. Surveying the area around my feet, I looked for the least soggy area and made a jump for it. "So, how do you know so much about the house?" I asked as he headed for the front porch.

"It's my mama's," he said over his shoulder before the screen door slammed shut and he disappeared inside.

His mom's?

Oh crap.

Meeting Mama

PAIGE

A WOMAN I assumed was Tatum's mom stepped outside the house, wiping her flour-stained hands on the front of a well-worn apron. "Hi, Paige, I'm Emily Montgomery." She extended a clean hand.

Wavy brown hair framed her face, and her blue eyes twinkled as she grinned at me. Apparently she knew who I was. There was recognition in her eyes, as well as a sort of giddiness in her demeanor. She seemed happy and inviting, a far cry from the welcome her son gave me.

"Hi, Mrs. Montgomery. Thank you so much for letting me stay here."

She nodded her head and waved a hand in my direction. "It's no trouble. No trouble at all."

"I really do appreciate it."

"Would you like some sweet tea?" she asked with a smile, and my own dropped a little.

"I don't know what that is," I admitted sheepishly.

"It's sweetened sun tea, dear. It's a Southern tradition."

"You sweeten it yourself?" I asked, feeling like a complete imbecile.

"You bet."

"Well then, I'd love some."

As she walked toward the front door, she stopped abruptly and turned to face me. "Oh dear, I hope you like dogs."

"I love dogs," I said, noticing the large chocolate lab behind the screen door, wagging its tail back and forth.

"Thank goodness. This here's Buster. He's a big love, but he gets in the way sometimes," she said. "Tell me something else, dear. Would you prefer to sleep in the main house, or would you like some privacy in the back house by yourself? I can get it fixed up for you, if you'd prefer."

I thought about it for a second, then said, "I'd love to stay in the main house with you, if you don't mind." I didn't want her going to any more trouble than I'd already put her through.

"That would be lovely. Truly lovely. Come on then," she answered before yelling, "Tatum Alan Montgomery, come help this young lady with her bag right now or so help me, God—"

"No, Mrs. Montgomery, it's okay," I started to argue, but Tatum appeared at my side and lifted my duffel with two fingers.

Buster bolted for me as soon as the door opened. I bent down and squeezed his face affectionately before scratching behind his ears. "You are so handsome, aren't you?" I planted a quick kiss on top of his nose, and he licked the side of my face. I laughed and stood up straight, noticing that Tatum was watching and waiting for me.

His eyebrows lifted as he walked away, his manly scent drifting toward me as I followed behind him. "Your room's in here. Mama's making dinner. She'll cook breakfast, as well. I'll order that tire first thing in the morning."

"I'm not in any rush," I offered, hoping to slow him down, but he didn't take the bait.

"Well, I'll try to get it here as soon as I can, but it might take a couple days."

I shrugged. "That's fine."

"The bathroom's across the hall." He pointed toward an open door. "Mama's room is at the end," he explained, then walked away. "Come on, Buster."

"Thanks," was all I seemed to manage at his indifference. I didn't consider myself an egotistical person, but when someone clamored to get as far away from me as possible, I'd be lying if I said it didn't give my ego a beating.

Glancing around at the sweet blue-and-yellow room, I smiled to myself. It was comforting and homey, the decor tasteful yet not over the top. It was everything I'd expect a Southern bed and breakfast to be.

Tossing my duffel bag on top of the queen-sized bed, I unzipped it and unpacked a few of my things on the dresser and nightstand. The bag was disorganized and nothing was where it should have been, but I didn't care as I rifled through it, searching for my stuff. Normally I was a complete neat freak, but the chaos of the past week had put my neat gene in check.

Not wanting to appear antisocial, I headed into the kitchen where Emily, aka Mrs. Montgomery, was rolling some kind of dough.

"Hi," I said, not wanting to startle her.

"Paige. Is your room okay?"

"It's perfect. How much do I owe you?"

She shook her head. "Oh, we'll deal with that later. Once you figure out how long you'll be staying."

I pulled out one of the white bar stools and sat down at the counter. "Tatum said it would probably only be a couple of days before he got the tire." I glanced around, wondering where he was.

His mom caught me and a smile reappeared on her face. "He went to go tow your car to the shop."

I nodded, embarrassed that she knew I was looking for him. "Mrs. Montgomery, I know I've got no business asking you for anything else after all you've done for me, but can I ask you for another favor?"

"Of course, dear, but I thought you were going to call me Emily."

I chuckled. "I'm sorry. I can't. My mom never let me call her friends by anything other than by their last name. Is it okay if I call you Mrs. Montgomery, or will you be offended?"

She stopped working the dough and turned to face me. "Offended? Oh, heavens no. I just wanted you to feel comfortable. Now about that favor. What do you need?"

"I really don't want it getting out that I'm here." I stumbled over my wording. "I mean, to the press and stuff. Is there any way to keep my being here private?"

Her face crinkled with worry before softening with what appeared to be understanding. "I won't tell anyone you're here. This is a small town, though, Paige. Word will definitely get out to the locals, but I'll see what I can do about keeping them quiet."

"I'd really appreciate that."

"I can't make you any promises, but I'll do my best. Tatum will too," she added.

"I'm not so sure about that," I said, and she tilted her head.

"Why would you say that?"

"I don't think he likes me much," I admitted honestly.

She waved a hand at me and said something that sounded like *pshaw*. "He's just going through his own stuff. He's harmless. All bark and no bite. It's not you, honey, it's him. That sounds like a blow-off, but it couldn't be more true."

I huffed out a hard laugh. "I do not believe that for one second," I said, emphasizing the word *not*.

Mrs. Montgomery tapped her fingers on the countertop. "Well, he's got you fooled then. Now tell me, hon. What are you doing all the way out here?" She leaned across the counter and reached for a pitcher of tea before pouring two glasses.

Pushing one toward me, she waited for my reply.

I sipped the tea. "This is so good," I said before taking another big gulp. "I just needed to get away for a little while. I think I'm having a breakdown or something." I managed an awkward laugh.

"You don't look like you're having a breakdown. But I did hear about what that boy did to you. I'm so sorry for that." She reached out and squeezed my hand before pulling away.

My heart pounded and I swallowed hard. "Thanks. It's okay."

"It's not okay," she said. "That sort of behavior is never okay. And from what I've seen of you, you don't seem like the type of girl to deserve it. Not that any girl deserves that sort of thing, I reckon."

I looked away, fighting to keep my eyes from watering. "Yeah, well, this isn't even really about Colin. It's about…" I paused, shaking my head from side to side as my breaths came out in a rush. "It's about everything else."

"I can't imagine what it must be like for you." Her tone conveyed a sort of compassion that I rarely heard when people talked about me.

"I don't want to complain, because I know I have an amazing life and I get to do things that most people only dream about." I was over-explaining, but I couldn't stop myself. Mrs. Montgomery was so warm and understanding, she reminded me of my mom, and I found myself opening up. "But sometimes things just aren't all they're cracked up to be. You know?"

"I can't say that I do. At least, not from your perspective."

I stopped myself from laughing at her blunt honesty. I'd been so used to people constantly agreeing with everything I said and saying the things they thought I wanted to hear, that her words were refreshing, to say the least.

"I just wanted to do something normal, and everyone in my life told me that I couldn't."

She glanced around at her surroundings as if seeing them for the first time. "Well, hon, this town right here is about as normal as you're gonna get. And I can't imagine what it would be like to be told what you can and can't do all the time."

"Like I said, Mrs. Montgomery, I really don't want to complain. Thank you for listening. And for letting me stay here." I'd already felt more at home and peace than I had since the news of Colin's cheating broke, but I wasn't ready to give my whole story to someone who could sell it in two seconds if the opportunity presented itself.

"It's no trouble, dear. No trouble at all. But I'm here if you need to talk about anything. Okay?" She smiled and then turned back toward the dough, lifting it and pressing it into a waiting pie plate, then crimping the top edges carefully.

"Thank you. That means a lot." Swallowing the rest of my tea, I dabbed the corners of my mouth with my finger, wondering if I could truly trust her or not.

"Now it's my turn to ask you for something. If you don't mind, that is." Her blue eyes pinned mine, and I couldn't help but notice they were the same shade of blue as her son's.

"Of course not."

"Have patience with him. That's all I ask of you," she said, then let out a light laugh.

"Um, okay?" I practically choked on the words as they left my lips. "Your son's not my biggest fan."

"You never know. Lightning could strike." She grinned and hummed a tune as she put the finishing touches on her pie.

Confused and unsure how our conversation had turned in this direction, I pushed through the screen door and sat down in one of the rockers on the covered porch. Birds flew through trees I didn't recognize, and a breeze gently lifted my hair. The air was sticky and humid, but I didn't mind it as the sun started to set. I found if I listened real hard, I could hear the sound of water splashing in the distance.

Being here for a couple of days wouldn't be the worst thing that had ever happened to me. I could definitely handle this.

I'm Such a Dick

TATUM

I TOOK OFF after showing Paige to her room; I had to get the hell out of there. Being near her, around her, surrounded by her scent and her long legs, it was all too much. My mind refused to think straight in her presence, and my dick completely took over all rational thought. All I could think about was pulling her against me and having my way with her. The pure physical attraction I felt toward the girl was off the freaking charts.

I wanted to kiss her, touch her, and make her moan my name all night long. Why the hell I wanted to do that, I wasn't quite sure, to be honest. Of course she was gorgeous, but I'd seen gorgeous girls before. It wasn't just that. Paige exuded a sense of innocence that I wanted to corrupt.

Shit.

Why does everything I say always make me sound like such a dick?

I didn't mean it in a bad way. I was intrigued by her innocence, a complete sincerity that I would refuse to believe if I hadn't witnessed it myself. Paige Lockwood's personality screamed "I'm a good girl," and that pulled me to her like a moth to a flame. Stupid analogy, but call me a moth.

I'd pretty much sworn off women after my ex-girlfriend dumped me for dropping out of college and moving back home. At the time she'd broken my heart, and I had stupidly convinced myself that I'd never get over her. It was funny the shit you believed when you were blindsided by love. Or what you thought was love when you were just a kid.

Looking back, I could see that what Brina and I shared wasn't real love. At least, not the kind that was worth a shit. I probably would have jumped in front of a train for that girl if she'd asked me to. Good thing it never came to that. My misplaced loyalty sometimes astounded me.

I drove to the shop and switched out my Chevy for the tow truck, then made my way to Paige's broken-down car all alone on the highway. I had to admit it was a nice-looking ride, and I wouldn't mind taking it for a spin when it was fixed. We don't get too many foreign cars in our town, and I'd never pass up the opportunity to drive one. Maybe I really shouldn't have acted like such an asshole to her. I'm betting she'd never let me drive it now.

Hitching the front of the car to the rig, I lifted the front end and made sure it was securely fastened to the truck before I cautiously towed it back into town. After pulling into the garage, lowering the car to the floor, and detaching the equipment, I started to close the shop's garage door.

"Hey, Tatum. Nice car," Brina's voice called out from behind me. I turned around to see her and her best friend, Celeste, stopped in the middle of the street, watching me.

I shrugged. "Thanks. It's not mine. Obviously," I added for emphasis. Brina had expected that my football scholarship would lead to big things for me...for *us*. And when it didn't, she was quick to opt out of our so-called relationship. I kissed my scholarship, college degree, and girlfriend good-bye all in the same week. It had been a really shitty week.

"That's too bad. So, whose is it? No one I know has a BMW," she asked, prying for information that was none of her business.

Little did she know that the last thing I planned on telling big-mouthed Brina was that Paige Lockwood's car broke down and she was staying at my house. That news would spread like wildfire, and the whole town would show up on Mama's front porch by dinner.

"Just a tourist. Got a flat," I said, trying to sound nonchalant so she'd take the hint and go away.

"That's not exciting at all." She pouted, tucking her hair behind her ear, and I wished she could see me rolling my eyes from where she was.

"I gotta go. 'Bye, Celeste." I purposely didn't say Brina's name, silently wishing she'd leave this town—and me—behind already. But I'd always liked Celeste. After Brina dumped me and shattered my heart, my pride, and my ego, Celeste had always been the one to say that I could do better, that Brina didn't deserve me. I'd always appreciated that, even if I never believed her.

"Bye, Tatum." Celeste smiled before whispering something to Brina, who then emphatically shook her head. "Coming to the kegger tomorrow night?"

I shrugged my shoulders. "I don't think so."

"Tatum, you have to join the land of the living sometime," Celeste complained, her bright red hair blowing in the breeze as she and Brina climbed into her car.

She was right, but my thoughts instantly went to Paige. I didn't want to leave her alone, and I sure as shit didn't want to bring her to something like that. I tried to imagine a Hollywood actress sitting on the tailgate of my truck while people blew shit up and acted like idiots.

Celeste leaned outside her open window. "Just think about it. Please. It will be fun. Like old times," she said before she revved her engine.

Old times were exactly the problem. I didn't get excited to hang out with everyone who never found their way out of this town. It used to be the thing to do when we were in high school, but high school was a long time ago. And I was over it.

"We'll see," I said noncommittally and they drove off, their hands waving good-bye in the air above the open Jeep Wrangler, its soft top stowed for the summer.

Locking the large garage door, I walked into the office and turned on the computer. I had to wait ages for it to start up and connect to the Internet, something I'd grown used to doing when it came to anything in my hometown. Life was slower-paced here, but I wasn't in any rush.

Paige's long tanned legs, brown hair, and her bright blue eyes filled my thoughts as my pants grew tight. I shifted in my seat, forcing my thoughts to her blown-to-bits tire sitting in my garage to calm myself down. Scanning my tire contact's information, I shot him an e-mail telling him what I needed so he'd get the request first thing in the morning.

Then I scanned the entertainment headlines, searching for any recent news on Paige. I wasn't sure what the hell had gotten into me, but even as that thought crossed my mind, I continued to search for any information on her. Typing her name into the search bar, I pressed ENTER.

Numerous reports of her leaving town showed up immediately, including a press release and an official statement from her management team. I found a few articles on her dipshit ex-boyfriend, Colin, and his feeble attempt at saying it all was a misunderstanding and there was no wrongdoing on his part. The reporter asked if he'd talked to Paige, and he said they were "working things out." Not only did I find that hard to believe, but I found myself getting pissed off at the very notion of it. This guy didn't deserve her, that much I knew, and as long as I was around, there would be no *working it out* between them.

I smacked my palm against my head. What was I thinking? What the hell did I care? I didn't know this girl. All I knew was that she was seriously hot and I liked looking at her. Irritated, I switched off the computer without another glance and stormed out of the office, locking it all up behind me as I left. My stomach growled, and I prayed I hadn't missed supper completely. I hopped into my truck and headed toward home.

Where Paige was.

Paige.

Damn it, I needed to stop thinking about her, stop thinking about anything that had to do with her. She'd be gone soon, and the last thing I needed was to get all caught up in someone who had no intention of staying, much less a freaking actress from California.

Reaching Out

PAIGE

AFTER DINNER, TATUM'S mom insisted on cleaning up, explaining that was how a bed and breakfast worked. She wouldn't let me help with anything. Tatum had shown up during the middle of our meal, his mood even worse than before, if that was possible. His mom offered to fix him a plate, but he rudely waved her off without even a glance in our direction and did it himself.

When he took the seat farthest away from me at the table, I suddenly wondered where his dad was and why they didn't come in from the shop together. When I asked, the table grew silent except for the clang of Mrs. Montgomery's fork as she dropped it onto her plate. Tatum's jaw clenched and his hands balled into fists, and I wondered what I'd said wrong.

As Tatum's face paled, his mom reached for her dropped

fork. "Tatum's daddy died a few years back."

Drawing deep on my acting skills to hide my shock, I offered a meek apology. Tatum jumped up and stormed away from the table, then dropped his dishes into the sink with a crash before he rushed outside. The screen door slammed behind him, and the sound of his boots stomping back and forth as he paced across the wood-planked front porch drifted through the open windows.

"I'm so sorry," I offered again.

Mrs. Montgomery leaned forward and whispered, "Not you, it's him, remember?"

I squeezed my eyes shut, not truly believing her words. "Do you think I should try to talk to him?"

"It's worth a shot," she said, giving me a sad smile.

I rose from the table slowly, unsure of how to handle this situation or him. The screen door squeaked as I pushed through it. When my eyes adjusted to the darkness, I noticed his silhouette as he sat on a porch step, his head in his hands.

"Tatum," I said softly, trying not to scare him off.

"Go away."

His sharp tone and rejection cut straight through me. I lowered my head and reached back for the door. Before stepping inside, I turned in his direction and said, "I just wanted to tell you how sorry I am. I didn't know. It must be really hard, and I bet you miss him a lot."

Without waiting for a response, I headed back inside and down the hall toward my room. Regret filled me as I realized that no matter what I did, it seemed like I couldn't do right by

Tatum. An internal battled waged in my head about whether it was all my fault. I wanted to yell at myself and determine why I cared so much, but I knew the answer. Simply put, I was that kind of person. I cared about others, no matter who they were or where they came from. I didn't find joy in causing others pain, and my curiosity had hurt Tatum.

After getting ready for bed and changing into my pajamas, I plopped onto the top of the bed and let my mind drift for a while. Realizing that I didn't have to wake up early the next morning and drive, I almost felt panicked. I couldn't remember the last time I had no plans or obligations.

I fought the urge to call Quinn or my mom, not really understanding why I was fighting it to begin with. Maybe I should send them a quick e-mail?

"Mrs. Montgomery?" I opened my bedroom door and yelled toward the kitchen.

"Call me Emily, Paige. Really."

"I can't do it," I yelled again and she laughed.

"Yes?"

"Do you have a computer I can borrow? I'd like to send my mom and best friend an e-mail letting them know I'm okay." I suddenly wished I'd brought my own laptop, but not being able to get online whenever I wanted was a blessing. Having no readily available Internet access meant that I didn't have to avoid looking at all the gossip sites and reading about my life as if I weren't the one living it. I knew for a fact that I didn't want to see what was currently being said about me.

She popped her head around the corner, curiosity alight on

her face. "Not using your cell phone?"

"I don't want to be tracked, and I can't trust that my agent wouldn't do exactly that. I'd really hate for them to show up when I just got here."

Mrs. Montgomery shook her head. "Your life is so crazy, I can't even imagine. The computer's in the back house with Tatum. Go on and head back there."

I leaned back in surprise. "Tatum lives back there?"

"Oh dear, I thought you knew."

"Maybe I'll just use it tomorrow after he leaves for work." The idea of seeing Tatum again after I'd just upset him didn't appeal to me. "I'm sure I'm the last person he wants to see right now," I mumbled, knowing that I couldn't bear to face him again after he'd just told me to go away.

His mom shook her head. "Don't be silly. Go on back there. I'm sorry about his behavior earlier. Losing his daddy hit him real hard." She tried to smile, but it didn't reach her eyes. "It hit us both hard."

"I'm really sorry for bringing that up. I feel so bad."

"You have nothing to be sorry for. You didn't know."

Still not sure this was the best idea, I pushed myself off the bed and made my way to the converted barn behind the main house. Knocking on the front door, I waited nervously for Tatum to open it. When he did, he stood silently in the doorway, shirtless, his hair wet, and I had to force my jaw to stay closed. Good Lord, this man's body could cause drool fests worldwide. Tatum Montgomery was a fine specimen of a man, and despite his unfriendliness and gruff personality, he made me all hot and bothered.

When I realized that I was staring instead of speaking, I looked up at his eyes, feeling the heat in my cheeks rise. "Your mom said I could use the computer, but I can come back tomorrow when you're gone if you don't want me around." I had turned to walk away when a strong hand gripped my wrist and pulled me inside.

"Come in," Tatum said, his voice sounding defeated.

I glanced down at where his hand held mine before tugging out of his grip. Part of me didn't want to break the contact, my skin tingling at his touch. I figured I'd probably let him lead me around town like that all day if he wanted to. Apparently I turned stupid when it came to good-looking men. Colin had already proved that. I sighed to myself and walked through the door he held open.

Once inside, I glanced around, amazed at how a barn could be converted into a guest house. It was adorable, with two bedrooms you could see from the living room, a bathroom, and a full-sized kitchen area. It was perfect.

"You live here?" I asked, already knowing the answer.

He nodded and led me toward a large desk near a window. "The password and stuff is here," he said, pointing at the sticky note stuck to the top of the monitor. "If you need anything, just holler."

"Thank you," I said before clicking the power button on and logging in. I wanted to e-mail my family and Quinn, but I didn't want to see all the e-mails directed toward me. I hadn't checked my voice mail or anything since I left that day; I'd gone on complete radio silence. And as much as I loved the idea of being cut off from everyone, I knew that eventually I'd have to pick up all the pieces I'd left scattered behind. I briefly wondered if this would be worth all the trouble in the end.

Logging in to my e-mail account, I noted two hundred fifty-three e-mails. Glancing quickly at the names of the senders, I realized that most were from my agent and Colin. Colin's e-mails were relentless at first, but had tapered off as the days passed. I assumed it was because I never responded to a single text message, phone call, or e-mail from him, aside from the one time when Quinn answered the phone for me. I looked at the date and noticed there hadn't been an e-mail from him in two full days. I expected my heart to ache with that fact, but instead it beat with relief.

Interesting.

Scanning the rest of the e-mail list for any from my parents or Quinn, I read them all hastily. My mom expressed concern for my well-being, but she just wanted me to be safe and happy. She was sad I didn't just come to our family home to get away, but she understood why that wasn't the best idea. She urged me to check in with her as soon and as often as possible.

Quinn already knew I was leaving, so her message was short and sweet:

Go find what you're looking for. And then bring some back for me.

I fired off a quick e-mail to them both:
Hi Mom & Quinn,

First off, I miss you both so much. Sorry for the combined e-mail, but I'd send you both the same thing anyway. Ha. So, I got a flat tire in Texas…or maybe it was Louisiana? I'm honestly not sure exactly where I am, but I wanted you guys to know that I'm okay. Better than okay, actually. This tiny town is charming, and I'm staying with a really nice family at their B&B. Can you believe there are no hotels here? Heck, there's not much of anything here. I've never seen a town so small before (unless it was a set).

"Tatum?" I shouted toward the other end of the house where he had disappeared to.

"Yeah?" he shouted back.

"Where the heck am I?"

He made an odd sound that could have been a laugh, but I couldn't be certain. "You're in Hanford, Louisiana, named after Francis Hanford the third, the man who first settled on this land."

"Really?" I asked.

"I'm dead serious, Princess."

"Princess?" I shrieked.

"It suits you," he yelled back, and my annoyance level suddenly raised significantly.

"It does not suit me. You don't know anything about me," I shouted before returning to my e-mail.

I'm back. Bet you didn't even know I was gone, did you? Had to find out what this town is called. It's called Hanford, Louisiana and it's apparently named after its first resident. That's sort of cool. Why does every other state seem to have so much more history than the one we live in?

Tatum says the tire will take a couple of days to get here, so I'll be staying with his mom at the B&B until then. Don't worry, she's super nice, and I know you'll both think I'm probably naive, but I trust her. My phone is still off, but I'll get you the phone number here so you can call me anytime, okay? Don't worry about me. Love you both so much. Thank you for letting me work through this. I appreciate your love and support. Mom, tell Dad and Stacey I miss and love them. Q, tell Ry I love him too. :)

Paige

She's No Princess

TATUM

AFTER PAIGE ASKED about my dad, I couldn't shake the memory of him from my mind. Everyone in town already knew what happened, had lived through it with me and my mom, so I rarely had to relive the specifics of that day. But sitting here now, seeing it all again fresh in my mind, I wanted to hop in my truck, drive away, and never look back. Losing my dad had been the defining moment in my life; it had changed everything.

I stalked back to my house after yelling at Paige, part of me feeling like a jerk for being so mean to her, and the other part in so much pain I could barely stomach it. I took a quick shower and stalked into the kitchen, my hair still wet and dripping onto my shoulders. Determined to numb the misery, I poured myself a double shot of Tennessee whiskey. A knock on the door interrupted my plans.

I assumed it was Mama, but she rarely knocked. When I opened it, Paige stood there waiting for me to invite her in, but I was too busy staring at her hot little body to say anything. She watched me, her eyes wary before she spoke. "Your mom said I could use the computer, but I can come back tomorrow when you're gone if you don't want me around."

She thought I didn't want her here. Little did she know that I wanted her everywhere. As she turned to walk away, I grabbed her by the wrist, stopping her from leaving. I yanked her back toward me, resisting the urge to pull so hard she'd crash into my bare chest and press her body up against mine.

I told her to come in and allowed her to squirm out of my grip. After showing her to the computer, I sulked back into my bedroom to give her space, or air, or something. Truth was, I didn't know what the hell Paige Lockwood wanted. From me, this town, or in general, but I had a feeling I'd be willing to give her whatever it was she was looking for. Hell, I'd help her find it. And hopefully it would include her mouth pressed against mine, for starters.

Damn, it had been too long since I was this attracted to someone, let alone someone I could see on my television anytime I wanted. Was Paige Lockwood, America's sweetheart, really in my house right now? And why wasn't I nervous around her?

She stayed in the other room on the computer while I sat in my bedroom, avoiding her. I wondered if she was looking up the things I'd just looked up at the shop. Did she want to hear what Colin was saying about her? Was she interested in all the Paige Lockwood gossip?

I started pacing back and forth in my room like a fucking lunatic. It was the only thing I could think of to distract myself from the fact that she was about fifty feet away from me wearing what I assumed was her pajamas. The second I opened the door to see her standing in those tiny shorts and tank top, I wanted to simultaneously pull her against me and shove her right back outside.

She'd gotten snippy when I called her Princess, which made me want to call her that more often. I liked getting a rise out of her; it made me laugh.

"Princess?" I shouted at her.

"Stop calling me that," she yelled back, and I fought back a smile.

"What are you doing online? Reading about all the people who can't live without you?"

She sighed loud enough for me to hear, before her voice lowered. "I was just sending an e-mail to my mom and my best friend."

There was a hint of sadness in her voice, and I wondered if I was being too hard on her. Walking from my room into the living room, I sat on the couch behind her and watched her typing.

"Did they know you were leaving?"

Paige jumped in the chair before turning around to look at me. She scanned my shirtless chest before moving to my eyes and locking on. "I told them both before I was leaving that I was going. But I didn't know where I was heading. My mom was probably worried sick, so I wanted her to know I was safe." She shifted uncomfortably. "I am safe, right?"

Unable to hold back a grin, I pushed up from the couch and walked straight over to her and leaned down. "Depends on your definition of safe." I slid my thumb across her cheekbone before I could stop it. "How long are you thinking of staying, Paige?"

Her eyes squeezed shut for a second as she sucked in a silent breath. I watched as her chest moved in and out, all the while fighting the urges that came with being a guy alone in a room with a ridiculously sexy girl.

Shallow much?

Opening her eyes, she looked up at me cautiously and stuttered, "I-I...don't know."

"Will you leave right after your car's fixed?" I asked, my agitation growing. I shouldn't care at all when she planned on leaving. I shouldn't be anywhere near a girl like Paige Lockwood, but here I was.

Here we are.

"I guess." She shrugged. "I'm not really sure why I'd stay longer."

Her response was like a bucket of cold water, helping me gather my wits. Feeling a little disappointed—and hating myself for it—I moved a safe distance away.

Can't Do Anything Right

PAIGE

NO MATTER WHAT I said, it was always the wrong thing when it came to him. Tatum had asked me how long I planned to stay here, but I really had no idea. Would I leave as soon as my tire was fixed? I had no clue. But why would I stay here any longer than that?

Did he want me to?

Did I want to?

I didn't have anywhere else to be, and I couldn't keep driving forever. Eventually I'd have to find my way back to where I came from. And drive there. Alone. The farther I drove away, the farther I had to drive back. Staying here for a little while might be as good an option as any. So why couldn't I just tell him that?

When Tatum moved away from me, storm clouds back in

his eyes, it occurred to me why I'd held information back from him. He ran so hot and cold that I didn't know what to expect from him, and I'd only known him for half a day! But when he touched me, I almost melted right into him. One simple touch from this guy, and I was drooling like a schoolgirl. I really needed to get out more.

Colin was beginning to feel like a distant memory as Tatum demanded all of my mental energy and focus without even trying. I was so caught up in his general hotness that it was all I could see. Of course I was still hurting over Colin, but being out of Los Angeles seemed to help tremendously. There was true peace in being let out of the cage. I would have never known this kind of serenity existed if I hadn't run away.

A subtle ping redirected my focus back to the computer. A new e-mail from Quinn appeared and I clicked on it, already smiling before I read its contents.

What's a Tatum and is it hot? And before you ask, YES, that's all I got from your e-mail. :)

I laughed out loud before glancing back at Tatum, who watched me with an eyebrow raised as I typed out a quick response.

Tatum's the guy who owns the mechanic shop. And had I known that guys like this existed outside of LA, I might have left a long time ago. Ha!

"Who are you chatting with?" His voice startled me, sending chills shooting through me, but I willed myself to stay calm.

"My best friend, Quinn," I responded without turning around.

"What are you two girls talking about?" he teased, but I was too embarrassed to admit the truth.

"Just letting her know where I am. And she might have asked who you were."

He pushed off from the couch and stood behind me as I quickly minimized the window on the computer screen, which made him whine, "I wanted to see what you wrote."

"I bet you did," I teased back, my earlier defenses lowering.

His breath was hot on my neck as his hands gripped the chair and brushed against my shoulders. "So, what did you say about me?"

I angled my head slightly and his face appeared in my view, way too close. Holding my breath, I said, "Nothing. Just that you were the guy who owned the shop that was fixing my car."

"Uh-huh," he mumbled before walking away and into the kitchen.

Reopening the computer window, I logged out of my e-mail and turned off the monitor. I stood up and headed toward the door, needing to get away from whatever this was. "I better go to bed."

"I'll let you know about the tire as soon as I hear back from my guy."

I nodded. "Sounds good."

"'Night, Paige," he drawled, and I fought the urge to walk over to him and wrap my arms around his waist and breathe him in.

"'Night, Tatum." I pulled the door shut behind me and stepped into the warm Southern evening, the sound of crickets serenading me as I headed back to the main house.

I WOKE UP the next morning refreshed and relaxed. It had been a dreamless night, free of stress, deadlines, and unkind memories of Colin. The sound of birds chirping and other insect noises I'd yet to become accustomed to greeted my ears. Reaching my arms above my head, I clasped my hands together and stretched, my body popping and realigning itself with my movements. The smell of muffins wafted into my room, and my stomach growled.

Rubbing at my tummy, I tossed the covers off and hopped out of bed. It was definitely weird not having anywhere to be, anyone to call, or anyone to report to. It was one thing when I had a vacation or a short break from filming, but this felt different. Maybe it was because I ran away. Or maybe it was because I was the one making decisions for what felt like the first time in forever.

While part of me had never felt so settled (and relieved), the other part of me hated sitting still. I'd never been very good at relaxing and doing nothing, but I decided to force myself to try. I deserved this. Hell, I needed this. And all of this peace would end far too soon if I allowed it.

"Good morning, Paige. I didn't want to wake you. I hope that was okay." Mrs. Montgomery turned to greet me from the kitchen as I plodded down the hallway in my shorts and tank top. Putting down the newspaper, she asked, "How'd you sleep?"

"Great. Thank you."

"Are you hungry? I made some muffins with the blueberries from outside, and I can whip you up some fresh eggs and bacon, if you'd like?"

"The muffins smell amazing. I don't need anything else," I said, reaching for one out of the basket on the counter. When I took a bite, the steam burned my mouth, and I fought the urge to spit it out all over the table. I swallowed, forced a smile, and asked if she had any milk, all while trying to appear semi-normal.

Laughing, she poured me a small glass. "I should have mentioned they were hot. Did you get to e-mail your family last night?" Her tone hinted at something more.

"I did. Thank you. I actually need to check my e-mail again, if that's okay?"

"Of course, dear. The back house is always unlocked. And Tatum's at work already. Probably trying to get you that tire, so you can get on out of here." Her face fell and she looked away for a second, then she brightened and patted my arm. "You should go see him if you don't have any plans."

I scrunched my face at her suggestion and said, "I don't

have any plans, but I don't think I should go see him either."

"Oh, I just meant that you should go ask about your car was all." Her cheeks turned rosy and I wondered what she was up to, but didn't dare ask.

"I thought I might walk around your property, if you don't mind." When Tatum brought me here yesterday, I noticed that the land seemed to stretch for miles. There was a path through the tall grass and trees that begged me to explore it.

"Of course. That's a great idea. The swimming hole's not too far down the pathway, if you want to go for a dip."

"Swimming hole? That's a real thing?" I probably sounded like a complete idiot, but that term was one I'd only heard in old TV shows and movies. I'd never actually heard it said in real life.

She let out a little chuckle. "It is very much a real thing. There's even a tree with a rope swing," she added, gently teasing me.

"I'm sorry. I know I sound stupid, it's just that I've never been anywhere like this before." I blew at my muffin before biting into it again, and chewed slowly.

"Sweetie, the last thing I think you are is stupid. But make sure you wear bug spray for the mosquitoes. Oh, and there's a beach towel in the linen closet next to your room."

"Thank you so much," I said after I swallowed. "Oh yeah, can I get your phone number so that I can give it to my mom and best friend?"

"Absolutely," she said as she moved toward the table. "I'll just write it down for you." She scribbled onto a piece of scrap paper. "Make sure you tell them to call anytime."

"I will. Thanks again," I said, looking around. "Where's Buster?"

"Tatum takes him to the shop sometimes. It's a shame too, because Buster loves that swimming hole." She extended her hand and I reached for the piece of paper.

"Does he go in?" I asked seriously.

"Does he go in? It's more like, can someone please keep Buster out of the dang swimming hole!" She waved her arms around for emphasis, making me laugh.

"Well, now I wish he was here. Might be fun to have a partner in crime." I tossed the last bite of muffin into my mouth.

"I imagine that someone else might be up for that job," she said, her eyebrows raised meaningfully.

"Mrs. Montgomery, stop it. Your son can barely stand to be around me, let alone want to be my partner in anything." I probably sounded flustered, but decided not to try to hide it.

She gave me a mock frown. "I thought we went through this already, dear. I realize you just got here, but I see the way my boy looks at you. I haven't seen that spark in his eyes since his daddy died. So if you're not careful, you might get a heck of a lot more than just a partner in crime during this vacation of yours." She sipped her coffee and eyed me over the top of the cup.

I measured her words carefully against my already unbalanced heart. Hearing them didn't register with my brain. None of it made sense. There was no way Tatum's eyes did anything except narrow with annoyance at my presence. Partner in crime? No way. He probably wished I'd just head on right out of town.

Unsure how to respond to that, I mumbled, "Well, I guess I'll go grab that towel now."

"I didn't mean to make you uncomfortable, Paige. I'm sorry." Mrs. Montgomery set her coffee mug down on top of the counter and took a step toward me.

"You didn't. I just…" I paused and shrugged. "I just think you're wrong about Tatum and me is all."

She nodded and waved me off. "You're probably right. Now, the swimming hole is about a ten-minute walk down the path. You don't need to stray from the path at all, it will lead you right to it. It's real peaceful, I think you'll enjoy it."

"I still can't believe places like this exist," I said with a smile.

"Surely you've been to the South for filming before, haven't you?" she asked as she tilted her head to the side.

I shook my head. "I have, but it wasn't like this. And I didn't get a chance to explore or go sightseeing, you know?"

"Well, you're here now. In the true South. Might as well enjoy it."

My smile widened. "I couldn't agree more."

No Rush to Leave

TATUM

FRESH COFFEE AND sandwich in hand from the café, I walked side by side with Buster down the narrow street back toward the garage. Buster was my dad's dog, and he used to bring him to work almost every day. The damn dog even had a giant puffy bed thing in the corner of the office. Dad used to say that the dog would sleep all day long, snoring away through the pounding and the machines. He used to think that was the funniest thing ever, the way Buster would sleep through life. But he loved that dog. And I loved my dad. It sucked without him here.

I pulled my old man's chair back from the desk, sat down, and turned on the computer. Buster whined at my side. "What's the matter, boy?" He did that sometimes now. He'd stare at me and whine like he was telling me some secret I couldn't understand, or he'd head over to the place where we found my dad's body, then lie down next to it. Damn near killed me when he did that shit.

Pushing the memory from my mind, I shook my head and sipped my coffee. Opening up the latest e-mail from my tire guy, I read his response carefully.

It will most likely take me a few days, maybe even a week to get that kind of tire in. Who the hell is driving a BMW in these parts?

I laughed to myself and wrote back:

Just a tourist. Take your time with the tire; she's in no rush.

Pressing SEND, I sat back. What the hell did I just write? Take your time? She's in no rush? Who the hell was I to speak for Paige? Clearly, I was the one who was in no rush to get her out of town. The bigger question was: Why?

A response pinged on the computer, and I winced at the e-mail's title:

You're in luck!

I clicked on the message to reveal the whole thing.

The tire will be in first thing tomorrow morning. I'll have it delivered by the afternoon.

I responded with a quick thank-you, then slammed my fist on the desk before grabbing my coffee cup. Tomorrow? The last thing I wanted was Paige out of my life by tomorrow. Thoughts of her leaving drove me half mad.

I picked up the phone and dialed Mama's number. When

she answered on the second ring, I impatiently tapped my pen on top of the desk and asked, "Hey, Mama, is Paige there?"

"I just sent her off to the swimming hole. Sorry, hon."

I stopped tapping. "Did she go there alone?"

"No. I sent her with all her friends."

Smartass. "Very funny," I snapped. "What if people are there, Ma?"

She sucked in a quick breath. "Shoot, Tatum. I didn't even think about that."

Even though the swimming hole was on our property, my high school friends and their little brothers and sisters would sneak on and hang out there most days in the summer. It wasn't like we didn't know they were doing it; we just didn't care. It never mattered before today if our water was the most popular hangout spot in the area.

"I'll head over there and make sure she's okay," Mama offered, and the fine hairs on my neck bristled.

"No. I'll do it. I don't want anyone giving her a hard time. With this hot weather, if she's alone, I doubt she will be for long."

"I'm sorry. I wasn't thinking. Did you hear about her tire?"

"It won't be here for a week," I said, the lie slipping easily from my mouth.

"Oh dear. She'll have to stay for a whole week then, huh? I hope she'll be okay with that," Mama said sweetly, but her tone told me she was up to something.

"I'll tell her when I see her. I gotta finish up some paperwork and make some phone calls before I head out. Talk to you later, Ma."

I hung up before she said anything, knowing I'd get an earful for that move later. Mama hated being hung up on and scolded me any chance she could about my Southern manners. I should have called her back to apologize, but right now I was too flustered to think about anything other than Paige. Anyone could be at the swimming hole, and she had no idea she might have some unwanted company.

I knew she wasn't some vulnerable and weak little girl, but something in me wanted to protect her. Maybe it was seeing her broken down on the side of the road, totally clueless about where to go or what to do. Or maybe it was knowing what her dickhead ex-boyfriend had done to her publicly that made me want to wrap her in my arms and lock her away. Hell, I didn't know what it was about Paige Lockwood, but I felt like I'd go to battle for her.

Scrolling through the rest of my e-mails, I answered the ones I could and made phone calls with updates to the rest. I finished up my paperwork, checked in on outstanding orders, and called it a day. Before I left, I put up the sign letting people know I was away from the office for the rest of the day. That usually meant I was either at home, or driving out of town to pick up a part or an order. It wasn't unusual for me to be gone for hours at a time on weekdays.

Everyone knew how to get a hold of me, and if anyone needed anything, I'd be right there. I handled a lot of farm machines and trucks, ordering new parts for the worn-out old ones and putting them in. The cars in this town seemed to last forever, but the machines tended to break more than they used to. Of course there were the typical new tires, oil changes, and the like, but most of the men here handled that stuff on their own. They would order the oil and tire from me, but as far as the labor went, they managed it themselves. It was when the big things happened, like engines and transmissions blowing, that I needed to get involved and get my hands dirty.

But the girls in town preferred to have every little thing done in my shop. Hell, they'd have me adjust their rearview mirror for them if I'd do it. I wasn't stupid enough to pretend I didn't know why; it just irritated me more than anything. I'd grown up with everyone here and had known them my whole life. That was the thing about a small town like this—it was hard to have feelings more than friendship for most of the people who lived in it.

After Brina dumped me, I'd never thought about girls much. Never gave any consideration to getting married, or having another girlfriend. I simply didn't care anymore. Girls weren't worth the heartache.

And I'd be lying if I said I didn't find it hard to trust again. Brina took every ounce of trust and belief I'd had in our relationship and discarded it like a piece of unwanted garbage. Talk about feeling worthless. It took me months to realize she was the problem, not me. But to say that I wasn't scarred would be another lie.

That relationship practically destroyed my sense of self-worth. I never wanted to feel like that again, so I didn't allow it. I kept myself closed off from everyone and I refused to open up. It was just easier that way. Keeping everything locked up inside was effortless when you didn't have anyone you wanted to share it all with.

Swimming Hole

PAIGE

I FOLLOWED MRS. MONTGOMERY'S directions and walked down the dirt pathway carved through her property. Plush green grass grew tall on each side of me and the trees were large, overgrown, and spectacular. I'd never been surrounded by so much greenery before. Los Angeles was mostly concrete and brown since we didn't get much rain. Not to mention the fact that people couldn't stop building things on every piece of available space there was. Seeing a landscape filled with so much color was awe inspiring.

In moments like these, I wished I were the creative type. If I were a painter, I'd stop and paint the scene around me. If I could draw, I'd sketch the way the tree branches dipped low and looked like arms bearing heavy loads. But since I could do neither of those things without putting out something that looked like it was done by a second grader, I simply scanned the area and committed it to memory. Sure, I could have pulled out my phone and taken a picture of it, but it wouldn't be the same. Sometimes a photograph didn't do a place justice the way physically being there did.

When the swimming hole came into view, I stopped and smiled to myself as the trees thinned out to reveal this perfect little area. It was like something straight out of a movie set. I realized I always compared everything to movie screens and sets, but that had been my life for the last seven years and had formed my frame of reference.

What Mrs. Montgomery referred to as a swimming hole was actually a bend in the river that was wider than the rest. The water slowed here, probably because it was deeper, and the banks were rounded, reminding me of a secluded lagoon.

Large rocks lined one side of the hole, and tree branches hung low over the water, nearly dipping in. The rope swing dangled in almost the middle of the water, and I realized that I had to climb out onto a tree branch if I wanted to reach it. The area around the water looked like it had been groomed to mimic a shoreline. All the small pebbles had been cleared and the sandy ground was smoothed out evenly. I spread my towel across it and lay down, listening to nothing but the sound of the water moving and the birds chirping.

My entire being relaxed as sunlight streamed through the tree branches and warmed my skin. Mrs. Montgomery was right. It was peaceful.

"Oh, hi. We didn't know anyone was here."

The sound of female voices startled me, and I practically jumped off the ground before I even opened my eyes. I glanced up to see two girls who appeared to be around my age looking down at me. Sitting up, I took inventory of the newcomers. One was blond, while the other was a fiery redhead. They were both striking in their appearance, making me wish I'd put on makeup this morning.

The girls inspected me from head to toe as I silently waited for the recognition to kick in. It was my experience that the majority of girls my own age knew who I was. Even if they weren't fans of my movies, they knew me anyway.

"Oh shit, are you Paige Lockwood?" the pretty blonde asked from behind her oversized sunglasses, her head tilted to one side as she elbowed her redheaded friend in the ribs.

I sucked in a quick breath and steadied the nervousness that suddenly surged through my body. I could have tried to lie to them, but I was never a good liar. "Yeah."

"Oh my gosh! I loved you in *Summer Rain*. It's one of my favorite movies!" the girl gushed.

My cheeks warmed and I mumbled, "Thanks."

"Oh my gosh, I can't believe it's really you. This is so cool!" she continued, and I didn't know how to respond. I was never sure what to say in situations like this where the person wasn't really asking a question, but more making comments. Fortunately, I didn't have to stumble for long before she cooed, "So, what's it really like to make out with all the hottest guys in Hollywood?"

That question I could answer easily. "It's not like you

think," I said with a smile.

"What do you mean? You've had like the hottest guys in all your movies. Kissing them has to be the best thing ever!"

I nodded. "But it's work. And you're not alone when you're filming these scenes that are supposed to be super romantic, you know?"

The blonde shook her head and said, "No. What do you mean?"

"We're surrounded by a ton of crew members. Someone's making sure the lighting is hitting us just right, and there's a guy holding a giant boom mic to pick up all our lines and sounds." I held my arms up to mimic what it was like to hold out the giant microphone on the heavy pole. "And there's the director and the assistant director, the makeup artists, wardrobe."

"Ew. That's a lot of people watching you make out," the redhead said as she scrunched up her face.

"Exactly." I nodded. "Not romantic. At all."

"Well, that stinks," the blonde said. "So, what are you doing here anyway?"

"My car got a flat, so I'm just here until Tatum gets it fixed."

His name slipped off my tongue with such ease, it almost surprised me as much as it did the blond girl. At the mention of him, her body language changed completely and her stance became defensive as she crossed her arms over her chest.

"Ah, so the BMW is yours, I take it?" she asked, her tone now overly sweet, but in a way that warned me to proceed with caution. "It's a really nice car. Tatum showed it to me yesterday at the shop."

The redhead glanced at her, then frowned and made a face.

"He showed you my car?" I asked, not quite believing her.

She nodded, her lips pressed together in a fake smile. "I'm sure Tatum will fix it up in no time. He's good at everything he does." Then she pinned me with a knowing look as she added, "If you know what I mean."

My skin prickled with her words and my chest felt like it was filled with bricks as I inhaled each breath. I hated what this girl was insinuating. It was ridiculous for me to care so much about a virtual stranger, but I didn't like thinking that Tatum belonged to anyone, much less this kind of girl. Jealous feelings flowed through me before I could think about where they came from or why they were there.

My emotions confused me. Just a few days ago I was mourning the loss of Colin and being humiliated by his actions, and today I was getting all jealous at the thought of a guy I didn't even know had a girlfriend. Who does that?

I wanted to reach inside my chest, pull my heart out, and have a frank discussion with it about its behavior. We needed to be on the same page, or at least in the same book.

The redhead extended her hand. "I'm Celeste and this is Brina. She's Tatum's *ex*-girlfriend." Celeste emphasized the ex part, much to Brina's dismay, and the bricks in my chest immediately burst, making breathing much easier.

"It's nice to meet you," I said with a smile. The last thing I needed was enemies, or crazy ex-girlfriends causing me any more personal drama.

"And I love all your movies. You're a great actress," Celeste added, sounding genuine.

I gave her a quick smile. "Thank you. I really appreciate that."

"Oh yeah, we're big fans," Brina chimed in. "I made Tatum watch all your movies. He was always—" Brina stopped short, her face twisted with whatever thoughts she was suddenly thinking. She didn't finish her sentence, and I didn't press.

"Thanks again. That's really nice of you both. And I definitely appreciate you making your boyfriends sit through my girly flicks," I said with a laugh.

"I don't ever remember Tatum complaining," Celeste teased, and Brina scowled at her.

"He hated when I made him watch your movies."

"They usually do," I said, trying to sound nonchalant, but my insides were bruised. The idea of Tatum hating what I did for a living hurt my feelings. Quinn was right; I was too sensitive.

Brina turned to flap her towel in the air before she settled it onto the dirt not far from mine. Celeste followed suit. "I hope it's still okay if we hang out here with you? We like to come here to lay out during the day when we can."

"It's fine with me. Some company would be nice," I admitted, although I didn't want this to turn into some sort of Q-and-A session that would be sold to the tabloids the second

I left town. I hated having to constantly be on guard and watch the things that came out of my mouth, but that was one of the harsh realities of the business I was in. Anything I said could be sold, misconstrued, or used against me if the person were malicious enough.

The girls lay down on their towels, then began to apply sunscreen to their legs and stomachs. "So, what are you doing all the way out in Hanford, Paige?" Brina asked.

I supposed there was no harm in answering that question. Tatum and his mom had asked the same thing. My deeper personal reasons were no one's business but mine, so I answered vaguely, "I just needed to get out of LA for a little while. And my car got a flat, so here I am."

"Oh yeah, we read all about what Colin did to you," Celeste said angrily.

"I think everyone did," I admitted, embarrassed.

"What a jerk. Who does that and thinks they aren't going to get caught?" she added.

I shrugged. "I don't know."

"Well, he's a real jerk, Paige. You're better off without him."

"Thanks, Celeste."

"But he's so hot. I bet he's an awesome kisser," Brina added before slapping her hand over her mouth. "I'm sorry. It just slipped out."

"She's always speaking before she thinks," Celeste said, then smacked her friend on the arm.

"It's okay. He is really good-looking. But that only goes so far when everything else about you sucks." I instantly wished I could inhale the words back into my mouth as my mind flashed to a tabloid headline that read "Paige Lockwood Says Everything About Colin McGuire Sucks!" I needed to be more careful.

"Did he ever write any songs about you?" Brina asked, and I actually laughed.

"No. Colin doesn't write his own music."

"Seriously?" both girls asked in unison.

"Seriously. Not a single lyric," I admitted, and felt good how that fact seemed like a slam against Colin. One more thing he didn't do well, or at all.

Celeste's eyes grew wide. "Wow. I'm shocked."

"Don't be. A lot of singers don't write their own stuff. I think it's more rare when they actually do."

"So, how long do you think you'll stay in town?" Brina asked.

"I'm not sure, actually." My thoughts instantly drifted to Tatum's body last night when he opened his door, shirtless and wet. Everything in me suddenly buzzed with energy and I longed to be near him, even if it wasn't what he wanted. I enjoyed the way my body reacted to his.

"Well, you should definitely come to the field party tonight," Celeste said.

"Oh yeah? What is it?" My interest was ignited. I'd never heard of a field party, but I assumed it was pretty much what the name implied.

"It's a giant party," Celeste answered.

"Oh my gosh, yes. Paige, you have to come. You'll love it," Brina added.

"What's it like?"

Brina sat up, her face filled with excitement. "Everyone drives their big ol' trucks out to the middle of the field. There's always lots of beer and dancing—"

Then Celeste chimed in, "The guys usually do keg stands and act stupid. Someone always gets in a fight—"

Brina cut her off. "But it's entertaining and just some good old-fashioned fun out in the open with no one else around. I guarantee you've never seen anything like it in LA, sweetie."

She might have called me sweetie, but I knew there was a thinly veiled insult behind it. Before I could think up a response, Buster bounded over toward me with a stuffed toy in his mouth. "Buster, what are you doing here?" I looked around as I patted his head, knowing he had been at the shop with Tatum.

Buster moved over to the girls and Brina shrieked, "Ugh, get away from me, Buster," as she shoved at the oversized dog.

"Buster, come here," I said, and he jogged toward me.

The leaves rustled and Tatum appeared in view. The smirk that appeared on his face as he eyed my bathing suit was quickly replaced with a sour look when he noticed the girls next to me. Buster sat at my feet as I continued to scratch him.

Brina jumped up, her body barely covered in the tiny black bikini she wore as she moved toward him. "Hey, Tatum," she crooned, pressing her chest against his and running her hand down his well-defined arm. His eyes looked past hers and locked onto mine.

I swallowed hard and tried to force myself to look away, but couldn't. My eyes refused to leave Tatum's, and I stopped the smile from forming on my lips as I watched him step away from her and remove her arm. "You girls aren't giving Paige a hard time, are you?" His voice was stern.

Celeste glanced at me before looking back at Tatum with a smile. "No, sir. We were just telling her about the party tonight and insisted she come along."

Tatum dropped his chin as he kicked at the ground. "Is that so?"

"It sounds like fun," I said, and he raised his head to look at me.

"So you want to go?" he asked, almost as if he couldn't believe it.

Brina moved toward him again and he put up a hand to stop her. She placed one hand on her hip and said, "You don't have to come along, Tatum. We all know how much you hate socializing these days. She can come with us. We'll take good care of her. Promise."

My insides twisted. The party had sounded fun and I did want to go, but not without Tatum. I wouldn't even consider going if he weren't there. There was no way I trusted Brina to be alone with me at some random party. Too many things could go wrong. If anyone wanted to set me up or mess with me here, I had a feeling it would be her.

"If Paige wants to go, I'll be the one who takes her," Tatum informed a now-scowling Brina.

"I'm pretty sure Paige can make decisions for herself. She doesn't have to go with you if she doesn't want to," Brina shot back, clearly pissed off for whatever reason. They both turned to look at me, while Celeste quietly observed the chaos. Maybe she was used to the two of them acting like this?

They all waited for me to say something, and I wanted it to be clear that my loyalties, however misguided, lay with Tatum, so I said, "If I decide to go tonight, I'll go with Tatum."

His mouth began to turn up into a smile before he bit it back and turned toward Celeste. "Is it at Luke's farm?" he asked, completely ignoring his ex.

"Like always," she responded with a tight smile. I could tell she was holding back a laugh. I realized in that moment that I liked Celeste.

As Tatum held out a hand to me, I instinctively reached for it as if it was the most natural thing on earth. Under normal circumstances I might have fought him on it, but Brina made me uncomfortable, and I sensed he didn't like me hanging out with her. He pulled me to my feet and I fought the urge to grip his hand in mine so tightly that he couldn't let me go. Instead, he released me easily once I was standing, and my body mourned the loss of his energy that trickled through me whenever he touched me.

After I shimmied into my cutoff jean shorts and threw on my tank top, Tatum grabbed my towel and motioned for me to follow him. "Bye, you guys. I guess I'll see you later." I waved at the two girls, who were leaning toward each other whispering something I couldn't hear.

"See you tonight. 'Bye," they both yelled before returning to their private conversation.

Tatum walked in front of me as he tossed Buster's toy for him to fetch. Once we were out of earshot, I teased, "Well, that was the quickest swimming-hole excursion I've ever had."

He stopped on the path and turned to face me, his expression serious. "Stay away from Brina, Paige. I mean it."

"She found me, not the other way around," I said innocently as he moved closer toward me. With each step he took, my heart thudded more painfully inside my chest. He leaned toward me, his lips mere inches from mine, and I held my breath in anticipation of what might come. Fighting my attraction for Tatum was a lot of work.

"You can't trust her," he whispered, and I prayed for him to close the space between us completely. Instead, he turned back around as I stood there dumbfounded, fighting for air.

Field Parties Are a Bad Idea

TATUM

SEEING PAIGE WITH Brina royally pissed me off. I had been so happy for all of two seconds when I first saw Paige in the clearing, her black-and-white bikini showing off way more skin than I ever thought I'd see. But then I noticed we weren't alone, and any happiness I felt evaporated into the hot and humid air. The last thing I needed was for Brina to go filling Paige's head with lies, stories, and her version of the truth.

"Paige, did you ask the girls not to tell anyone you were here?" I asked, suddenly remembering that Paige was trying to recover from heartbreak and she needed space.

She shook her head, her long brown ponytail moving with it. "I figured if we were going to a party tonight, that's sort of pointless. Don't you think?"

Buster ran back to my side, toy in his mouth, and I grabbed it and chucked it across the field. "Shit." Why'd they have to go and tell her about the party?

"What's wrong?" Paige's eyes narrowed and she looked genuinely sad.

"I don't like the idea of everyone knowing you're here. After this party, Paige, the whole town will know you're here. And then who knows what else will happen after that."

"Is that really a bad thing? I mean, will they tell? Can't we ask them not to say anything to anyone?"

"We can try, but I'm not sure it will work. Most of the people here are good folk. But this might be too much for even them to handle. It's more excitement than we've had in years."

I laughed because it was true, but my chest ached at not being able to promise her privacy. Paige being here would be front-page news of our newspaper, if we had one.

"Give me a minute," I said, handing Paige her towel before running back the way we'd come, leaving Paige standing in the middle of the field with Buster jumping around her.

Jogging back toward the swimming hole, I prayed Brina and Celeste hadn't left yet. The last thing I wanted to do was have to call Brina on the phone. I'd done a pretty good job of avoiding that task since we'd broken up. I entered the clearing and saw them lying on their towels, chatting away.

"Oh, Tatum. You came back." Brina sat up immediately, her blond hair falling down around her shoulders. I hated that my dick twitched at the sight of her. What my dick should do is curl up inside itself and run away screaming. If there was ever truth to the rumor that guys' penises acted on their own accord, this was the proof. *Earth to penis, this one's bad news. Down, boy.*

"I just wanted to ask you girls to please keep the fact that Paige is here to yourself. She really needs the privacy right now, and she wants to relax without any of the typical craziness."

"What do you care?" Brina whined, and I wished someone would knock some sense into her.

"I care because Paige is a nice girl. She's just trying to catch a break, and if her agent or whatever finds out where she is, he'll come get her and make her go home." I didn't know why I spilled this much personal information, but I needed them to know how important it was that they keep their mouths shut.

"I won't say anything to anyone," Celeste said. "And if you guys come tonight, I'll help keep everyone else quiet about it too."

"Yeah, Tatum. No one's really going to care that she's here. I mean, they'll care," Brina said slowly, "but no one will want her to leave."

Celeste laughed. "Brina's right. They'll all just want to be friends with her."

I shook my head, the list of cons for taking Paige to the party growing with each word they spoke. "Well, just don't say anything. Please? I'm asking nicely."

"We already said we wouldn't. God, Tatum, I always knew you had a thing for her. Every time we'd watch one of her movies you'd—"

I cut her off. "I don't have a thing for her, okay? I barely even know her."

"You sure seem to care an awful lot about someone you barely know," Brina added with a frown, then lay back down on her towel and turned her head away.

I kicked at the dirt and tried to stop feeling so damned frustrated, but dealing with Brina made everything ten times worse. Stalking away, I balled my hands into fists before releasing them. I refused to let Brina affect me. Seeing Paige ahead in the distance waiting for me, I broke into a jog as my anger dissipated.

"Sorry. I wanted to ask them to keep quiet about you being here."

Paige smiled and I stared at her mouth. Like, I couldn't take my eyes off her full lips and I wanted to feel them, taste them, have them pressed against mine.

"What'd they say?" she asked, her voice interrupting my inappropriate thoughts.

"They said they would."

"That's a good start, right?"

I think she gave people more credit than they deserved, but I didn't want to disappoint her. "Yeah, it's a good start." I smiled back at her, and even though it didn't seem possible, her smile grew larger. She was so damned optimistic, and it made me want her even more.

We walked side by side the rest of the way to Mama's house as my insides tore in two. One half wanted to stop overthinking everything in my life and enjoy whatever time I had with Paige doing whatever she'd allow me to do with her, while the other half refused to let down its guard. I didn't handle being hurt well; I'd learned that from experience. But weren't some people worth the risk?

I wasn't so sure.

As we neared the house, I was no closer to an answer.

Partying in the South
PAIGE

WITH ALL THE excitement of Tatum crashing my swimming-hole party and making me leave, I'd completely forgotten about my car. I didn't even think to ask him about when the tire would be in. And the honest-to-God truth was that at the moment, I didn't care at all. I'd stay here all summer if I could. And I think I'd like it. I liked the way he acted like he was protecting me. With Tatum, it didn't seem self-serving; he seemed to genuinely want to keep me safe. Part of me didn't know how to reconcile that in my head. I could count on one hand how many people truly cared about me.

After changing out of my bikini, I walked into the kitchen to hear Tatum and his mom talking about me.

"Tatum. Take her to the field. It will be fun for her," his

mom insisted, and Tatum grunted.

"You grunt a lot," I said, announcing my presence.

"What?" He glanced at me from the corner of his eye.

"That sound. You do it a lot when you're irritated. Or maybe you just do it a lot around me because I irritate you."

He looked away. "You don't irritate me."

"Coulda fooled me."

His head finally turned in my direction and his blue eyes pierced right through me. "I already told you I'm not good at making small talk."

"Tatum, stop snapping at her and apologize this instant!" his mom yelled before smacking him on the back of the head.

"Sorry."

"I did not raise you to be so impolite to a guest, or to a woman for that matter," she said, and stomped a foot on the floor for emphasis.

"You're right, Mama."

Seeing his relationship with his mom only made him hotter in my eyes. Who didn't swoon over a man who respected his mom?

"It's okay, Mrs. Montgomery, clearly he can't help himself. I'm sure you did the best you could." I felt awful for Tatum's mom getting caught in our crossfire, but I headed into my room and closed the door before I could take it all back.

The screen door slammed shut, followed by a light knock on my bedroom door. A woman's voice called out, "Paige, can I come in?"

"Of course," I said from my bed. When Mrs. Montgomery walked in, I apologized immediately. "I didn't mean to say that to you. I was just trying to get to him."

She smiled warmly. "I know, but I still wanted to apologize for my son."

I waved her off. "Don't. I'm getting used to it."

"You absolutely are not. And you shouldn't have to." Her Southern accent grew more pronounced the more upset she got. "No gentleman treats a lady that way. Not in my home," she said hotly.

"I don't think he means it. And I don't think he can help it when it comes to me," I admitted to her.

"You might be right." She laid a warm hand on top of mine and squeezed it gently.

Longing to change the subject, I asked, "So, what do girls wear to these field parties anyway?"

Her face lit up. "Ooh! The girls either wear shorts or dresses. It's so warm in the evenings that you can wear what you wore that day. But they usually cute it up some."

I smiled back. "I think I have some things that will work."

"What size shoe do you wear?"

I looked down at my feet, as if they would give me the answer. "Seven."

"I think I might have a pair of boots that will fit you if you want to wear them."

"Cowboy boots?" My mood perked up.

"Yep."

"That would be amazing. Thank you."

When I beamed at her, she hopped off the bed. "Be right back."

A moment later I heard the sound of boxes falling and crashing. Before I could shout to ask if she needed my help, she was back in my room holding the most beautiful pair of brown leather boots I'd ever seen. Granted, I'd never really looked at boots before, but these were amazing.

"These have never been worn," she said. "They were a gift, but unfortunately they didn't fit. Too small."

I reached out and brought the boots to my nose, inhaling while closing my eyes. "These smell so good." Then I froze, wondering if I looked like a total creeper sniffing someone else's footwear. My cheeks burned as I tried to cover for myself. "Uh, was that weird? I'm sorry. It's the leather."

Mrs. Montgomery laughed. "I do it all the time. There's nothing like the smell of new leather. Aren't they gorgeous? I love the detail."

Gold rivets adorned the boots, and a tan stitched design weaved from the top to the bottom. No less than four varying shades of brown were visible and I had no idea why, but Mrs. Montgomery told me it was because each pair was handmade and the leather was worked throughout the process in a way that created the numerous shades.

"I love everything about them."

"Try them on," she insisted.

"Do I wear them with socks?" I asked, feeling once again like a complete idiot. "I'm sorry I ask such stupid questions all the time."

"They're not stupid, Paige. How would you know? And yes, you wear them with socks."

Grabbing a pair of white cotton socks, I pulled them on and slipped my feet into the waiting boots. They seemed snug at first until I stood. I walked around the room, the heels of the boots clicking against the hardwood floors. "They are so comfortable. Who knew?"

"Do they fit? They look great!"

"I think they fit. They feel good." I wasn't entirely sure how boots like this were supposed to feel. Obviously my toes didn't go into the pointy part, which I assumed would be as uncomfortable as all get-out.

"Great! Then you'll wear them tonight to the party," she said before pushing herself off my bed.

I widened my eyes. "Are you sure?"

"Absolutely. They sit in a box in my closet. They deserve to see a night out."

"Thank you so much," I said, then enveloped her in a warm hug.

A LITTLE LATER, I walked around the back of the main house toward the barn. When I knocked on the door, memories of last night flooded my mind. Tatum had taken over my brain and turned me into some horny teenager. I'd been around good-looking guys my whole life, but this…this was different. Tatum was smoking hot, but he was real. And his genuine nature, no matter how brutally honest, pulled me to him even more.

"Hi," he said as he opened the door.

I looked into his deep blue eyes and said, "I'm sorry about earlier." Why was I apologizing again?

"Me too."

With that out of the way, I asked, "Do you think I could use the computer again?"

"Of course," he said, holding open the screen door. I brushed past him as I entered and forced myself to keep walking when all I wanted to do was turn around and run my hands all over his well-formed chest.

Sitting down at the desk, I noticed the computer was already on, so I logged back in to my personal e-mail. My mom had e-mailed, wanting all the information for where I was staying, including full names and addresses. She told me if I didn't have them, to get them. I wanted to roll my eyes, but she was right to want that stuff, and I quickly typed out an e-mail telling her everything I knew about where I was and who I was spending my time with, including the phone number to Mrs. Montgomery's house.

And then I sent Quinn the same e-mail with the same information, plus a little extra. I told her all about Brina and about the field party. I told her that I wished she were here, experiencing all of this with me. E-mailing her wasn't the same as hearing her voice, so I told her to call me soon.

I continued to ignore the other e-mails from my agent,

manager, publicist, and everyone else, figuring that they could all wait until I was ready to deal with them. It surprised me how good it felt to claim some of my power back, although a small part of me felt like I was just avoiding everything and that avoidance didn't really equal power.

While I was relieved to have left town, I also felt cowardly. As if running away was a weak move, even if it had been necessary. And I convinced myself that it had been absolutely necessary to leave. I imagined myself sitting in a corner in my apartment all alone, rocking back and forth, if I hadn't gotten out of there when I did.

I logged off and turned around, searching for Tatum. He was standing in the kitchen watching me, but his eyes had a faraway look about them.

"So, about tonight…" I started, and watched as his eyes blinked and refocused.

"What about it?"

"I wanna go."

"Have you thought about this, Paige? I mean, really thought about this?" He crossed the space between us and stood in front of me.

"What is there to think about?"

"The repercussions of your actions, maybe? That going to this party might ruin everything for you?"

I let out an exasperated breath. "Tatum, just stop."

"Stop what?" he asked as he tucked his hands inside his jeans pockets.

"You're trying to control me, and that's exactly why I left

LA in the first place. I don't need more people in my life telling me what I can and can't do."

"I don't want to control you. I just want to protect you," he said, and the sincerity of his words took the edge off my anger.

"Protect me? I don't need you to protect me. I just want to do something normal. But I don't want to do it without you. Please come with me tonight."

He looked conflicted as he pondered my request. I didn't want to fight with him, but I would in order to get what I wanted. And right now, I craved normalcy. I longed for something typical. And a Southern field party was something I wanted to experience.

"Okay."

"Okay?" I repeated with a slight smile.

"We'll go."

"Yay!" I hopped up and wrapped my arms around his shoulders without thinking, my body pressing against his in every place it could. I felt him harden against me as he quickly pushed me away. "Sorry," I said quickly, feeling stupid, but secretly turned on by what had just happened.

"We'll head out after dinner," was all he said before leaving me standing alone in his living room.

I knew Tatum was attracted to me. I could see it in the way he looked at me, but he apparently had far more self-control than I did. He had indifference down to a fine art, and every time he hit me with it, I felt dumber and dumber.

"Tatum?" I shouted toward his bedroom, and he poked

his head out from the doorway with his eyebrows raised in response. "Any word about my car?"

Changing the subject seemed to be a good idea. Maybe if we focused on something else, he'd stop running away from me.

"The tire's going to take a week to get here," he said flatly.

"A week?" I honestly didn't care, but my surprise made my words come out sounding as if I were annoyed.

He blinked, then said deliberately, "It's a specialized tire, so it's taking extra time. I can put a rush on it if you need to get out of here sooner. I'll go to town and pick it up or—"

He was shutting me out again; I could see it written all over his face, so I shook my head and interrupted him. "No. It's okay. I was just surprised, but you know I'm not in any rush."

Did he know I wasn't in any rush?

Well, he did now.

AFTER CHANGING INTO my dark brown sundress that went perfectly with Mrs. Montgomery's leather boots, I accessorized with some turquoise jewelry and was all set to go. When I stepped out of my room, I found Tatum waiting for me wearing a pair of dark blue jeans and a black sleeveless shirt. His arm muscles bulged with definition, and his baseball cap was on backward, covering his dark brown hair. He looked as hot as hell, and I wanted to meet the hell maker.

Tatum examined me from head to toe, hesitating on my legs for a moment, long enough for me to catch him doing it. I smiled, happy he liked what he saw, even if he'd never admit it.

We walked together toward his truck, then Tatum opened the door for me and Buster suddenly pushed me aside and tried to jump in. "No, Buster! Go lay down," Tatum shouted, and Buster retreated toward the house. "Sorry about that."

"It's okay," I said before hopping into the truck and tugging down the hem of my dress.

Tatum sat in the driver's seat and cranked the ignition. The truck's engine roared and he shifted into reverse. Before he let his foot off the brake, he turned to me, his fingers mere inches from my shoulder. "You look really pretty. The boots suit you."

"Thanks. You look really nice too." Our eyes locked for a moment before he looked out the back window.

The drive was painless, but quiet. Country music played softly on the radio as I took in my surroundings, constantly making little sounds of wonder when something new to me came into view, which was often.

Tatum pulled the truck onto a gravel drive and drove for what seemed like miles before we passed the first house. "Is this it?" I asked.

"That's just their house. We're heading out into the field. Still have a little ways to go yet." Tatum smiled and continued staring ahead.

Eventually there was a break from the rows of crops where a plowed dirt field sat looking out of place. "Why is it," I started to ask but didn't know how to word my question. "Do things not grow out here? I'm confused."

"They plow it for us to party on," he said, as if it was the most natural answer on earth.

"You plow perfectly usable crop space away to party on?"

"Oh, Princess," he said with a deep, throaty laugh. I loved the laugh but hated the nickname, so I frowned. "They aren't using this part of the field, so they keep it plowed so we can come out here."

"Okay," I said with a shrug, still not really getting it, but accepting his answer all the same.

It was well before sunset and plenty of people were milling around with red plastic cups in their hands. Lifted trucks of all shapes and sizes sat parked in a circle, their tailgates down as country music blasted from someone's speakers. A crowd was milling around one of the trucks, and I noticed there was a keg in the back of it.

"How do we see later? Or do we all just hang out in the dark together," I asked, feeling like an idiot.

"Most of us turn on our headlights," Tatum answered.

"Ah, gotcha."

"In the winter we have bonfires. But not when it's hot at night like this."

"How do you guys keep the fire from burning up the nearby field?" I was slightly concerned with this situation.

Tatum smiled. A real, full-on, genuine smile, and I wanted

to tell him to never stop doing that. My attraction doubled each time those lips curled upward. "The fire pit gets set up in a pile of dirt so there's nothing for it to burn except the wood. And we always carry plenty of water in case things get out of hand. But we've been doing this for years. The fire burns itself out eventually."

"You guys have never…not once…lit the town on fire?" I tilted my head and raised my eyebrows. "Or this farm?"

"Cross my heart." His hands gestured across his chest and my eyes followed.

"So are you taking me around to meet everyone, or will they come to us? How does this work?"

"It's a party, Paige. Everyone is gonna be pretty social. And seeing as how you're a new girl and you're with me, we're going to draw plenty of attention tonight." Worry lines deepened between his eyebrows as he turned his baseball cap around and pulled it low.

I looked up and noticed a group staring in our direction. "They're already looking over here."

"It's not because of you," he said, "at least not yet. I haven't been out here in a couple years."

"How come?"

"I just haven't wanted to be around everyone since my dad died. I sort of felt like when I quit college, I'd let the whole town down," he admitted, and my heart pinched for him.

"I'm sure that's not true."

"I'm not. You ready for this?" He gestured with his head toward the group now making their way toward us.

"Yep!" I answered with excitement in my voice.

And I honestly felt that way...at first. Then the group of people reached us. The guys shook hands with Tatum, saying things like "It's been too long" and "Good to see you, man." And before they asked him who I was, they all stopped and stared. Their eyebrows pulled together as they tried to figure out why I looked so familiar.

I started to shift my weight from foot to foot before the whispers kicked in, and I heard "Paige Lockwood" mentioned in every other breath. This was the sort of thing I was used to. Most people reacted this way when they saw me in public.

"Tatum, who's your friend?" a guy with blond hair asked.

"Troy, this is my—" Tatum fumbled a little before recovering. "Paige. Paige, this is Troy."

I extended my hand toward the guy, who brought it to his lips and kissed the top of it. Laughing, I pulled my hand back and shook my head.

"It's nice to meet you, Paige."

Tatum's face reddened. "Knock it off, Troy," he said, glaring at his buddy.

"What? I was just saying hi." Troy lifted his hands, palms up in innocence, but Tatum looked genuinely upset.

"You okay with all this?" Tatum whispered in my ear as his hand settled possessively on the small of my back.

"Yeah. I'm fine," I said, loving the way his hand felt.

"Are you Paige Lockwood?" Troy asked, and the crowd around us grew quiet.

I nodded instead of saying yes, and he promptly asked if

we could take a picture together. He pulled out his phone and I leaned in toward him, my head resting against his as he took a selfie of us.

Tatum looked around at the group that was now chirping with excitement and squabbling about who was next to take a picture with me. "Okay, listen up. Paige got a flat tire and she's staying in town with us until I get the damn thing fixed. All we ask is that you don't post about her being here. Not on Twitter, or Facebook, or InstaStupid or whatever the hell else you kids are playing on these days."

The crowd laughed and one of the guys hollered, calling him an old man as Tatum continued. "Please don't ruin this for Paige. If you post about where she is, she'll have to leave."

He leaned toward me. "Do you care if they post the pictures after you're gone?"

"Of course not," I said.

Tatum pulled me close, then addressed the group again. "Feel free to post the pictures you take with her after she's left town. But not before. I don't want to have to kick anyone's ass tonight," he finished, looking me in the eye before planting a kiss on my cheek.

What the hell?

Dear Lord, please make him do it again. And then again. And then he can move straight on to my mouth and never stop. Ever. Tatum may have lost his mind, but don't help him find it. Not if it means he'll stop kissing me.

I decided to address the crowd as well. I didn't want Tatum to be speaking for me when I felt like I should be the one explaining myself to them.

"Like Tatum said, no one knows where I am right now, and I really want to keep it that way. I love your town and I'm enjoying spending time here. I'm not quite ready to leave, but if it gets out that I'm here, I'll have no choice. So I just want to thank you all in advance for respecting my privacy. I really appreciate it. And once I do head back to LA, feel free to post our pics together wherever you want." I smiled broadly, making eye contact with everyone who surrounded me.

The group immediately shouted their approval and then swarmed me for pictures and autographs. Everyone was incredibly sweet, but they were overwhelming as well. Hollywood was such a foreign concept to them, in the same way that their way of life was to me. They had a ton of questions that they weren't afraid to ask. Anything personal I politely refused to answer, but questions about living in LA and my work, I happily answered. I understood the appeal and figured that I'd do the same thing if the shoe were on the other foot.

"Paige, do you want something to drink?" Tatum's voice shouted over the questions being tossed at me.

I knew he meant alcohol, but I honestly didn't want to let my guard down in this situation. "Do they have sweet tea? I've grown kind of fond of it," I said as I gave him a huge grin.

"Sweet tea it is, Princess!" he shouted before taking off.

More laughter and shouting came from somewhere behind me, and I turned in time to see Brina and Celeste exiting a Jeep Wrangler. They both looked amazing. When Celeste caught sight of me, she waved like crazy and I waved back. The group surrounding me turned to see who I was waving to, and a few whispers accompanied the revelation.

"Hey, girl! So, what do you think?" Celeste asked with a big smile before giving me a quick hug.

"Is everyone here so good-looking? I mean, really!" I said, deliberately complimenting everyone within hearing range.

"It's the curse of the South. Gorgeous people stuck in the middle of nowhere with no one to find them." She laughed, tossing her head back, and her fiery hair fell from around her shoulders and spilled onto her back.

"You made it." Brina leaned in to give me a quick hug and my defenses sharpened.

"Yep."

Brina looked me up and down before commenting, "Nice boots."

I looked down. "Oh, thanks. They're Mrs. Montgomery's."

Her eyes widened as her lips pressed tightly together. She turned to look at Tatum, who was busy talking with a group of guys, drinks in hand. When he didn't acknowledge her, she turned back to me. "It's nice that you get along so well with her."

I wasn't sure what she meant exactly. Was she hinting that she and Mrs. Montgomery hadn't gotten along when she dated Tatum? I couldn't imagine that, so I dropped it, hoping I could ask Tatum about it later.

A strong hand found its way onto my lower back once again and I leaned into it after making sure it belonged to

Tatum. "Here's your tea." He handed me a red plastic cup filled to the brim.

"You didn't spike this, did you?" I asked playfully, peering up at him through my eyelashes.

He took a swig of his beer before winking. "Want to get out of here?"

"But we just got here," I said, disappointed. "And you're drinking."

"No. I meant here," he gestured to the crowd still surrounding me, "away from the crowd and picture taking."

I looked around, wondering what exactly he had in mind before I agreed, not that it really mattered. I'd follow Tatum anywhere he wanted. "I guess."

"Come on." He reached for my hand and interlaced our fingers before pulling me away. I waved my cup at Celeste, who had a smile ten feet wide plastered on her face, and Brina, who wore a scowl about the same size.

"Where are we going?" I whispered.

"Just over to my truck."

We walked to the back where Tatum lowered the tailgate and placed our drinks on the ground. He spread out a thick blanket he had brought across the bed of the truck, then hopped in. "Hand me the drinks, please," he drawled, and I happily obliged. Putting them down, he reached out a hand to pull me up. Two beanbag chairs were pressed against the cab of the truck, and he straightened them out before sitting down on one and patting the other one for me.

I plopped down next to him and looked up at the

darkening sky. I'd never seen so many stars before and it was barely dusk. LA had too many lights that drowned out the night's sky almost completely. Even during nights when I thought I could see a lot of stars, it was nothing compared to this. I found myself wishing again that a camera would do any of this justice, but I knew it was up to my memory to capture the view and hold on to it.

"It's beautiful out here," I said before turning to look at Tatum.

"It sure is," he said, looking straight at me.

I felt myself blush as I wished he'd let me wrap myself up in his arms. The kiss on the cheek made me want more from him, but I was too scared to initiate anything physical. Tatum could make me feel amazing and wanted one second, and discarded the next.

"So, are you having fun yet?" He leaned his head against the back of his makeshift seat.

"I am. Everyone's really nice."

He grinned. "They didn't leave you alone the second they found out who you were. How many autographs did you sign, Paige? How many pictures did you take?"

I shrugged my shoulders, not knowing or caring what the answer was. This type of thing was part of my job, and I was used to it. But there was a niggling in the back of my mind. A realization had forced its way through and I frowned.

"What's wrong?"

"Just thinking," I admitted and forced a slight smile.

"About what?"

"Nothing. Everything. I don't know." I shrugged, stumbling on my words, my thoughts, my emotions.

"Why are you really here?" he asked. "There's more to the story than what you've told me."

"Of course there's more to the story. We've barely talked at all. I mean, I try to talk and you get all pissy and shut down."

He looked away briefly. "I know. I just…"

"You're not good at making small talk. I know. You've told me that one already," I said for him. "More than once."

"That wasn't what I was going to say. Smartass," he teased.

"Oh." I didn't hide my surprise. "What were you going to say then?"

"I was just going to say that I have a hard time opening up to people."

It was a small admission, but I felt like I'd just gotten to break ground on a new development project. Tatum had just smashed the first cinder block, and I planned on knocking down all the rest. One at a time, if that was how he needed it to be.

Leaning a little closer, I said, "I know we don't really know each other, but I'd like to get to know you better. I mean, I'm going to be here for at least a week, right? Can't we be friends?" I deliberately used the *F* word, hoping to put him at ease. Privately I hoped that his concept of friendship included hot-and-heavy make-out sessions in his converted barn. Knowing how proud Quinn would be of me and my dirty thoughts, I stifled a laugh.

"And here I was, thinking we already were, Princess." Tatum winked at me and I suddenly wanted to sock him in the eye. And then kiss it to make it all better. Seriously, what the heck was going on with my hormones?

"You have to stop with the princess stuff," I huffed. "I don't hate much, but I think I hate that." I ran my fingers through my long hair and tucked it behind my ears before taking a sip of the tea.

"Prove to me you're not one then, and I'll stop." He took another gulp from his cup.

"You're so irritating," I snarled, even though I wasn't really mad.

"But you like it," he said before leaning into me, his shoulder pressed against mine. I did like it, but I refused to admit it.

"Can I ask you something?"

"Go for it," he said as he poked me playfully in the rib with his finger, and I squirmed.

"That day when you picked me up. You said you knew who I was, right?" I wasn't sure why I was bringing this up now, or why it even mattered. I think I simply wanted to continue chipping away at his armor and let him know that he could trust me. Which I was aware, was ridiculously ironic.

"Hell yeah, I knew. I told you that."

"Then why were you so mean? I tried to shake your hand and you wouldn't even touch me." I thought back to when I first hopped into his truck.

Tatum laughed as he took a sip of his beer. "Paige," he said solemnly as he turned his face to look at me. "You had just bent over and I couldn't stop staring at your ass. I got—" He paused, apparently trying to choose his words carefully. "—excited. I figured touching you anywhere else would only fuel my situation."

"Oh," was all I could muster up for a response. I hadn't expected that answer. I liked that I turned him on, but wasn't sure what to do with that information. Maybe I should bend over every time he was in range of my ass so I could render him stupid and speechless? I almost laughed at the crazy thoughts swirling in my head.

"Sorry. You asked and I didn't want to lie." He smiled before turning his attention to the emerging stars.

"No. I appreciate your honesty." I followed his lead and stared up at the darkening sky.

Watching the blue fade away, I was mesmerized by the streaking oranges and pinks in the distance that eventually lost their battle to the night. The sky was one of the darkest I'd ever seen, and the multitude of stars was amazing, almost hypnotic in their glow.

"I don't hate your movies, by the way." His voice broke through my silent star-gazing and I smiled without moving a muscle.

"Thought you didn't watch chick flicks," I teased, already knowing differently.

"I don't. But Brina used to make me watch them with her all the time."

"I'm sorry. I'm sure that must have been painful for you," I said mockingly.

He sucked in a quick breath. "Look. Your movies were the only ones I never bitched about having to watch. I don't know why, but you're one of the few Hollywood actresses whose heads I don't want to rip off," he said, and I was slightly taken aback.

"Care to share who else's head you like attached to their body?" I asked, wondering what other actresses he liked besides me.

"No. I don't. But I will tell you this, and probably only because I've been drinking. Brina used to tease me all the time about you. She used to say I had a thing for you. Eventually we stopped watching together any movie you were in."

My smile grew even wider. "So," it was my turn to poke him in the ribs, "did you have a thing for me, Tatum? Like what you saw on the big screen?" I giggled.

"This conversation is over," he snapped, but his tone wasn't unfriendly. I dropped it, but the idea of Tatum liking my work and my movies warmed me from the inside out.

I wasn't sure how long we stayed side by side, our bodies pressing against each other with nothing but the sound of our breathing between us, but I knew damn well I wouldn't be the one to break our connection or our silence. It was the most comfortable stillness I'd ever experienced.

Until it ended.

"I can't believe that Paige freaking Lockwood is in our hometown," said a guy who had wandered along with his girlfriend next to the truck. "Tatum, you lucky son of a bitch, keeping her all to yourself!" The guy lifted his arm to give Tatum a high-five, but couldn't reach him.

His girlfriend grinned at me, her teeth flashing white in the darkness. "Paige, it's so nice to meet you. I love all your movies. You're so pretty in real life. And so skinny. What's LA like? Is it as amazing as it seems? Do you see movie stars everywhere you go? Wait, what am I saying." She paused and then giggled. "I mean, you're a movie star, so of course you do!" The girl rattled off questions quicker than I could answer them, so I just smiled and waited for her to stop.

"You said you wanted normal," Tatum whispered while the girl continued to talk.

"This isn't really normal," I said as the realization dawned on me that he had a point.

Tatum shot me an amazed look. "Paige, when will you realize that you aren't normal? Your life isn't normal. You want something you'll never truly be able to have. People are always going to treat you differently because of who you are. You have to accept that."

I didn't respond; I couldn't. I hated that he was right. His points were making too much sense and it scared me.

Tatum eventually cleared his throat and the girl stopped talking when he said, "Paige, I'd like you to meet Luke and Jessica. This is Luke's parents' farm. And Jessica has been his girlfriend since we were about thirteen."

"Twelve!" they both yelled in unison before giving each other a sloppy kiss.

"It's nice to meet you both. Luke, I love your property. It's beautiful. And Jessica, thank you for all the compliments. You're super pretty too."

Tatum leaned over the side of the truck bed and waved them closer. "Will you both do us a favor?" he whispered, acting like he was letting them in on a big secret. Luke and Jessica leaned in close. "Don't tell people that she's here, okay? I already asked everyone earlier to keep it quiet, but I don't know where you two lovebirds were."

They laughed and started to say something, but Tatum interrupted. "And I don't want to know. But listen, we can't have it getting out that Paige is in town or she'll have to leave."

"Oh no! Don't leave!" Jessica giggled, reaching for my hand.

"Don't ever leave! Marry Tatum and stay here forever so we can all be best friends," Luke slurred as he tried to regain his balance.

Brina's bitchy voice cut through the night and my back stiffened. "Like that would ever happen. Paige Lockwood, Hollywood royalty, marry small-town, going-nowhere, biggest-disappointment-in-three-counties Tatum Montgomery? Why on earth would she ever do something as stupid as that? She could have anyone she wanted."

I turned to look at Tatum, but he was too busy shooting daggers at Brina through narrowed eyes. Reaching out my hand, I placed it on his bicep, but he shrugged it off. Swallowing the hurt that followed, I searched for the right words, desperately wanting to help.

"Cut it out, Brina. I'm sorry, you guys. She's drunk, don't listen to her." Celeste maneuvered around her best friend and tried to pull her away.

"I might be drunk, but that doesn't mean what I'm saying isn't true. Tatum, you think you could ever keep someone like her? What a joke," she spat out, venom dripping from every word. "You couldn't even keep me."

"Thank God for that." The words tumbled out under his breath and I gasped.

Brina narrowed her eyes at him and crossed her arms over her chest. "What did you say?"

"Last time I checked, no one was beating down your door to take you out, so why don't you leave me the hell alone?"

"You were supposed to get me out of this town, Tatum! You promised we'd leave it behind and have a real life. But you're still here and I'm still here and neither one of us is ever getting out and it's all your fault!" She started to cry and I couldn't believe the scene that unfolded around me. Talk about a made-for-TV drama.

"Celeste," Tatum growled. "Get her out of here. Now."

"No! You can't make me leave," Brina shrieked as she fought against Celeste's hands trying to tug her away.

I sucked in a deep breath before speaking, my tone firm. "Brina. Go home. You've said enough."

She lowered her head at my words. "You don't really like him, do you? You can't possibly." She stopped talking as Celeste wrapped an arm around her and led her away. "There's no way Paige really likes Tatum, is there, Celeste? That would never happen. Not in a million years. Not even in one of her movies. Right?" Her voice faded as Celeste pulled her out of earshot.

"Well, that was fun," I said, trying to lighten the mood, but Tatum was fuming. His chest heaved in and out and he breathed heavily through his nose. I hated that he was hurting. I felt protective of Tatum in what I assumed was the same way he seemed to feel protective of me.

"Tatum?" I said softly. "Tatum, please. Look at me." When he slowly turned his head to face me, his gaze low as I placed my hand on his thigh, I said, "It doesn't matter what she says. It doesn't matter what she thinks. You can do whatever you want and be whoever you want. If you want to leave this town, then do it. But don't let her words bring you down. Don't let her define you."

"You don't even know what you're talking about," he said in a low, hurt voice, "so how 'bout you just don't talk."

I drew in a deep breath, then said calmly, "Don't do that to me. Don't be a jerk when all I'm trying to do is help you."

"I don't want your help, Paige. I didn't ask for your help. I don't need your help. I'm not a charity case," he growled, his voice still low.

"I never said you were. You're impossible, you know that?"

"Well, thank God you won't have to deal with me for very long. Once you leave here you can go back to Hollywood and forget you ever met me. Your life can go back to normal and you can forget I exist."

I brought my free hand in front of my face and squeezed back the tears that formed in my eyes. "You don't actually believe that, do you? You think for one second that I'd just forget you?"

"It doesn't matter." He looked away as he pulled off his cap and ran a hand through his hair.

"It matters to me." I squeezed his leg, half-surprised he allowed my hand to stay there.

Tatum pulled his cap low over his forehead, then shot me a glance and said, "Get in the truck, we're going home."

I didn't move, and he couldn't make me.

Ex-Girlfriends

TATUM

BRINA'S WORDS HAD struck a chord, picking at a wound that had been festering inside me for the last three years. I had promised to take her out of our tiny town and build a life in a bigger one. I'd made myself that promise, as well. What I hadn't planned on was my dad dying and how my life changed so drastically in the moments after he took his last breath. How Brina could ever blame me for that, I'd never know. And honestly, I couldn't give a shit, but the things she said about me and Paige were exactly why I couldn't allow myself to get close to Paige.

It had been so easy to start lowering my walls with Paige tonight. She had made it so effortless. At least, until Brina came around and gave me the harsh reminder that I had so clearly needed. Paige Lockwood would never hook up with a small-town guy like me, and any thoughts I conjured up in my head to the contrary were a crazy man's way of thinking.

Why would Paige choose me when she could have her pick of any guy she wanted in the whole damn world? Who in their right mind would ever choose someone like me when they had options like that? No one, that's who.

When I'd admitted to Paige earlier that she had been one of the only actresses whose head I didn't want to rip off, I hadn't been completely honest. Truthfully, she had been the *only* actress whose head I didn't want to rip off. All the others annoyed the living shit out of me. Matter of fact, the whole idea of Hollywood irritated me, and I was getting pissed off just thinking about it.

Everyone there seemed so entitled and lived a life that I felt almost shouldn't be real. Should people really be that privileged while the rest of us worked our asses off every day to make ends meet? Those elitists lived their lives, getting the world handed to them day after day, not sparing a single thought for what the rest of us had to do just to survive. Why did people who already had so much get rewarded with more when so many others had so little?

Paige and I weren't just from two different worlds; we were from two different galaxies. I would do well to remember that.

"Well, thank God you won't have to deal with me for very long. Once you leave here you can go back to Hollywood and forget you ever met me. Your life can go back to normal and you can pretend I don't exist." She clearly needed the same reminder that I'd just been given. Our worlds couldn't be more different, and she had to have realized that. She would be going back home soon, leaving me and this town behind.

Paige moved her hand in front of her beautiful face, and I thought I saw tears glistening in her eyes. I knew I was acting like a complete dick, but I needed to keep up the charade. If Paige saw through me, I'd be done for. If she called me out, I'd beg for her forgiveness on my knees if that was what she needed. I wanted her, but I knew I couldn't have her. This conflict was tearing me up inside. Or maybe it was the beer.

"You don't actually believe that, do you? You think for one second that I'd just forget you?" she asked me. Her voice almost caused me to break my resolve.

"It doesn't matter." I reached for my hat and pulled it off. I needed to keep my hands occupied so they didn't reach out for her and blow it all to hell.

"It matters to me." She squeezed my leg and I ran my fingers through my hair, tempted to yank on it.

"Get in the truck, we're going home."

She didn't move. She just sat there like a defiant little princess. "Goddamn it, Paige, get in the truck!"

"No," she said firmly, her gorgeous face scrunched up in a scowl that didn't suit her one bit.

Frustrated, I shook my head and looked away. "Stop it, Paige."

"Stop what?"

"Stop acting like we're in some movie that has a happy ending. We're not. And it doesn't." We both needed that reminder. At least, I sure as shit did.

Paige finally moved to climb into the cab, her face filled with hurt. I wanted to apologize to her, but couldn't find the strength or the words. We drove back to Mama's house in complete silence; I'd even turned off the radio. I couldn't handle country music lyrics right now.

When I pulled in front of the house, Paige opened the door and jumped out before I turned off the ignition. As I watched, she raced through the screen door and didn't look back. She wanted nothing to do with me, and I didn't blame her.

THE NEXT MORNING I arrived at the shop to find some deliveries waiting for me at the back door. After unpacking the supplies and parts, I got a call saying that Paige's new tire would be arriving around three. I pretended to be nonchalant about the delivery, but I was half-tempted to tell them to hold off and deliver it, say…never.

When her tire arrived, I sighed before rolling it into the garage, frowning at it while Buster whined in the background. Debating about whether I should hide it or put it on her car, I finally decided to do my job and put it on. That didn't mean I had to tell her that her car was fixed, but at least it would be ready for her when she was ready to go.

I jacked up the BMW and removed the ruined old tire.

While I was there, I figured I'd better check the brake pads, rotors, and other parts connected to the wheel. Once I decided that everything looked fine, I put on the new tire, tightening the lug nuts and making sure everything was in working order. After sliding out from the car, I lowered it to the ground and wondered for a moment if I should hide it. I had a tarp I could throw over it so no one would know it was ready.

Shaking the crazy thought from my head, I swallowed hard as my chest ached at the sight of her perfectly drivable car. A car that she could get in right now if she wanted and drive away from here—and me—forever.

Shit.

I wasn't ready for her to leave my life yet. No matter how much I fought her or myself on it, I didn't want her to go. I'd tried to push her away, tried to keep myself from her, but it wasn't what I wanted. Nothing about Paige being away from me was even remotely close to what I wanted.

What I did want was that perfect little mouth against mine, that bikini-clad body in the swimming hole with me, and every single thing that Paige would let me have. But how could I tell her that after the way I acted last night? When it came to this girl, I acted like a complete asshole ninety percent of the time. The other ten percent I acted like a pure idiot.

I didn't know what to do, so in typical asshole fashion, I decided I'd head over to the bar after dropping Buster off at Mama's. I'd drown my sorrows in some good old-fashioned moonshine.

A One-Bar Town

PAIGE

AFTER LAST NIGHT, I knew things had changed between Tatum and me. I had convinced myself that we were making progress and that his defensive wall was lowering, but then Brina opened her big drunken mouth and made him worse than he was before, if that was even possible.

Side note: It was.

When I walked into the living room, I heard Mrs. Montgomery on the phone with someone. "Oh yes. You've raised a wonderful daughter. She's such a joy. You too. I'll go get her." She turned to yell for me, and I smiled knowing my mom was on the phone.

I practically ran to grab the receiver. "Hey, Mom!"

"Emily seems nice. I'm so relieved," my mom said.

"She is," I said with a smile. "Super nice."

"I have to admit, Paige, I feel so much better knowing that you're in one place rather than driving across the damn country all alone. I had to talk your father off the ledge more than a few times."

"What do you mean? Is Dad okay?"

"He is now, but he wanted to get in the car and drive until he found you. He's been really concerned."

I closed my eyes. "I'm sorry, Mom. Tell Dad I'm sorry too. And tell him not to worry. I promise I'm okay. Actually, I'm more than okay. I sort of love it here."

"We're your parents, Paige. We'll always worry. It's our job. But I'll tell him, and he'll be as relieved as I am. Talking to Emily was a huge help."

"I'm glad," I admitted, hating that my family was feeling stressed with my absence. My fame caused them enough issues without my adding more.

"So, how are you doing? Are things okay? What's going on with your work and stuff?"

"Honestly...I don't know. I haven't answered any e-mails except for yours and Quinn's, and I haven't turned my phone on since I left. Has anyone tried to call you?"

"Jayson's called here once, but I convinced him that I didn't know where you were or how to reach you."

"Did he believe you?"

"I doubt it. But who cares. It's not like he can get anything out of me that I don't want him to," she said with a laugh.

"Thanks, Mom."

"You're welcome. By the way, Stacey accepted the offer

from NYU. You might want to congratulate her when you have a chance."

My stomach clenched. I was happy for my sister, of course, but there it was, that old jealous feeling rearing its ugly head again. "Is she there?" I asked, knowing that my feelings had nothing to do with my little sister and everything to do with my own personal issues.

"No, she's at work."

"Okay. Well, tell her I said congratulations and I'm super excited for her. I'll call her when I can."

"I will. And Paige?"

"Yeah?"

"Try and relax a little while you're there, okay? Enjoy this time away. Lord knows when you'll get it again."

I sighed. "I will. I love you. 'Bye, Mom."

"Love you too, honey. 'Bye."

When I hung up, Mrs. Montgomery looked up from where she was sitting at the table, sipping some tea and working on a crossword puzzle. "Your mama sure seems like a nice woman." She smiled, her accent once again noticeable in comparison to my mom's voice.

"She is. She's been really great since my career started."

"I didn't know you had a sister. What were you congratulating her for, if you don't mind me asking."

"Oh, she finally picked a college," I said, "NYU. I'm really proud of her, actually."

Mrs. Montgomery slapped the table with her hand. "Well! If that isn't just the greatest news. How wonderful for her!"

"It is. She's worked really hard to get in." I was truly proud of my sister. She deserved this, and she deserved my support.

"I bet you miss her," she said softly.

"I do. But I started working when she was little, so we didn't get the chance to be really close the way some sisters are, you know? And then she pretty much grew up without me."

She waved a hand, dismissing my concerns. "None of that matters, Paige. You'll be as close as two peas in a pod as adults if you both allow it. It's the grown-up stuff that really counts. Marriage and kids and all that. You'll see."

I smiled, strangely comforted by the notion. "I hope you're right."

MRS. MONTGOMERY LET ME borrow her car, and she gave me directions to the one and only bar in town.

"Don't be scared about how the bar looks on the outside, okay? It's incredibly old and it's a little farther out near the railroad tracks."

I raised my eyebrows and made a face, pretending a fear I didn't feel. "It sounds perfect," I said, knowing full well that getting out of this house and away from this property for a little while was just what I needed.

"Aren't you worried about people recognizing you?"

"After last night, I feel like I've already met half the town, and the rest probably know I'm here by now. No sense hiding anymore." I paused. "I mean, I still don't want anyone to say anything about me being here, but I keep telling myself I want to do normal things. I need to follow through." I smiled, and she gave me a quick hug before shooing me out the front door.

The bar was a little farther out than anything else in town, just like Mrs. Montgomery said it would be. When I walked inside, I immediately spotted a group of people I'd met last night at the field party. Celeste's fiery red hair caught my eye as my hopes for a peaceful evening dissipated with my assumption that Brina had to be nearby.

Celeste caught my eye and waved me over, giving me a hug as I joined their group. "Brina's not here. She's nursing a wicked hangover," she said, and I immediately felt better.

I grinned. "Is it bad that I'm happy about that?"

She gave me a knowing look. "Not at all. I'm really sorry about everything she said last night. She had no right, and she was way off base."

"It's not your fault."

"I know, but she's my best friend so I feel responsible for her."

I nodded, knowing I felt the exact same way about Quinn. If she ever did anything crazy, I'd want to apologize for her too. I missed Quinn so much. She'd know exactly what to say and do in this situation, and if she'd been there last night, she would have sent Brina home in tears from the verbal lashing she would have given her.

"But that one's been here for hours." She pointed over at the other side of the bar where I caught sight of Tatum's muscular frame.

"Have you been here for hours?" I asked with a laugh.

"I dropped someone off earlier and noticed Tatum's truck. When I came back about an hour ago, his truck was still here."

"Probably avoiding going home since I'm there."

"Looks more like he's trying to drink his problems away." She looked between us. "Come on, I'll buy you a drink."

I hesitated, almost saying no, but the whole point of coming to the bar in the first place was to get a drink. "I should be buying you the drink," I offered.

"Why? Because you're a big movie star? I have a job, you know," she said with a smirk.

"Actually, I don't know. What do you do?" I asked, following her toward the dark oak bar and stools.

"Oh, I do hair. We don't have a salon here in town, so I do hair out of my mama's house most days. It's not much, but it pays the bills. And I really love it."

We sat side by side as the bartender meandered over, drying a glass. He was an older gentleman with salt-and-pepper hair and a mustache to match. "Evening, Celeste. And who's your friend?"

"Hey, Mitch, this is Paige. Paige, this is Mitch. He's been here forever."

"Forever's a long time, young lady," he said, and waved a scolding finger at her.

Celeste pretended a pout. "I didn't mean anything by it. I

love you, Mitch. You know I love you."

"Oh, I can never stay mad at you, honey. What can I get you ladies?" He put down the glass and leaned both hands on the bar in front of us.

"I'll have a whiskey sour," Celeste said, and I nodded.

"I'll have the same."

"You ever had one before?"

"Nope."

She laughed. "You'll like it, it's sweet."

Mitch put the small drinks in front of us and waved Celeste off when she tried to pay him. "On the house," he mumbled, slinging a towel over his shoulder and walking toward the other end of the bar before I could thank him.

"He always does that," she said before taking a drink and placing some dollar bills on the bar in front of us.

I sipped the concoction carefully, unsure of what to expect. The sweetness and bitterness hit my tongue all at once before I realized it wasn't half bad. "It's good," I said as the liquor traveled down my throat and warmed my stomach.

"Told you. I usually move on to straight whiskey after a couple of these."

I almost spit out my drink. None of my friends drank straight liquor, and I couldn't imagine the appeal. I definitely needed additional flavorings with my alcohol consumption.

Celeste pushed off the bar stool and I followed suit. We walked over toward the pool tables and stood side by side.

"Can I ask you something?" I asked, feeling comfortable with Celeste's up-front and honest nature.

She leaned against the wood railing. "Of course."

"You've known Tatum a long time, so what's his deal? I mean, I honestly think he hates me."

Celeste glanced over at Tatum and a smile lifted her lips. "Don't be silly. Tatum's one of the good ones. Probably one of the best, honestly. He and Brina were together all through high school, and he was a big football star. Brina wanted to leave this town and Tatum was her ticket out. But when his daddy died, and he gave up his college scholarship to stay on and help his mama run the shop..." She sighed and added sadly, "Well, Brina, she gave up on him too. Said that he wasn't going anywhere anymore, and she didn't want someone who was content with staying here and being a mechanic."

My jaw fell open and I consciously closed it tight and continued to listen. I hadn't liked Brina before, but now I hated her. As in wanted-to-punch-her-in-the-face-and-tell-her-what-a-horrible-person-she-was hated her. I also couldn't comprehend how someone like Celeste could be such good friends with someone like Brina.

"How did you stay friends with her after that?"

"She's been my best friend since we were five," she explained. "I hated what she did to Tatum and I told her that, but I couldn't stop being friends with her because of it." She leaned toward me. "But honestly? I've never really looked at her the same since she did that to him."

"Yeah. That would change things for me too." I tried to understand Celeste's reasoning, not certain I'd be able to stay friends with someone I'd lost all respect for.

"He has a big heart, Paige. It's just been broken so deeply that he doesn't trust that well anymore. Plus he knows you'll leave him, and so he's trying his best to be tough and act like he doesn't care. You could probably ruin him forever and he knows it."

I turned to look at her. "What are you talking about? He runs so hot and cold with me that I have no idea how he feels."

She giggled. "For such a smart California girl, you're sure not that observant." She nudged my arm and nodded her head in Tatum's direction, where he was shooting darts with his friends. "Just watch," she said.

And I did. I watched as it was his turn to throw the darts. I watched as his arm pulled back before he aimed and let the tiny dart fly through the air until it stuck inside its cork target. And I fought the urge to sidle up behind him and wrap my arms around his muscular waist, nuzzle into his shoulders, and hold on for dear life.

He turned his head in my direction as he took a swig from his bottle of beer. His eyes met mine before they jerked away, and Celeste laughed. "He's been doing that since you got here."

I let out a little snort. "He has not."

"He most certainly has. He knows your every move, Paige. And not because he doesn't care. It's because he does."

"He is so frustrating!" I complained as Brina waltzed in the front door like she owned the place, her gaze darting around the room. "Looks like someone's feeling better," I whispered to Celeste.

"I highly doubt it. I bet someone tipped her off that you and Tatum were here. She can't handle it, she's so jealous."

"She still has feelings for him, doesn't she?"

Celeste shrugged. "I honestly think it's more a case of she doesn't want the guy, but she doesn't want anyone else to have him either. Know what I mean?"

"Yep." I knew exactly what she meant. I figured that was pretty standard when it came to breakups, not that I was an expert or anything.

"I also think it's worse because she doesn't have a boyfriend. If she had someone in her life, she might not care so much about what Tatum was doing." She tilted her head. "Then again, you're the first real threat she's had. It's not like Tatum has even talked to a girl since Brina dumped him."

We stopped talking as Troy walked up to us. "Hi, Celeste. Hi, Paige."

We both said hi back, then suffered through an awkward silence as Troy shuffled his weight between his feet and avoided our eyes. Finally he looked up at me and mumbled, "Uh, Paige. Would you like to dance?"

I looked between Tatum, who was focused solely on my interaction with Troy, and Celeste, who was practically shoving me onto the dance floor, before I said, "Sure."

The music was slow and Troy pulled me close. I stepped even closer, our bodies moving in unison to the beat. It was immature of me to attempt to make Tatum jealous, but I needed to force some sort of reaction out of him. If Celeste was even remotely right about him, I'd waited about as long as I wanted to for him to make a move.

Closing my eyes, I pretended Troy was Tatum, only he wasn't nearly as tall or as well-built, but it was the only way I could stomach being this close to someone who wasn't Tatum. My daydream was interrupted by Troy pulling away from me and my body suddenly going cold. My eyes flew open to see Tatum's blue ones glaring at me, his face twisted in anger. Or maybe it was disgust.

"Come here," Tatum bit out. "I want to talk to you." He grasped my upper arm and I jerked it out of his grip.

"Don't manhandle me!" I shouted.

He leaned in close to my face, his voice barely above a whisper, but his tone unhappy. "I don't like it."

"You don't like what?" I snapped back, my tone mimicking his.

"Don't dance with my friends like that," he practically spat at me.

"Like what?" I placed a nonchalant expression on my face, wanting to push his buttons.

Tatum pulled off his baseball cap and ran his hand irritably through his hair. "I don't want you dancing that close to anyone but me."

"Then why don't you ask me to dance instead of brooding all night?"

"Is that what you want, Paige? You want to dance with me?"

I huffed out an annoyed sigh. "You can't possibly be this stupid."

"Tell me what you want!" he yelled, all his composure completely blown.

I glanced around to see people watching us, then lowered my voice as I admitted, "You already know what I want."

"Do I?"

"Don't you?"

"Stop playing games."

"I'm not playing games. You know what I want. You're the one who keeps fighting it," I said, tears welling up in my eyes as my frustration built.

"Say it. I need to hear you say it," he said, his voice breaking as if his very life were at stake.

"You two are creating a scene. Maybe you should leave."

Brina's nasal voice cut through the tension that surrounded us, but we ignored her as our gazes remained locked. Tatum and I continued to stare at each other, chests heaving with emotion.

"Go away, Brina. This doesn't concern you," Tatum ordered tersely.

He waited for the sound of her boots shuffling against the wood floor to signal her departure before he stepped a little closer and pleaded once more, "Say it, Paige. I need to know."

"Need to know what? How much I want you? Is that what you want to hear? Because I do. I'm so attracted to you and I've wanted to kiss you for forever, but I never know what you want or how you feel. I'm drawn to you, Tatum, in ways that make no sense to me at all. Sure, we're from two completely different worlds and I'm pretty sure we can never work out, but right now," I said, pausing to take a deep breath. "Right now I don't care. Now all I care about is getting you to finally freaking put your lips on mine, and feel your hands against my skin. Because I want you. I want you so—"

Tatum quickly closed the little distance left between us and pressed his lips against mine, moving them slowly at first, as though he was taking his time in tasting every inch of me before the hunger spread. My lips parted at the feel of his tongue pressing against them, begging for entry. At once we became frantic, devouring each other like the moment might be lost forever if we stopped. Tatum cupped one hand around my ass while shoving the other in my hair and holding on for dear life. I wrapped my arms around his broad shoulders and squeezed, digging my nails into the skin beneath his shirt.

"I'm sorry I haven't been nice to you," he said softly against my mouth, trying to kiss and talk at the same time.

"Shut up." I gripped the back of his neck and forced his mouth back against mine. I didn't want him going anywhere, and I'd be damned if I let him get away before I was ready. Our mouths continued to feast on each other as our tongues slowly moved in and out. This was hands down the best kiss of my life, and I completely forgot we had an audience until the clapping and hooting started.

"Shit." Tatum pulled away slowly before giving his friends an embarrassed wave and pulling me out of the bar.

I couldn't keep my hands off him as I ran my hands over

his shoulders, his chest, his back. Screw my celebrity status; I didn't care what anyone thought. I wanted to touch all of him at once.

The warm night air greeted us as we burst through the bar's double doors. Tatum pulled me toward the side of the building where the streetlights didn't shine as brightly. Pushing me against the wall, he tangled his fingers in my hair and pulled my mouth toward his. His tongue demanded my attention. He moved from my mouth to my neck, where he sucked and kissed me tenderly. His fingers splayed across my back and held me tight.

"You're gonna break my heart," he confessed against my ear.

I gasped and pulled away slowly before responding carefully, "I think you might break mine."

"I don't ever want to."

The hunger in his eyes should have scared me off, the passion and intensity reflected there unlike anything I'd ever experienced before, either on screen or off. Looking at him now made me question whether any feelings I'd ever experienced before had been real. It almost felt as if they'd been acted out on a set or scripted for good publicity. But this...

Right here.

Right now.

With Tatum.

It was as if my world violently came to life around me in that moment, as if I'd been living my life before in black and white, and now everything was suddenly lit up in vibrant Technicolor. Tatum woke me up from the slumber I didn't even realize I was in. This was the most alive and real I'd ever felt in my adult life.

The Kiss That Erases All Others

TATUM

KISSING PAIGE WORKED me up into a frenzy. I'd been trying to deny my feelings for her and shove any sign of them back into the hole in my chest where my heart once lived, but tonight had been too much. She pushed me too far. Seeing her body pressed against Troy's took all of my willpower. I wanted to rip him limb from limb just for touching her.

An immature notion, I know, but I still felt that way.

Once the craziness took over my body, I knew I needed to confess some things to her. Paige needed to hear that I didn't want her dancing with anyone else. I didn't want her touching any other guy in this town. Hell, I didn't want her touching any other guy in any town. Ever again.

Note to self: Good luck with that request.

When Paige told me she wanted me, I nearly lost it right there in that bar. She'd said the words I hadn't allowed myself to think when it came to her. I'd spent so much of my spare time convincing myself that a girl like Paige would never be interested in a guy like me. How many hours had I wasted being foolish?

No more.

She was still talking, and all I wanted to do was silence her. So I covered her pretty little lips with mine. They were so soft, and her tongue tasted like whiskey and sweet-and-sour mix. I'd never enjoyed the taste of whiskey as much as I did in that moment. I wanted to drink her in forever. My life before kissing Paige had just ended. Kissing her changed everything, and I knew it the moment her lips touched mine.

"You're gonna break my heart," I told her, wanting her to know how hard I planned on falling for her.

She gasped and pulled away from me. My mind instantly went to worst-case scenarios, and I figured I'd just blown the whole thing. Hoped I enjoyed kissing her, because I'd never get to do that again.

"I think you might break mine." Her words sent fireworks shooting through my chest and ricocheting across my heart.

"I don't ever want to," spilled from my lips, and damn if I didn't mean it. Every single word.

"Take me home, Tatum."

If I thought for one second that I couldn't be more aroused, I was instantly proven wrong with those words. I wanted her. I'd wanted her since I first laid eyes on those long tanned legs, but I couldn't go that far. Not tonight. Maybe not ever.

Pressing my body against hers, I cupped her firm ass in my hand and squeezed. She let out a quick sigh that worked me up even more. I had to detach my real brain from the one in my pants, so I sucked in a deep breath and said, "We gotta take it slow, Princess."

Then she growled.

Paige literally stopped rubbing her hands all over me and growled. And I laughed and almost begged her to do it again. The growling part.

"Don't call me that. Seriously, Tatum. Don't," she warned, but my eyes fell on her lips and all I wanted to do was suck them into my mouth and nibble.

"Fine. I won't. But still. I can't go throwing you into the sack the first chance I get."

Her eyes closed and she smiled. "Throwing me in the sack? You're so Southern."

"No shit, sweetheart."

"Well, I wasn't asking you to take me to bed, *Princess.*" She smirked as she threw my nickname for her back at me. Then her voice softened. "I just want to be alone with you. You know, without worrying about someone watching or being photographed."

Feeling like an idiot for forgetting who I was kissing, I suddenly became aware of our surroundings. "Shit. I'm sorry. I didn't even think about it." Even though we were in my hometown, I scanned the doors and windows of the bar, looking for prying eyes.

"Why would you? That kind of crazy only happens to me. And to be honest, even I forgot all about it when we were inside." She leaned up on her tiptoes and pressed a kiss against my nose.

Who the hell does that? Apparently Paige Lockwood does, and I'd be damned if I said I didn't enjoy it.

"Let's go home, babe," I told her, "but you've gotta drive."

While I was nowhere near hammered, I'd been at the bar long enough this evening to know better than to get behind the wheel. Having one or two beers was one thing for my one-minute drive home, but spending hours at the only bar in town was another. I liked to think I knew my limits, although everything was in question since this girl drove into my life.

"I have your mom's car," she announced and I threw my head back in surprise. Mama didn't let just anyone take her car. Hell, she'd never even let me take it, but here she was, letting Paige Lockwood drive it around town.

"We'll just leave my truck here and I'll come get it in the morning." I started to walk toward Mama's little red sports car as Paige got into the driver's seat.

Once she pulled onto my dirt road, I started fidgeting. I couldn't wait to get Paige out of this car and into the barn. Once at the house, she turned off the ignition and we both stepped out of our seats and into the night. I hurried to her side, reaching for her hand, and pulled her toward the back of the house. "Wait, let me put your mom's car keys in the house first."

"No way!" I almost yelled, but then recovered. "She'll know you're back but you're not home, if you catch my drift." I wanted Paige in the barn with me, but I wasn't sure I wanted Mama to catch on to that fact. She wasn't stupid or naive, and come tomorrow morning, she'd be asking me a ton of questions that would make me want to rip all my hair out. What was it with females and questions?

"Tatum." Paige pulled me to a stop and faced me. "Your mom has been pushing me toward you since I got here. I have a feeling she won't mind."

"She has not," I argued halfheartedly, wondering if my mom would really do that.

"Oh yes, she has," she said before dropping my hand and opening the front door. Paige's cute ass disappeared into the darkness before immediately reappearing. She was back at my side, pressing her lips against my cheek before I could argue.

We walked in a hurried pace toward the back house. I never locked the door, so I pulled at the screen first and held it open for her. When she walked through the door, I smacked her ass and she screamed.

"That hurt!"

"Good," I teased, not really meaning it, but liking the sound that came out of her mouth. It had been a long time since I'd been with a woman…in any kind of way.

As I wandered through the entryway, she tried to block me with her petite frame. She threw her arms around my neck and leaped onto me, wrapping her legs around my waist.

"I've been waiting forever for you to kiss me," she said as she planted kisses on my mouth, my cheek, my neck.

"If it's any consolation, I've wanted to kiss you since you hopped into my truck," I mumbled through my lust-filled haze.

She leaned back slightly, her weight shifting in my arms. "Nope. It's no consolation at all."

I tore my eyes away from hers and locked onto her pretty lips. Her tongue darted across the bottom one before she pressed her mouth against mine, her tongue entering without any hesitation. I stroked her tongue with mine, pulling away a little to nip gently at her lips. She fisted my hair as I cupped her ass and her back with my hands. Most of me wanted to throw her down on my bed and bury myself in her, but the other part of me had to fight for self-control.

I pulled away from her kiss and lowered her gently to the floor. "I need a second, babe." Her chest heaved as she struggled to even out her breathing. We were both filled with want for each other, and I found some comfort in that fact.

"What's the matter?" she asked as I stepped away from her.

"I'm not...I'm not ready for this. Between us. I just can't go there yet." I'd been so attracted to her since the moment I laid eyes on her, and I'd wanted to kiss her for just as long. But my willpower was only so strong and if I didn't take a few moments, I'd throw her on the couch and lose myself to her before I took another breath.

Her face broke out into a grin. "Well, isn't this ironic?"

"What's that?"

"The guy telling the girl we have to slow down. That happens…oh, about, never?" When I laughed, she reached for my face, her hands cupping my cheeks as she pulled me toward her. "We'll go at your pace," she said in a mocking tone before planting a quick kiss on my mouth.

"Yeah, we will. You know I'm worth the wait," I teased back.

Paige moved toward the couch and sat down before patting the cushion next to her. "We don't have to do anything, Tatum. We can just talk, if you want."

"I don't want to talk, Paige. I've been dying to kiss you, so I plan on doing just that. And I want to do a lot of it. I just can't go further than that with you. Not tonight. I hope you're okay with that."

It was official. If they gave out man cards when we were born, mine would certainly be revoked right about now.

"Of course I'm okay with that. I almost don't know what to think, to be honest." She fluttered her eyelashes and a small smile appeared on her face. "Usually guys are clamoring to get into girls' pants. Not just mine, but any girl."

"Trust me. I know. I'm still a guy. And the guy part of me is dying to get in your pants," I admitted before leaning over her and covering her body with mine.

I held my body over hers, before turning on my side so both of us fit. Pressing my hand against her back, I pulled her chest against mine as I willed my focus to remain intact. I swore I felt the blood leave my body and congregate in my pants, as if to mock me and test my resolve. Knowing it was useless to fight my growing erection, I attempted to ignore it.

My dick was like a knock-knock joke, constantly throbbing against my zipper until I answered its call. Trying to distract myself, I weaved my hand through Paige's long hair. It was so soft, my fingers slid right through it. Slowly I brushed my fingertips along her neck as I moved them up toward her cheek. Then I traced her upper lip with one finger, surprised when her tongue darted out and licked it slowly. I closed my eyes and my entire body stilled as she tilted her head and began sucking my finger into her mouth.

"Jesus Christ, Paige," I muttered, and she instantly pulled away, releasing my finger.

"I didn't think good Southern boys talked like that," she said, looking at me with her eyes all big.

"That's because you believe all the movies you star in."

"Well, the stereotype has to come from somewhere," she said as her eyebrows pulled together.

"Yeah. Hollywood." I framed her face in my palms and pulled her against me. "And girls like you."

My lips ached for contact with hers. My hands longed to be touching any part of her skin. The electricity that buzzed around us had nothing to do with alcohol, and I knew it. It had been there since day one, I'd just tried to ignore it.

There was no way I could ignore anything that had to do with the girl in my arms. Not any more. And I wouldn't even bother trying.

I Feel Red

PAIGE

KISSING TATUM HAD been electrifying. When I wasn't in contact with him, I missed the high. My entire body felt like it was linked to his by tiny invisible cords connecting us in a million different points. Whenever he pulled away from me to collect himself, the cords stretched and my body ached against the strain.

I'd never experienced such red-hot intensity. No one had ever made me feel so connected to them before. Not even Colin, and I'd been head over heels in love with that guy. Maybe I'd just been head over heels in stupid with him?

I realized that I was still learning about myself, my heart, and those who wanted a piece of it. It was a fair assessment that I'd loved Colin, but not in that life-changing way. A part of me probably always knew that Colin was temporary. My heart realized we wouldn't last forever, so it only loved him with as much as it allowed me to give. Or maybe I was just plain crazy and reading way too much into my current emotions.

After sneaking into the house last night, I crept into my bed and tried to make as little noise as possible. Mrs. Montgomery hadn't said a thing so far, so I didn't think she realized I'd been having a make-out session with her only child.

Pulling on a pair of cutoff white shorts and a blue tank, I walked into the kitchen the next morning where Mrs. Montgomery always seemed to be. She did a lot of cooking and baking, and had been asking if I wanted to learn how to make a few Southern staples. I told her I did, seeing as how I didn't have anything else to do except daydream about her son's lips.

"Mrs. Montgomery, is there a phone at Tatum's place?" I asked, hoping that the answer would be yes because I needed some privacy.

"There is." Her eyes narrowed in a way that should have warned me that she knew more than she was saying, but I pretended to be oblivious.

"Is Tatum back there?"

"He's at the shop already."

"I need to make a couple of phone calls, if that's all right with you, and I just wanted some privacy. Is that rude?" This woman had gone out of her way to make me feel at home, and telling her that I needed to be alone felt like I was betraying her trust, or accusing her of being untrustworthy.

"Of course that isn't rude. You go on back. Take all the time you need." She waved me off. "And here, take a muffin." She tossed another freshly baked muffin at me and I caught it with both hands, surprised I didn't smash it into a hundred pieces.

"When I come back, you'll show me how to make that pie?"

"I won't start it without you." She smiled and sipped from her coffee mug.

I walked to the back of the property toward the barn and opened the front door. Yelling Tatum's name just to make sure he was gone for the day, I relaxed when I heard nothing but the sweet sound of quiet. I scanned the living room for the phone and spotted it sitting on the counter in the kitchen. Reaching for it, I dialed Quinn's number and held my breath as it rang.

"It's about damn time," Quinn answered, and I smiled.

"I know. Sorry."

"Don't be sorry. Tell me everything," she insisted.

Leave it to Quinn to not even care how long it had been since we last talked. She wasn't the type of best friend to hold a grudge like that, and she wasn't needy. We could go for weeks without speaking, and nothing would feel off. Not that we would ever do that; I just knew that we could.

"Quinn, I'm dying here," I breathed out before plopping down onto the couch.

"What are you talking about?" she demanded, her tone

turning serious. "What's the matter?"

"Sorry, not in a bad way. This guy. My God."

"The Tatum one?"

"Yes. The Tatum one," I repeated as my mind filled with memories of last night.

"Oh my gosh, you little slut! You slept with him, didn't you?"

"No!" I yelled back, my fingers picking at strands of fabric.

"Well, why not?" she huffed. "Dude, send me a pic of this guy! I'm dying to see him."

"You'd approve," I informed her, knowing that Quinn would absolutely think Tatum was worth doing whatever it was I was doing with him. "But listen—" I started to say before she interrupted.

"Me first. Colin's in town. He's been asking about you. Tried to talk to Ryson, but he got scared when Ryson started cracking his knuckles and threatened to deck him. Colin ran away. Like literally, ran away." She laughed and surprisingly, my insides didn't ache at the mention of Colin's name.

I was fully aware that not much time had passed since Colin and I had broken up, and that I should still be hurting to hear any news about him. But it was in this moment when something inside me clicked. I realized that Colin now belonged to my past, and that was where he would remain. My future would never include him.

"You still there?"

I cleared my throat. "I'm here. I...I don't care about Colin. At all. I need to tell you about Tatum. And about all these feelings I'm having."

"So, quit stalling and tell me then."

"You're the one who… Never mind! You don't understand." I searched the recesses of my mind, trying to find the right words to explain my Technicolor emotions. "Ugh! Quinn, it's like if we associated ourselves with colors and how those colors felt, I'd be red. Oh sweet Lord, I'd be red."

"You'd be what?"

"You know, like that damn Taylor Swift song."

Quinn hummed the melody to "Red" before saying, "So this guy is like driving a car down a nowhere street? Is that what you're saying?"

I huffed out a quick laugh. "First of all, that is not how the song goes. At all. Second of all, no. But being around him is like being surrounded by so much color. So much feeling."

"So much red…he makes you angry?"

I shook my head, not sure if she was teasing or seriously confused. "No. Damn it, Quinn! He makes me feel like I've never felt before. It's intense. *He's* intense. But it's like everything around me bursts into the most vibrant glow when he's around. He makes me *feel* red."

"I still have no clue what you're talking about, but I like it. Did you ever *feel red* with Colin?" she asked, mimicking me.

"No. Not like this. Not even close. This makes everything with Colin feel so superficial. I can't explain it." I blew out a breath and sank deeper into the cushions on the couch.

"Well, try to explain it in color then. How did Colin make you feel?"

I laughed and blurted out the first color that came to mind. "Pink. Colin made me feel pink. He was light and fluffy, but nowhere near as serious or intense as he'd like to think he is."

"That's 'cause Colin's a pussy," Quinn blurted out, and I slapped a hand across my own mouth as if I were the one who'd said it.

"Quinn!" I yelled through my fingers.

"What?" She laughed. "He is. You even said it. He makes you feel pink. What kind of man makes you feel *pink*?" she said pointedly.

"The metrosexual kind, I guess? I don't know. Think about Ryson." I paused and she moaned. "See? Ryson makes you feel in color. And I'm sure it's not pink either."

"He does make me feel in color. Horny colors. He makes me green! Like an M&M!" she said with a moan.

"Gross."

"You're gross."

"No, you're gross. Now, stop thinking about green M&Ms and help me!"

"Help you what? Sounds like you've got a good thing over there in wherever the hell you are again."

"It has been a nice break from reality."

"But you have to come back," she said, and the truth hit my stomach like a boulder crashing off a cliff.

"I know," I said sadly as I hugged a throw pillow and tucked it under my chin.

"But not yet. You don't have to come back right now, Paige."

"I know that too. But I can't stay here forever. And then what?"

"Then what, what?" she asked, and I could picture the face she was making in my head. I knew her face was pinched as she tried to read my mind and guess what I was about to say before I said it.

"I mean, what do I do about Tatum? I really like him."

"Then you enjoy him. Enjoy every cotton-picking minute you have with him. Do they say that there? Cotton-picking?" Quinn amused herself as she continued. "You'll enjoy him. And you'll take some damn photos of him for your best friend!"

"You really are no help."

"Eh. Apparently my superpowers don't work on you when you're in another state. Who knew?" A loudspeaker blared in the background and I tensed as I heard Quinn's name being paged. "I've gotta go. Call me later, okay? I love you. Take pictures!"

The line went dead. Quinn was on the set of her newest movie, and I must have caught her during a break in filming her scenes. Thankful that I'd caught her at all, I placed the phone down and brought the pillow to my nose. It smelled like Tatum, and I breathed it in for a moment. Feeling a little foolish, I set it down and got up. I hung up the phone and made my way back to the main house, where Mrs. Montgomery waited for me to make the pie.

On the way back to the house, I stopped on the porch and daydreamed about kissing Tatum. If I thought Tatum had consumed my thoughts before, I was wrong. Every moment I wasn't around him, I wanted to be. A giant had awakened inside of me. A giant who wanted one thing…Tatum's mouth.

"Girl, get in here. What are you doing out there?" Mrs. Montgomery called out from the side window, and I coughed, startled by her shouting.

"Be right in," I called back before heading inside.

Tatum's mom walked me through the motions of making a pie crust from scratch. She showed me tips and tricks to getting the edges just right, and how to make it perfectly flaky without being dry.

I really enjoyed the process of creating something in this way. It relaxed me. I didn't cook much back in LA because I didn't have the time and besides, I rarely ate at home. Doing this forced me to realize just how many meals I ate in restaurants and out of craft service trucks on set.

When I got back, I'd be adding that to the list of things in my life that needed to be changed.

Reliving Old Memories

TATUM

I COULDN'T WAIT to get home from the shop and see Paige, but I didn't want to appear overanxious or smothering, so I played it cool. Well, as cool as a guy could be called when he raced through the screen door and practically sprinted into the house.

"Tatum, honey. Slow down," Mama warned. "Where's the fire?"

I glanced at Paige, but she turned away. The fire was in my pants, my hands, my chest. It was everywhere, but I wasn't about to tell my mother that.

"No fire, just starving." I stared at Paige, whose gaze had returned to mine as I licked my lips. She blushed and mouthed, *Stop it.*

"Well then, get over here and help me set out the food,"

she asked, and I obliged.

Dinner was pure torture. Having to keep my distance from Paige when all I wanted to do was reach out and touch her…well, it damn near killed me. She sat across from me, her hair up in a sexy ponytail, and the width of the dinner table put her too far away from me.

I willed the wood to disappear into thin air so nothing separated us. This girl had me feeling so many things that I'd pushed aside for too long, I didn't even mind it.

As soon as I'd swallowed my last bite of food, I tossed down my napkin and said, "I'm gonna take Paige over to my place to watch a movie. That okay?" Paige's mouth fell open slightly, but Mama couldn't wipe the smile off her face.

"I don't know what you're asking me for. Paige is a grown woman," Mama said gruffly, still trying not to smile.

I turned to Paige. "That okay with you?"

"Sure. You sure you don't mind?" she turned to ask Mama.

"Of course not, dear. Why in heaven would I mind?"

"I feel like we're ditching you," Paige said with a frown, and I wanted to grab her and kiss her for being so damned sweet.

"Don't be silly. You two go have fun. Don't worry about me." Mama waved us off before heading down the hall before we could say another word to her.

I leaned close to Paige and whispered, "I've thought about kissing you all day." She bit her bottom lip and smiled, then I pulled her out of there as quick as I could.

The second we stepped onto the porch, I pressed my lips against hers. She tried to pull away and gestured toward the house, but the porch light was off and it was dark. I knew Mama couldn't see us at all, not that that would have stopped me anyway. This girl had bewitched me, and I didn't care who saw me kissing her. Even Mama.

"So, what do you want to watch?" Paige asked as she looked at the DVDs stacked on my shelf.

"I was kidding. We're not watching anything."

"Why not?" She turned around with a huff and crossed her arms over her chest.

"If you want to keep up the charade, then pick something out for us to not watch. I'm going to kiss you, Paige. I'm not going to watch a damn movie with you."

"So we're just going to spend the rest of the evening kissing each other? That's your big plan for the night?" Her eyebrows pinched together, and I instantly wanted to fix whatever I'd said wrong.

"I hadn't thought past the kissing."

"Well, I have," she said, and I couldn't fight back the smile that spread across my face.

"Let me hear it."

She grinned like a Cheshire cat before launching into my arms. "Just kidding. I can't think about anything but kissing you either." Her lips pressed against mine before they parted and her tongue slid inside.

I licked her bottom lip, pulling it into my mouth as I sucked on it gently. Kissing her was like free-falling off a cliff that had no end. I floated in a world filled with nibbling and licking and sensations I'd fought off even thinking about for the last few years.

My insides felt like they were on fire, suddenly awake after being numb. You'd think that my heart would be rusty, that it might need a few beats to get used to the idea of wanting someone after being closed for business for so long. But no, not my heart. It started beating to its own rhythm the second we saw her, instructing my body to feel, want, and need— three things I hadn't experienced in years. This girl sitting right here called to me. I was a ship about to crash into oblivion on the rocky shore, and she was a beacon of fire, determined to save me with her light. And oh, what a beautiful light it was.

After making out for a while, I pushed her away. She laughed while I focused on my breathing. This girl tested all my resolve. I grabbed us each a beer, and we sat across from each other on the couch in my living room.

"So you'll stay on your side of the couch, and I'll stay on mine? Is that how this works?" she said playfully, pushing her toes against my feet.

"Yep. You keep your perfect little lips over there away from mine. You're like a temptress."

"A temptress, huh? Well, that's a heck of a lot better than a princess."

A laugh escaped from my throat. "You like being called Princess. Admit it."

She shook her head vigorously. "I don't. I really don't."

"Why not?"

"'Cause it sucks!" she insisted. "It insinuates all sort of stupid things that I don't like or relate to. I know I'm an actress, and I get way too many things for nothing, but I'm not that kind of person. I wasn't raised that way. I work really hard."

"But that's just it, Princess. You think being an actress is hard work," I said, then instantly wished I could take back the words.

She sat up straighter and cocked her head. "I know to someone like you it probably sounds stupid. I'm not up at the crack of dawn plowing fields or baling hay or growing corn. But I do work hard. Please don't pretend like you know what it's like to be me."

"You're right. I'm sorry." Feeling like a complete ass and desperate to recover, I asked, "Why don't you tell me?"

"I work really long hours. I have obligations to more people than I can count. I can't leave my house without someone following me or taking my picture. I know that's not hard work, per se, but it's hard emotionally," she said emphatically. "When I'm filming, we usually film all day long, from first thing in the morning until nine or so at night. And if we have a night scene to shoot, I'm there until whenever that finishes, which sometimes isn't until two or three in the morning. There's a lot of sitting around and waiting, but it's not like I can go to sleep or go home. I have to sit there until they're ready for me. And not mess up my hair or ruin my makeup in the meantime." She stopped suddenly and growled, "Damn it."

"What?" I asked, and had to stop myself from pointing out to her that she just swore for the first time in front of me.

"I'm trying to tell you that I work hard, but everything I'm saying is just stupid. None of it sounds hard. I have to memorize lines and get into character and be really good at what I do. But I know that my job is a luxury. I know how lucky I am."

"You do more than just act, though. I mean, you're all over the place."

"I am. I have meetings constantly. I'm reading scripts all the time, deciding if I like certain parts or not. I also have to do a ton of publicity for all of my movies, as well as personal publicity. I like the image that I have, and I work hard to make sure it stays that way."

She took a sip of her beer before continuing. "I have to be really particular about what events I attend. I need to know who is putting on the event, what it's about, who else is going to be there, where it's at, and that kind of thing. I also have to pick and choose where I hang out and who I hang out with. All kinds of things that most normal people never even have to consider because they don't wake up with their antics from the night before plastered all over the Internet and the supermarket tabloids."

She sighed. "I'm not complaining because I knew it was part of the deal. It's just more work. And it never ends. I never get to walk away and say, leave the office at five p.m. and turn my work off when I get home, you know? My work and my reputation and the things that I do are a 24/7 job. It never stops. I never shut off."

"That would be hard," I said slowly, realizing that only certain people could handle that sort of life.

"Don't make fun of me," she snapped.

"Shit, Paige." I reached across the couch for her knee and squeezed. "I wasn't. I wasn't at all. I think it sounds like a lot of unnecessary shit to deal with. And I have no idea how you're still such a good and kind person."

That got a smile out of her, a big one, and I wanted to pat myself on the back. "Thank you, Tatum. I try really hard to stay grounded. Being raised normal made all the difference, I think."

"Raised normal?"

"I just mean I wasn't raised in the business. Sure, I've been doing it since I was fourteen, but that also means that I had fourteen years of complete and utter normalcy, unlike my best friend, Quinn, who was raised in the business. She has no idea why I miss the things I miss, or want the things I want, because she never had that in her life and it doesn't appeal to her."

"But she's your best friend, so she can't be all that bad," I said, knowing exactly who she referred to. Quinn Johnson was hot as hell. Nowhere near as hot as Paige, though. Quinn was blond, and I had a thing for brunettes. At least I did now.

"Quinn's amazing, but she's had hard times. She just went through them all before we found each other. If I had known her when she doing the stuff she was doing, we wouldn't have been friends."

"You don't think so?"

"No way. I don't stay away from drugs and all that sort of stuff to be a good role model. It's just not my scene. I'm not into it. I don't like it, and I don't want to be a part of it. So I stay away from the people whose lives are ruled by it."

"Your parents must be really proud of you."

"They are. I think." She scrunched up her nose. "They don't really treat me any differently. And they don't play favorites between me and my sister."

"Wait," I said. "You have a sister?"

"Yeah."

"Younger or older?"

"Younger. She's graduating from high school in a few weeks."

"I had no idea."

"And here I thought you knew everything about me," she said with a wink.

"The only thing I really know about you is that your lips are my kryptonite."

"So you want to stay away from them?"

I inched closer to her. "I never said I was Superman."

I crawled across the couch and hovered above her body. Reaching for her beer, I placed it on the floor and leaned my face toward hers. Closing my eyes, I crushed my lips against hers and tucked my arm under her waist, lifting her body up against mine. She wiggled her hips and rubbed herself against the hardness in my pants. I stopped myself from moaning.

Our tongues were melding together as I nibbled and bit at

her. The way her hips raised into me, I couldn't stop myself from grinding against her. I worked myself into a frenzy with all the gentle grazing, teeth biting, wet tongues kissing, and hips rubbing.

Pulling my mouth away from hers, my hips continued to grind into her warmth. Her mouth fell open, and I forced myself not to grab her again. I pushed up from her, smiling at the effect I had on her.

"Oh good Lord, Tatum. You can't just do that to me!"

"But I did." I smirked before moving back over to my side of the couch. I wasn't sure why this thought popped into my head, and she might get mad as hell at me for asking it, but now that she was sitting here like this, I suddenly found myself wanting to know. "Can I ask you something?"

"Of course," she said as she ran a finger across her bottom lip.

"Since you mentioned your reputation and all that, remember those tabloid reports about you and that director?"

Her sweet expression immediately dropped and turned sad. "Remember? How could I ever forget."

"Was it true?"

"Tatum!" she yelled. "I was seven-freaking-teen. And he was forty-five!"

I shrugged. "I'm sure that kind thing happens in Hollywood all the time."

Her eyes narrowed. "First of all, ew. Second of all, it might happen sometimes, but it didn't happen with me."

"Not an ounce of truth to it at all?" I was pushing her and

I knew it.

"I was naive then, far more naive than I am now. But no. Nothing happened between us. And I probably would have freaked out and cried in a corner if it did."

"So people can just say whatever they want in the news and tabloids? It doesn't have to even be remotely accurate?"

She nodded. "Pretty much. As long as they say they got their information from a *source*," she drew quotes in the air, "they can write whatever they want."

"That's wrong. And screwed up. I don't like it." I found myself getting defensive of her innocence again. Imagining Paige at only seventeen years old, dealing with that kind of thing, made my blood run hot.

"It was horrible. Those reports. Those lies. They broke up a marriage. And for what? It wasn't even true. It wasn't even close to true." Her lip started to tremble, and I knew I'd lose it if she cried.

Please don't cry.

"The guy's wife didn't believe him?"

"No. And I even talked to her. Here I was, little teenage Paige going up to this grown woman, trying to tell her nothing happened and that I would never do something like that. You know what she said to me?"

"What?"

Paige sniffed. "She said, 'That's what I used to say too. We all do things to get ahead in this business, Paige. He might have been your first, but I'm sure he won't be your last. Enjoy your career.'"

"What a bitch," I snarled.

She chuckled. "I should have needed therapy after that fiasco."

"I'm sorry that happened to you."

Her face finally softened, and the Paige I was growing to adore was back. "It was a long time ago. But thanks."

"Random question," I said as more thoughts filled my mind. She tilted her head, giving me the silent okay to continue. "Did you ever think about suing them? Can you sue the tabloids?"

"That's one of the worst parts. You can sue a tabloid or a news outlet, but all the obligation is on you."

"What do you mean?"

"Well, like we just talked about, they can pretty much say and write whatever they want to sell papers, advertising, however it is they make their money. They can do whatever they want. But if I wanted to defend myself in court, I would have to prove that their words caused me to lose money. Like if they defamed my character, I would have to prove that their defamation cost me. Either I stopped getting job offers, or I lost roles I was up for. Things like that. But I would have to prove that all those things happened *because* of the articles and claims made by them. Gosh, am I making any sense at all?"

"You're making sense, but the situation doesn't make any sense."

"I know. They can print complete and utter lies, defame my character, and I can't really do anything about it. I have a publicist and she puts out the fires if necessary, but that whole affair thing. God, I wanted to sue. I wanted them to stop. But I didn't lose work because of it. Only sleep, tears, pride, self-worth. Nothing that stands up in a court of law."

"It shouldn't be like that. They shouldn't be allowed to do that kind of stuff."

"But it makes them so much money, why would they ever stop?"

Frowning, I admitted, "I'm starting to get angry, Paige."

"Don't. It's not worth it. I've been doing this long enough that I've got it under control, for the most part. They don't say many bad things about me. I'm lucky in that regard."

"Lucky? You don't do anything for them to talk about. You don't do anything wrong."

"I know. And that's exactly why. There hadn't been anything dramatic written until—"

"Until Douchepants cheated on you." I finished her thought for her, and she lowered her head.

"Yeah. That was mortifying. *Is*"—she looked at me—"*is* mortifying."

I leaned toward her, placing my hand on her knee. "He's an idiot."

"True," she said with a smile.

"Do you miss him?" It was another loaded question, but this detail was more recent. Forget my simply wanting to know…I *needed* to know.

"Missing him is the easy part. I don't. At all. We were both so busy and rarely in the same place at the same time, that there isn't really a lot to miss. I'm more angry at myself, to be honest. I feel like I was a complete idiot and I should have known better."

I nodded. "That's how I feel about Brina. Like I should have known she was just using me the whole time."

"How could you have known something like that?"

"How could *you*?"

"I don't know," she admitted with a little shrug. "I just feel like I should have."

"Me too."

We stayed silent for a minute, maybe more, letting the similarities of our experiences sink in. At least, that was what I was doing. I'd never expected us to have much of anything in common, but I was learning how wrong I was.

"Will you tell me what happened with your dad?"

I sucked in a breath. Was I ready to head down this road? If I didn't drive down it now with her, when would I? Talking about this would never be an easy conversation to have, but I wanted to be open with Paige. She needed to know this side of me, and understand the moment that had altered my life.

"I came home for Thanksgiving break. Mama had dinner ready, and we were waiting on my dad to come home. He was late and wasn't answering the phone, so Mama asked me to run to the shop and go get him."

I looked away from Paige's eyes, staring firmly at the wall behind her before meeting them again. Reliving that day hurt like hell, but I'd do it for her. My throat felt thick and it was hard to swallow, but I continued.

"I pulled my truck up to the shop and saw all the lights on. Thinking everything was okay, I yelled for him to wrap it up and come home to eat before Mama killed him. The music was playing and Buster was whining, but my dad didn't respond. I walked through the office and into the garage when I saw him lying there. The truck he had been working on had fallen off the jack and was lying right on top of his body. All I could see were his legs and a pool of blood."

I lowered my head and started shaking it back and forth. "I didn't know what to do, so I tried to lift the truck. Like with my bare hands. I tried to tried to get it off of his body, but it wouldn't budge. I screamed for him, shouted his name, but he didn't move. I fell to my knees at the front of the car to see if I could pull him out somehow, but that was when I saw that his chest was crushed and a piece of metal had pierced through his stomach. That's where all the blood came from. I knew he was gone, but I refused to believe it and I didn't want my mama to see him like that, so I ran to Doc Tracy's house. I don't even remember running there, but apparently I did. I don't remember most of what happened after, but my God, Paige. I wish every day it didn't happen. I wish every day that I'd gone to check on him sooner."

Paige reached out and intertwined her fingers with mine. Squeezing them, she brought my knuckles to her lips and placed a kiss against them before bringing my hand to her lap and holding on tight.

"Doc Tracy said there wasn't anything that I could have done. That he most likely died instantly, but those words never seem to make a difference. You can hear them a hundred times, but your brain refuses to believe it. What if I'd shown up ten minutes earlier? What if Buster had run home to get me, like the damn dogs do in movies? What if, what if, what if..." My voice drifted off as the pain came crushing back.

Paige squeezed my hand. "I'm so sorry, Tatum. I'm so sorry that you lost your dad like that, and that you were the one to find him."

"I'm glad it was me and not Mama. I don't think she could have ever recovered from seeing him like that. The funeral was bad enough."

"So after he died, you never went back to school?" She adjusted herself on the couch and sat up straighter against the back.

I sighed. "I went back. But only to quit the football team, drop my classes, and get my stuff." She nodded as if my words resonated deep within her. "What are you thinking?" I asked.

"That I would have done the same thing," she admitted with a shrug.

"Really?" I couldn't believe it.

She continued to nod. "I think so. I mean, on one hand, school would have been a great distraction, but I couldn't imagine leaving my family after a tragedy like that. I'd want to be home. I'd feel like everything else could wait."

"That's exactly how I felt. I didn't want to play football anymore. I didn't care. And who was going to run my dad's shop and support our family? My mom? She's not a mechanic. And no one in town was interested in buying it. The shop has been in our family for generations. It seemed like the right thing to do."

"I completely understand."

"Brina didn't."

"I heard a little about that from Celeste," she said, and I instantly bristled.

"Yeah. I realized later that Brina was just using me as her get-out-of-town ticket. And when that fell through, she wanted nothing more to do with me." I blew out a loud breath. "I thought she really cared about me. I don't understand how someone can fake something like that for so long."

"I'm sure she wasn't faking all of it. She can't be that cruel," Paige said, giving Brina the benefit of the doubt, even though she didn't deserve it.

"Who gives a shit? No more talking, Paige," I said, the weight of our discussion bearing down on me. I was exhausted emotionally, but I needed her more than ever.

"More kissing?" she asked through puckered lips.

"Lots more kissing. Stay here with me tonight."

"I thought you weren't ready for that?" She pulled her head back in surprise, and I wondered what exactly she was thinking.

"I just want to hold you in my arms all night, if that's all right with you."

"It's more than all right," she breathed out before standing and reaching out her hand for mine. She led me into the bedroom, kicked off her shoes and looked at me. "What do you normally sleep in?"

"Nothing," I said with a big smile.

"I figured. But what will you be sleeping in tonight?" She walked over to my dresser and opened up the top drawer before closing it. Opening up the drawer beneath it, she smiled and pulled out a pair of my workout shorts. I assumed they were for me to sleep in, but she unbuttoned her jean shorts and dropped them to the floor. My eyes fixed on her bare thighs, her hips, and the tiny piece of red cotton covering her skin. She pulled my shorts on over her underwear and I blinked.

Her hands gripped the bottom of her tank top and pulled it over her head as she walked toward my closet and flicked through my hanging shirts. Long brown hair hung down her back, and I realized spending the night just sleeping was going to be more difficult than I had imagined.

"Where are all your T-shirts?" she turned and asked, her breasts practically busting out of the top of her bra.

"Dresser," I mumbled, watching every move she made. When she pulled out a Texas University shirt and slipped it on, I hardened even more. Seeing her dressed from head to toe in my clothing was a ridiculous turn-on.

"Your turn," she said softly as she reached for the bottom of my shirt. It was such a bold move, but it felt right in her hands. I lifted my arms above my head as she pulled it off and tossed it to the floor near her discarded clothes.

This was a side of Paige I didn't even know existed. This

Paige was confident and bold and seemed completely unafraid, while I stood there half-terrified, feeling like my soul had been stripped bare and laid out in front of her. I hoped she'd be gentle with it.

Once she reached for the button on my jeans, I stopped her and did it myself. I trusted Paige but I was emotionally spent, and having her unbutton my jeans crossed the line from where my sanity and self-control lived. I wanted Paige in my arms. I needed to feel the closeness between us after what I'd just shared with her, but I wasn't ready to push the boundary. Yet.

"I know this probably seems crazy to have you here like this and not…" I paused as I pulled the covers back on my bed. "Well, you know."

"It's not messed up. Do you have any idea how many times a girl would just like to be held, or have an amazing talk like we just did and have it *not* end up in the bedroom? I'm happy to spend the night with you. I'm even happier that it has nothing to do with sex. You have no idea how much of a relief that is for a girl." She climbed in bed beside me, my shirt hanging well past her hips. "Especially for someone in my position."

My emotions still raw, I pulled her against me, still thinking about my dad and feeling vulnerable. She rested her head against my chest and I kissed the top of it. "Thank you. For understanding."

"Thank you. For not being typical."

"Yeah, I'm definitely not normal. Pretty sure I'm broken,

or damaged, or maybe just clinically insane."

She looked up at me. "Pretty sure you're amazing. And I'm lucky to have found you."

"Pretty sure you're just as messed up as I am," I teased, before finding her lips and kissing her until I could barely stay awake.

A New Kind of Trust

PAIGE

MY EYES FLUTTERED open as the weight of someone's arm reminded me that I wasn't alone in bed. Memories of last night flooded through my mind, and I smiled as I buried my face in Tatum's arm. I tried to turn over, but I couldn't move. His body pressed against mine as he held me so tightly.

It was in that moment that I started to freak out, realizing that his mom would know I had spent the night with her son.

"Oh my gosh, Tatum," I said, trying to shake him awake. "Tatum, wake up."

"What's up, babe?" he mumbled.

"Your mom."

"What about her? Is she here?" He shot up.

"No. But she'll know I spent the night. Oh my gosh, she's

going to kick me out of your house." I dropped my head into my hands and closed my eyes.

Tatum wrapped one of his arms around me and squeezed. "She's not going to do anything except probably bake us both more pie. She'll be pleased as punch."

"Pleased as punch?" I said, turning my head slightly.

"It's a Southern thing. It means happy."

"How do you know?"

"You saw her face last night. She lit up like a Christmas tree when we said we were hanging out together. I think she's been waiting for this since I first brought you home and warned her not to freak out."

"You warned her not to freak out? About me?"

"Well, yeah. I couldn't just waltz in the house with you and not warn her. I am a gentleman, after all."

"Is that what you call it?"

"What would you call it, Princess?"

I growled and frowned at him. "I hate you and I'm going to make up some stupid nickname for you that you hate. And I'm going to call you by it all the time. Because I'm twelve," I said with a fake scowl.

"Sorry, punk."

"But seriously, Tatum, I don't want to disappoint your mom." I hated the idea of her being upset at me.

"She's not going to be disappointed. You're reading way too much into this," he insisted.

"By the way, what's the deal with my car?" Not that I cared, I just figured I'd ask so I could pretend I needed to know.

"Oh." He turned his face away briefly before looking up at the ceiling and shrugging. "I'm, um, never fixing it."

I laughed. "That's just rude, Tatum Alan Montgomery."

"Is it?" He leaned over me, his mouth quirking up into a devilish grin. I wanted to smack his arm, be playful, or say something witty, but all I could see were his shoulders and the way his arms flexed as he held himself above me. Nothing in my life had ever been sexier than this moment.

"You see something you like?" Tatum winked as my focus returned to his face.

"A lady never tells," I said coyly.

"And you, Paige Lockwood," he kissed my nose, "are most certainly one of those." With a grin on his face, he rolled off of me and got out of bed. "I'm starving."

I moved to get out of bed and change into my clothes when I froze. "Tatum, seriously. I'm putting the same clothes back on and doing the walk of shame. Into your mom's house!"

"You'd better bring some of your clothes over here then," he said as he walked out the door, and my heart melted. I stayed on his bed for a minute, collecting the puddle of myself until I turned solid enough to move again.

Pulling open the porch door, I prayed that Tatum's mom wasn't in the kitchen, or anyplace where she could see me. But the smell of breakfast cooking hit me in the face, and I knew I was in trouble. Mrs. Montgomery turned her head at the sound of the door creaking open, and I pinched my lips together and offered her a tight smile.

"Morning, Paige," she said with arched eyebrows.

Crap. I was so busted.

"Morning. I'll just, uh," nerves fluttered through me, "be right back." I rushed into my bedroom and quickly changed into some clean clothes before returning to the kitchen for breakfast.

Sitting down at the table, Tatum couldn't wipe the stupid smile off his face as his mom kept looking between us.

"I'd really like to take you both out to dinner tonight if that's okay," I said. "You do have a restaurant in town, right?" I searched my memory, trying to recall if I'd seen one, but I was certain they had to have one.

Tatum laughed. "We have one café."

Mrs. Montgomery smiled. "You don't have to do that, Paige, but it's kind of you to offer."

"You both have done so much for me since I've been here. And Mrs. Montgomery, you haven't stopped cooking or baking since I arrived. I'd love to let someone else cook for you for once. Please?" I put my hands together in prayer and stuck out my bottom lip.

"So you don't like my cooking? Is that it?" Mrs. Montgomery teased, and as I opened my mouth to argue, she stopped me. "I'm kidding, Paige. That sounds nice. I'd love to go out."

"Yay!" I said a little too enthusiastically, and Tatum rolled his eyes.

Rubbing my full stomach, I hoped that my day with Tatum

would consist of more talking much like last night. My thoughts felt somewhat pushy in a sense, but I hoped he was on the same page as I was. As we washed the dishes from breakfast, I nudged my hip against his upper thigh, shoving him over a step. He turned and splashed water from the sink at me, and I squealed.

"All right, you two. I can do the dishes. Get out of here." Mrs. Montgomery came up from behind us and took the plate from my hand.

"No, really. We can do it," I argued.

"You'll make a mess of my floors and I'll have to mop them. Get on out." She reached for a towel and tried to smack Tatum with it.

"Let's get out of here before she beats us to death." Tatum squirmed to get away from her well-aimed swipes. He ran outside, Buster on his heels and me not far behind. "Wanna go for a walk?" he suggested, and I felt my face light up.

"I would love that."

The heat wrapped itself around me with each step, making me wonder if people got used to it. I still wasn't. Tatum reached for my hand and rubbed his thumb across my palm. Buster wagged his tail and followed behind before Tatum shooed him away and told him to stay put. The dog whined, but stopped walking and plopped down right in the dirt.

"So, where are we going?" I asked when I realized we weren't headed the same direction as the swimming hole, and I hadn't been to any other part of the property before.

"You'll see when we get there."

"That's helpful."

"You'll like it," he assured me, and I believed him. It made me realize that when Tatum said something, I knew it was true. For some reason I implicitly trusted him.

We walked through a wide-open field and directly into a line of trees. The sun disappeared as we stepped under the canopy of oversized branches and green leaves. Tiny rays of sunlight would stream through the space in the trees when they could, forming what looked like roads to the sky. Our steps echoed into the space around us as branches and old leaves crushed under the weight of our feet. My sandals slapped against my feet, and somewhere along the walk, I'd started counting the clip-clap sounds they made.

"Are we almost there?" I asked, breaking the vocal silence.

"Almost." Tatum smiled, and I noticed that his usual stress lines looked less pronounced. He looked happy.

Was it because of me?

Pulling me through the trees, it seemed that he knew exactly where to head. All the trees looked the same to me, and heaven help me because if Tatum ditched me in here, I'd never find my way out. I'd be lost in the land of sunless forest forever. And then I'd die there.

A few more steps and the trees thinned out, the forest opening up into a meadow with tall grasses. I spotted something out of the corner of my eye and knew this was where he was taking me. A swing hung motionless at the edge of the darkened woods and the brightly lit meadow. The tree that held it was large at its base, with sweeping branches that almost touched the ground in places. It looked like something straight out of a picture book, the way the light hit it on one side.

I smiled at Tatum. "Do I get to swing on it?"

He nodded. "Let me look at it first. I tightened the rope not too long ago, but I want to make sure it will hold."

The swing's wooden seat was strung up on each side with some weathered rope that I assumed was once white. I followed the rope upward until I saw where it met the tree branch and looped around. "Who made this?"

"My dad. He used to bring me with him when he would gather up fallen tree limbs for firewood. He made me that swing as a reward after I'd looked for as many pieces of wood that I could find." Tatum's expression looked wistful. "After I'd put all the wood in a pile, he'd push me on this swing for hours. It was probably only twenty minutes, but it felt like hours. I loved this swing."

"I would have too. What a great memory." I reached out for his shoulder and gently squeezed. He turned and pulled me against him, his arms strong and tight around my body. I could feel every movement his chest made as it moved in and out against me. The weight of his chin rested on top of my head, and I knew he was battling through some emotions, so I stayed quiet. We stayed like that for a few breaths before he let me go.

"He would've loved you. He woulda told me I was out of my league, but he woulda loved you," he said, his lips forming a half smile.

I smacked his arm. "Stop it."

"It's true," he said as he tugged on the ropes and inspected the wood. He hopped onto the seat and bounced a little before deeming it safe for me to ride. "All ready, milady."

I curtsied. "Why, thank you, good knight."

Tatum's hands gripped my waist as he lifted me like I weighed nothing and placed me square on the wood plank. I shuffled and scooted my butt back a little farther, then shouted, "Ready!"

"Ready for what? Don't you know how to swing?" he asked, standing in front of me.

I cocked my head to the side and extended my legs, trying to reach for his goodies. "I know how to swing, all right, and you'd better watch out. I've got one heck of a leg stretch," I teased.

"Don't you kick me, woman." He moved behind me, completely out of view. Firm hands pressed against my back before they shoved at me. I squealed as the swing flew forward and I was soaring into the trees.

"Tatum, it's so pretty! It looks like I'm flying through branches and with the trees!" I cried out in delight as he pushed me higher and higher, each forward movement sending me more and more into a state of bliss. My hair flew all around me, covering my face before blowing away again. I felt like I was soaring, and I wanted to thank the heavens for giving me the wings to fly.

Glancing back at him, I asked, "So, what did you want to do after school? I mean, did you want to play professional football for a living?"

"Not really. Playing football helped pay my tuition, and without that scholarship, my parents would have gone into serious debt to get me into school. Football was a means to an end, from my perspective."

"But did you enjoy playing, at least?"

He laughed. "Oh, hell yeah! I loved it. I just didn't want to do it forever."

"Well, if you didn't want to play football, then what did you want to do?" As the swing fell to where Tatum's hands would normally reach for me, I braced for the contact, but it didn't come. I turned to look at him and made the swing go crooked as it moved forward again, wobbling from side to side.

"I'll tell you after you tell me more stuff about you," he said.

"What do you want to know?" I offered, wondering what he would ask and if there wasn't anything I wouldn't honestly tell him.

He pulled the swing to a stop and leaned toward me like he was going to confess a secret before asking, "Why were you really driving across the country? Was it all because of Douchepants?" Reaching for my hand, he grabbed it, planted a kiss on the top, then pulled me back and sent me swinging again toward the trees.

"No," I shouted immediately before pondering on where to start exactly. "I just needed to get away. I'd been telling my team that I wanted to go to college for a few years now, but they kept putting me off. It was always 'Not now, Paige' or 'You can do that later,' you know?"

Tatum nodded that he understood, and I continued. "But I finally realized that later was a day that was never gonna come. They were never gonna let me stop working to go to school. And then my little sister started applying to colleges and hearing back from them, and now she's getting ready to move on with her life and move out."

"And you were jealous?" he asked, his tone understanding and not judgmental.

"I was. I was totally jealous. Stupid, right?" I slowed my kicks and waved Tatum's hands off as the swing came to a slow stop.

"Not at all. Most of us are raised as products of our environment. A lot of the kids here are raised to take over their family farms, or run a shop, or something. But I'm sure where you grew up, everyone planned on going to school and then going to college. We all follow these paths that are set before us, whether we realize we're doing it or not."

It felt like a light bulb clicked in my brain as I stared at Tatum. "You are so right. So, so right. I always assumed that that was what I would do. I would graduate from high school and go to college. I'd never planned on being an actress or anything like that. All that stuff came out of nowhere."

Tatum nodded. "But the things you'd wanted back then, you still want now. It's like having unfulfilled dreams. Or parts of your life you always thought you'd have and then they got taken away from you. The want doesn't go away simply because the opportunity did." He shrugged, obviously completely getting it. Maybe because he'd lived it too.

"How'd you get so smart?" I kicked playfully at his leg with my foot, and he grabbed on.

"How'd you get so dumb?"

I opened my mouth to say something in response, but all I could do was laugh. And then I couldn't stop.

"Your turn," I told him through my laughing fit.

"For what?" He raised his eyebrows and smirked at me.

"To tell me what you wanted to do after college."

"I can't."

"You can't tell me?" My stomach instantly tensed up. I had just shared so much of myself with him, and he didn't want to share this with me?

"Not here. I'll show you when we get back to the barn."

Curious, I was practically dancing in my seat with impatience. "Let's go back there now then."

"Nah. Not yet. You're not done flying through the trees." He pushed at my back again and I sailed into the humid air.

"I can't remember the last time I've been on a swing. How come we forget how fun they are?"

"We forget all kinds of things once we grow up. But I knew you'd like it."

As I pumped my feet, my brown hair blowing all around me as I floated, I thought about how quickly my relationship with Tatum had changed. How all it took was one kiss in the middle of a bar to change everything between us.

I recognized how truly happy I felt being here with him in

these moments. The feeling felt new, different somehow. Was I stupid to want it to last?

College Applications

PAIGE

WE HEADED BACK through the woods hand in hand before walking into his mama's house, saying hi, grabbing a sandwich, and going right back out the front door. Mrs. Montgomery's gaze dropped to our locked hands, and she smiled before making eye contact with me. I blushed and bit back the grin that tried to escape, but failed. I wanted to talk to her about all this, but right now wasn't the time.

Back in the barn, I started to head over to the couch to sit down, but Tatum stopped me. "Nope. Go over to the desk and turn on the computer."

Narrowing my gaze, I gave him a questioning look. "Why?"

"Don't argue with me or I'll call you that name you hate."

I grumbled and he laughed, then walked away as I pressed

the button to start the aging PC. Placing a plate with a sandwich in front of me, as well as a glass of sweet tea, Tatum nodded toward the screen. "So?"

I didn't get it. "So, what?"

"Where do you want to go to college?" He folded his arms across his chest as he waited for my response.

"Where do I what? I don't know!" I shrieked a little too defensively, and he threw his hands up in surrender.

"Don't bite my head off, Paige. I'm asking you a question you should already know the answer to, don't you think?"

Heat crept up my neck and flooded into my cheeks. I felt like an idiot. I'd talked and fought for the chance to go to college for so many years, but I'd never actually taken any of the steps to do it. I looked away from Tatum's knowing stare. "I'm not sure where I want to go."

"Well, figure it out." He pointed to the Internet icon.

I paused for a moment. "I always thought I'd want to get as far away from everyone as possible. But now I don't think I'd be happy if I went that far away. Is that stupid? Do you think I'm a wimp? I bet Quinn would call me a wimp," I said, babbling.

"Why would I think you're a wimp?" His hand caressed my arm and chills appeared.

"I don't know. It's just that I've been fighting with my agent over this for so long. And now that I'm actually thinking about doing it, I don't think I want to go away at all."

Tatum squinted at me. "What do you mean you don't want to go away?"

"I just mean that I still want to go to college, but I think that I actually want to do it in LA. I don't want to completely give up one thing for another, and I've worked too hard to build the career I have to just walk away from it. And I don't want to, but I also want something normal. I want to go to college and do college things. I guess I just want it all," I said slowly, realizing that I didn't want to give up on acting completely.

Actually, I wanted options and I wanted control, in all areas of my life; I was tired of everything being decided for me. There had to be a way where I could have all the things I wanted without losing my career.

"Makes sense to me. You want to control your destiny. You want to have a say in your life. And you should."

"So should you," I added, realizing now more than ever that our situations, while completely different, had similar themes.

"I wouldn't even know where to start anymore. I've been out of school for so long, basically doing nothing but running Dad's shop. What the hell would I major in? What would be the point?" His voice sounded so deflated, it tore at my heartstrings.

"Well, what did you want to do before? You never did tell me."

"Don't laugh, all right?" he warned before getting up off the couch.

"Okay," I said slowly as he walked away.

Tatum reappeared and sat on the couch with an acoustic

guitar in his hand. "I love to play. My dream was to write and produce music," he confessed, and I was dumbfounded. I had never seen this coming. Tatum had never even hinted at me that he loved music or wanted to have anything to do with it.

"Have you written anything? How well do you play? Do you sing too? Will you play something for me?" The overload of questions spilled from my lips as my curiosity and excitement built.

Tatum settled the guitar on his lap and began to strum a hauntingly beautiful melody. Lyrics filled the space between us as he sang along to the words he wrote, although not always loud enough for me to understand. I sat there staring at him, the red feeling inside me starting to burn. This incredible man who had been through so much had the most beautiful singing voice and talent, and I'd had no clue.

When he finished playing, I closed my mouth and smiled. "Tatum, you have an amazing voice. You can really sing."

He lowered his head briefly before looking into my eyes. "Thanks, but I don't like singing and I'm not comfortable singing in front of an audience, obviously. But I love writing the melodies and sometimes the lyrics. The way everything comes together and creates this piece of music that no one's ever heard before..." His eyes danced with excitement. "It fires me up."

"I can tell."

"So, what did you think?"

"You're incredibly talented. And I'm not just saying that because I like kissing you. I really mean it."

He leaned forward and sat his guitar on the floor. "You like kissing me?" he teased, his lips inching closer.

"Did I say *like*?" I sucked my bottom lip between my teeth. "I meant love. I love kissing you," I said before pressing my mouth against his. My tongue darted between his lips and met his as I moved toward him. He lifted me out of the chair, his hands splayed across my ass and my lower back, and I wrapped my legs around him.

Tatum moved us to the couch and I sat straddling him. I pressed my hips against the hardness growing beneath me, my body yearning for his. Our mutual confessions made me feel closer to him, and I wanted to shred every bit of clothing that kept our skin apart, but even I knew it was too soon. My hips moved faster as our mouths matched the rhythm I was setting. I silently wondered how far he'd let me push him before he told me to stop.

I didn't have to wait long. "Damn it, Paige. You're so distracting," he said as he moved his lips away from mine.

"Me? You're the distracting one with those blue eyes and those lips." I licked and nipped at his bottom lip.

"Get your hot little ass back over to that computer and pick a college. Or two. I don't care, but narrow it down and figure out where you want to go. We're on a mission."

I refused to move. Folding my hands across my chest, I arched my eyebrows at him.

"What? Why are you looking at me like that?" he complained.

"I'll go look at colleges on one condition."

"What's that?"

"That you figure out what to major in, or how to put that amazing talent to work."

He dropped his chin and closed his eyes. "Don't make this about me, Paige."

"This is about both of us. About not giving up on dreams we once had."

"I don't remember those dreams anymore," he said, sounding convincing, but I refused to believe him.

"Don't lie to me, Tatum. But most of all, don't lie to yourself."

He huffed out a long breath. "I think I'd like to write and produce music, but I'm not a hundred percent sure. I've never done it before, but if I had a passion for something, I think that's where it lies."

"Tatum, that's brilliant! I know people. I could introduce you to Walker Rhodes or anyone else in the business you wanted to meet." My enthusiasm echoed throughout the small place. "Except Colin McGuire because, you know," I paused, "screw him. Don't sell him any of your songs either, or I'll disown you."

He put one hand in the air as he shook his head. "One step at a time. And I don't want your help. If I ever do something like this, Paige, I have to do it on my own." He reached for his guitar, and I noticed his hands shaking.

"Don't be so proud. I didn't want to give you a handout," I lied. I'd totally give him a handout if it meant he could follow his dreams. I'd owe favors to Walker, Madison, or anyone who could help him. Even Jayson. "I simply meant that I could introduce you to people who might have some helpful tips and realistic feedback to offer. They've been in the business, so they can speak from experience and give you the rundown on what to expect. That's all." I sent up a silent prayer, hoping my words would calm him down.

"I'm sorry." He sat down next to me and placed his hand on my knee. "Thinking about doing this is scary. Hell, just thinking about it is terrifying."

"No kidding! How do you think I feel? I've wanted this for so long, and it's always been out of reach. I think subconsciously I always thought that's where it would stay. Out of reach, just a dream, something I wanted but would never get to have. And now that I'm actually thinking about pursuing it, it's scary as hell. What if I fail? What if I hate it? What if this, what if that?" I grabbed my head with both hands and squeezed, overwhelmed by the mere thought of achieving this goal that had been nothing but a pipe dream for so long.

Tatum reached around my shoulder and pulled me against him. I breathed in his scent and instantly relaxed. "You'll be great," he said. "And if you hate college, then you'll stop going and it won't be a big deal. You will have tried the one thing that's been haunting you for years. It's a hell of a lot better than never trying and never knowing. You're not wimpy, Paige Lockwood. You're one of the bravest girls I've ever known."

No one had ever said those words to me before. At least not in a way that made me feel like I could no longer breathe, or that my heart might explode. My eyes welled up as I fought to keep the tears at bay.

"No crying, babe. I can't take it," he said with a smirk as I swiped at my eyes. "Not from you."

"Then stop saying things that make me emotional," I choked out, trying to smile.

"Never."

Tatum leaned forward and pressed his lips against mine, and all thoughts of college, dreams, and goals were wiped from my mind in an instant.

Dinner with Mama

PAIGE

AFTER EVERYTHING TATUM and his mom had done for me, I wanted to treat them to a meal in town. Part of me wanted to cook and show off what Mrs. Montgomery had taught me, but the realistic part didn't want to risk my screwing it up. If Tatum's mom had to save me in the kitchen, that would have blown the whole point of me trying to do something nice for her. She happily agreed to going out, and Tatum didn't seem to care where we ate as long as we did. I decided right then and there that guys never stop growing.

Without leaving town, we only had one option: the café. I hadn't eaten there, but I'd seen it from a distance and knew it was small and homey. I dressed for comfort in a pair of ripped jeans and an oversized tan Diesel tank top. Mrs. Montgomery let me keep her boots in my room so I pushed my feet into them, smiling the whole time. Somewhere in this escape, I'd become the kind of girl who had fallen in love with a pair of cowboy boots. Grabbing my long hair, I swept it up into a ponytail and left wispy pieces falling around my face. I felt like a country girl when I looked in the mirror, and I had to admit that I liked it.

Heading into the living room, I spotted Mrs. Montgomery sitting on the porch, rocking back and forth in one of the wicker chairs. Buster sat at her side. I joined her as we waited for Tatum.

"I'm wearing your boots again, if that's okay?"

"Of course it's okay." Her gaze swept the length of my body before stopping at my feet. "They look adorable on you. You have such great style."

"Perks of being a celebrity. Free clothes and stylists to help dress you."

"Do you get a lot of things for free? I mean, I suppose you would."

I nodded. "I do. Way more than I could ever wear. You'll have to come raid my closet sometime," I offered with a wink.

She gave me a grin. "I just might take you up on that."

I smiled, thinking about her and Tatum visiting me in Los Angeles. "Have you ever been to California," I asked as she continued to rock in the chair.

She laughed out loud. "Honey, I've never even left the state. Tatum's daddy took him to visit schools and I stayed here. We planned on taking in a game after the holidays, but...well, that didn't end up happening."

Her face pinched and I knew her heart was hurting thinking about her late husband. I hated seeing her in pain, so I tried to cheer her up. "After I leave, we'll have to work something out where you can come visit. I'd love to show you LA and Malibu."

Tatum's footsteps interrupted our chat and she leaned in to whisper to me, "I've always wanted to go to Hollywood."

"What are you two whispering about?" He stopped on the porch stairs and stared at us both as my eyes drank him in. His jeans always fit him so well, and tonight's pair was no exception. The sand-colored shirt he wore actually matched mine, and I wondered if he noticed. The sight of his arms and shoulders caused my pulse to pick up.

Tatum's mom pushed up out of the chair and stood. "None of your business. Hey, you two match. You look real cute together."

Tatum glanced at his outfit before looking back at mine. "We do match."

"Go change," I said teasingly, and pointed toward the barn.

"You change," he huffed back in response.

"I was ready first." I placed one hand on my hip and pretended to snarl.

He cracked a smile. "I'm not changing. Neither are you. Let's go eat." He reached for my hand and I grabbed it tightly.

The three of us couldn't fit into Tatum's truck comfortably, so we followed behind his mom as she headed toward her car. "Do you want me to drive, Mama?"

Mrs. Montgomery waved her hand around, as though his suggestion were words she could slap out of the air. "You are not driving my baby. You get your behind in the backseat like a gentleman and hush up," she demanded as she opened her door.

"You've been told," I whispered.

"No shit," he said as he pushed the seat forward to squeeze into the back. I felt bad that Tatum's large body had to sit back there, so I moved my seat as close to the dashboard as I could to give him more legroom.

The car came to a stop next to the bowling alley, which had a diner attached to the side. "This will be nice, Paige. Thank you. It's been far too long since I've been out of the house for a meal," Mrs. Montgomery confessed.

"It's my pleasure. Really."

Tatum squeezed my hand as we approached the diner's glass doors. Our bodies moved in sync before he held the door open for his mom and then for me, giving my butt a quick smack as I walked in front of him. The diner wasn't crowded, but every person in the room turned to stare the second we entered. I figured that the news about my being in town had gotten around a while ago and that it wouldn't cause any problems, but I quickly realized that they weren't only looking at me.

"Maybe this was a bad idea?" I said apologetically toward Mrs. Montgomery.

She leaned toward me. "It's not you, dear. It's me. And Tatum holding your hand probably doesn't help."

"Emily. Tatum. Young lady I don't know. Sit anywhere," an aging waitress shouted from behind the long white counter, and I stifled an uncomfortable laugh. Three men sat on bar stools watching us, and I shifted toward Tatum, feeling a little uncomfortable. He wrapped an arm around my waist and pulled me against him.

Mrs. Montgomery slid into a corner booth away from the majority of prying eyes and forced a smile. "I don't get out much since Tatum's daddy passed. It was just too hard at first. Not just to leave the house, but to leave the bed," she said with a sigh. "But this is good." She nodded, as if trying to convince herself. "This is a good step. These are my friends and I've ignored them for far too long."

I sat next to Tatum, silently listening as his mom confessed things I was certain she usually never talked about. Before I could feel guilty for forcing her out of the house, she assured me with a smile that this had been a great idea. I wasn't entirely convinced.

When Tatum rested his hand on top of my thigh, I both relaxed and tensed at the same time. He had this calming effect on me that mixed with his ability to turn me on with just a touch, which of course caused complete chaos inside my body. Excitement tore through half of me while utter comfort settled the other half. It made zero sense, but I chalked it up to the Tatum Effect and all that feeling "red" he seemed to do to me. Quinn would have a field day with that.

Air blew past me as someone stopped abruptly in front of our table. "Hi, y'all. I'll be your server tonight."

I looked up to see Brina standing there glaring at us with a notepad and pen in hand.

"Hi, Brina, I didn't know you worked here," I said sincerely.

Her face soured as her voice turned bitter. "It's not like we're friends, so how would you know?"

"Be nice, Brina," Mrs. Montgomery said in a warning tone.

"Can I get y'all anything to drink?" She tapped her pen repeatedly.

"I think we'll all have some tea," Mrs. Montgomery said before Brina turned on her heel and stomped away.

"Do you think she'll spit in them?" I whispered toward Tatum's mom.

"She most certainly better not or I'll be paying her mama a visit. What happened to that girl? She used to be so nice."

Tatum's grip on my hand tightened. "She wasn't ever nice, Mama. She's a fake. A fraud. A phony."

I squeezed Tatum's fingers before letting go. "She's not worth it," I reminded him, and he leaned over, placing a kiss on my cheek.

"Do we get to talk about this now?" Mrs. Montgomery waggled her finger between us, and my cheeks warmed.

"I hope it's okay. I meant to talk to you." I glanced at Tatum. "Alone. I just—"

"Paige." She reached across the table for my hand. "It's more than okay. You've brought light to my son's eyes again and a smile to his face. It's been too long since I've seen either."

Tatum squeezed my thigh and nodded in agreement at his mom's words. A smile spread across his face, and my eyes instantly filled as I fought to keep back the tears that threatened to spill. I refused to be the girl who cried at dinner because some nice words were spoken about her. Focused on holding back my emotions, I'd almost forgotten my manners. "Thank you, Mrs. Montgomery. That was really nice of you to say."

"I wasn't being nice, dear. I only speak the truth. So, thank you."

Tatum's mouth breathed against my ear, "She's right. You've made me believe in love again. I'd all but given up any hope for it existing before you came along. Thank you for reawakening my heart."

I ducked my head, and the tears I'd fought so hard to stop from falling spilled down my cheeks. I quickly wiped them away as Brina sauntered over to our table. Perfect timing.

"Make her cry already, Tatum? Great job, sweetheart," she snapped as she placed the three drinks on the table.

"Brina Marie Ward, I know for a fact that your mama didn't raise you to have such a smart mouth. I'll ask you one last time to act like the Southern woman you were raised to be before I start lodging complaints. And you know how much I'd hate to do that." Mrs. Montgomery cocked her head to the side and smiled.

Brina straightened her back and lowered her head. "Yes, ma'am. You're right. I apologize. I'll be back in a minute to take your order." She quickly shuffled away.

"Wow. That was impressive," I said, somewhat intimidated by Mrs. Montgomery's attitude.

"Here in the South, we know how to make you feel about this big." She held her fingers almost an inch apart from each other. "And we do it all with a smile on our face."

"You ladies scare me," I admitted with a tight laugh.

"Me too," Tatum chimed in.

Dinner was uneventful and Brina didn't act out anymore. Matter of fact, she barely spoke to us unless absolutely necessary. I think Mrs. Montgomery scared her. After paying for the check and tipping Brina more than she deserved, I noticed Tatum's eyebrows pull together as his eyes got that faraway look in them.

"What's the matter?" I asked.

"I think I left the office door unlocked at the shop. I need to run there real quick and make sure I locked it all up."

"This is a dangerous town. You should definitely dead bolt everything," I teased.

Mrs. Montgomery chuckled. "You two go check on the shop, and I'll go wait in the car," she offered with a smile.

"Thanks, Mama. We'll be right back," Tatum said before giving her a quick peck on the cheek.

As we closed in on the shop, I noticed the side door hanging completely open. "Tatum, you didn't even close the door!"

He shrugged. "I was in a hurry."

"For what?" I asked as we entered the dark space.

"To see you." He wrapped an arm around my lower back

as his lips met mine softly, his tongue gently begging for entry. I opened my mouth, allowing him in and greeting his tongue with my own. I wrapped my arms around him and hugged as I deepened our kiss, his lips all over mine, tasting me, wanting me. But then he broke our kiss just as slowly as he started it. "Stop distracting me."

"Me?" I pretended to growl and walked through the office door out into the garage. Even in the dark, my eyes immediately found my beautiful black car, gleaming as it sat in one of the garage's two bays. I walked around it, noticing all four tires were intact and in place.

"Uh, Tatum?" I shouted toward the back office where he was doing God knows what.

"Yeah?"

"Is this my car?" I asked, knowing full well that it was.

"Yeah," he drawled out.

"How long has it been fixed?" I asked with a small smile playing on my lips.

He exited the office and stared at me before answering, "Pretty much since you got here."

My mouth fell open. "What?"

Tatum stalked toward me, wrapped his arm around my waist, and pulled me against him. "I didn't want you to leave. I still don't."

His lips came down on mine and I lost myself in the feel of his tongue slowly exploring my mouth. His heart raced and beat against my chest, filling me with more passion. A moan escaped my lips as I leaned closer, my hands pulling at the back of his neck and winding in his hair.

"I miss you when I don't see you," he murmured against my lips, and I pulled back slightly to make eye contact with him.

"Me too," I admitted before closing my eyes and pulling his lips back toward mine. A few moments later, we started for the exit, hand in hand. "Wait." I stopped short and his hand jerked against mine. "I want to bring my car back to your house."

"Now?"

"Why not now?" I paused before waggling my eyebrows and adding, "I'll let you drive it."

"Really?" His eyes lit up.

"Really. I'll head back with your mom and you can bring my car back with you."

"Deal." He placed a quick kiss on my lips before grinning wide. "Let's go home, babe." He said like it was the most natural thing in the world and I nodded, as if his home was where I belonged.

My Girl

TATUM

PAIGE'S BMW WAS a dream to drive. It was the first time that I wished my house was a hell of a lot farther away from the shop—and that the drive there included hairpin turns and well-paved roads where I could floor it like I was on a racetrack. The car hugged the road and made even the simplest of moves feel effortless.

It was official. I was jealous of a goddamn car. And the girl who got to drive it whenever she wanted.

When I pulled into the driveway, I made sure to slow down to a snail's pace so the gravel kicking up wouldn't chip away at her paint. Paige stood out on the porch with her hands on her hips, a big-ass smile on her beautiful face.

"Waiting for me, darlin'?" I said as I slid out of the car.

"Always," she shot back, and sprinted down the steps and

into my arms.

I strode toward the porch with her in my arms, reaching down awkwardly to pet Buster's head as he danced around us. This girl drove me crazy in the best of ways; I couldn't get enough of her.

"How'd you like driving her?" she asked, her arms wrapped around my neck.

"She handles like crazy. I'm in love." When her body went rigid in my arms, I had to backtrack. "With the car, I mean. I'm in love with your car."

Paige let out a little snort. "Figures."

"I'm only a man, honey. Can't blame me."

"Oh, I don't. It's typical. Men and their cars."

"Actually, it's your car. But I'll take it off your hands if you're tired of it," I offered, knowing full well she'd never say yes.

"You wish. That's my baby. I'll drive that thing till one of us dies."

I leaned in and whispered, "Let's hope it's the car."

Her fragrance intoxicated me. I had no clue what it was, but she just smelled like Paige. I wanted to bottle it up and put it on my nightstand.

Weird, I know.

Reaching for Paige's hand, I pulled her toward the barn, the feel of her fingers idly stroking my knuckles turning me on. The simplest things this girl did seemed to awaken every part of me.

We walked through the door and I flipped on the light

switch. She glanced at the computer, making me wonder if she wanted to use it.

"Have you been online lately?" I hadn't been online at all since she'd let me kiss her. Personally, I couldn't give a shit what was being said about her when I knew the truth. And I'd rather be physically around her than read about her on my computer screen. Real-life Paige was a million times better than online Paige.

"I applied to a couple of schools, but that's about it. I haven't checked my e-mails or anything, though. The only people I really care about know where to find me." She smiled, and it brightened her whole face.

"Quinn and your family?"

"Yep."

"So, tell me about the schools. Where'd you apply?" My curiosity was piqued, and I wondered why she hadn't mentioned it until now.

"UCLA, USC, and Pepperdine. That's all for now. I figured I'd research some more later, but it was a good start."

"Those are all really good schools."

She shrugged. "I know. And honestly, I probably wouldn't even be able to get in on my own, but since…" She paused and blushed a little. "Well, since I'm me, there will probably be some strings pulled in the admissions office."

"Is that a bad thing?" I asked, not entirely sure how I felt about the situation. Had it been someone other than Paige, I would have thought they were a spoiled brat getting whatever they wanted because they were famous. And it would have annoyed the living shit out of me. But since it was Paige, I didn't feel as irritated. Which made me a hypocritical dick who was okay with double standards. I should make a T-shirt.

"It's not really a great thing," she said. "I mean, it does sort of suck that I'll most likely get into all those schools because of who I am, not because I truly earned it. But I want to go. And I want to go to a good school, so I'm not above asking for help getting in." Her face scrunched in an adorable way as she frowned at me. "Does that make me a crappy person?"

I let out a laugh. "No, it doesn't. You're aware that you're asking for help. And you don't act like you deserve all these things for nothing. Nothing about you is crappy, Paige. Except maybe your taste in ex-boyfriends."

"Hey!" she squeaked out, her eyes wide and her jaw hanging open. "What about my taste in guys now?" She deliberately ran her gaze up and down my body, and I wanted to throw her over my shoulder and spank the sass right out of her.

"Still questionable," I said teasingly.

She shrugged. "Can't win 'em all."

"I'm proud of you." I walked over and wrapped my arms around her waist, then pulled her against me and dipped my head to kiss her soft lips.

"Thank you. That means a lot. So, where'd you apply?" she asked with a wink.

"You're hilarious."

"I mean it, Tatum. You shouldn't let all that talent go to

waste. You won't let me give up on my dreams, so I can't let you give up on yours."

"My dreams aren't as easy as yours," I said, and instantly wished that I could take the words back as her relaxed stance turned defensive and she pulled out of my arms.

"Easy? Oh, that's right, everything's easy for me."

"That's not what I meant, Paige. It's just—" I bit back my words, unsure how to fix this. "Shit, I'm sorry. I'm an idiot. Please, I just meant that I don't even know where to start anymore." I closed the space between us, not wanting my stupid mouth to ruin the night.

"You're just scared," she snapped, and my temper flared.

I stared at her, a battle of wills brewing between us. Instead of fighting her, I nodded. "You're right. I am," I admitted as my defenses crumpled.

"I know it's scary. Change is scary. And going after your dreams is terrifying." She walked into the kitchen and leaned her arms on the countertop.

"I'm comfortable in my failure." I sat on top of the coffee table and positioned myself to face her, even though she was across the room.

"You're not a failure."

"I think deep down I know that. But I've tossed everything I want aside. I've let my whole life simmer on the back burner for so long. And I think the honest-to-God truth is that it's just easier that way."

"Of course it's easier. It's always easier to *not* try, to *not* rock the boat, to *not* put yourself out there," she practically shouted. "Of course it's easier to stay complacent and pretend you're happy when you're just content. There's a fire that burns inside you, Tatum—I've seen it. I've seen it when you play the guitar and you talk about music. It would be a real shame to let that fire burn out instead of feeding it."

Throwing my head back, I closed my eyes for a moment before refocusing on her. Her words were powerful, and part of me couldn't believe she was talking about me. When was the last time anyone had said something so inspired—and meant it in reference to me?

I shook my head. "You know what you want to do. You want to go to school and find that normal life you've been searching for. But nothing else in your world has to change if you don't want it to. Everything in my life has to change. Every single thing."

"That's not necessarily a bad thing, is it?"

"I don't know. I don't feel ready."

"When will you ever feel ready? Every day that passes is just more time you're losing and can never get back."

"I know."

"Tatum," she said in a soft, pleading voice, but my gaze stayed glued to the floor. "Tatum," she said a little louder, and I looked up at her. "I don't mean to push you. I just really think you'll regret it for the rest of your life if you don't at least try. I think you'll eventually hate yourself for it."

"Because you hated yourself?"

"I didn't hate myself, per se, but I definitely regret not doing all of this sooner. Maybe I thought my desire for college would go away eventually. I don't know, but it never did. It's like a part of me that is this living, breathing thing. It wants to be recognized. It wants to be fed. That's what I think music is for you. But I guess I could be wrong."

I shook my head. "You're not wrong."

"You of all people should know how precious time is. That every day we're given is a gift and not something to be taken lightly."

My thoughts drifted to my father. Would he be proud of me and the man I became? I knew he would be. But would he want more for me and want me to follow my own dreams? He would want that as well.

With a sigh, I said, "Okay, I'll do some research tomorrow. It's a small step, but that's probably how I'll need to approach this."

"It's better than no steps at all." Paige smiled and moved over toward me. She dropped to her knees and rested her forearms on my thighs. "You can do this, Tatum. You can do anything you set your mind to. I truly believe that."

Her head tilted up as her lips met mine in the sweetest kiss. I opened my mouth and drank her in. Paige's hands wrapped around the lower part of my back, her fingers digging into my skin, and I pulled her even tighter against me. She couldn't get any closer, but that didn't stop me from trying. I slid my hand up the small of her back and traced her curves before settling on the crook of her neck. When she moaned into my mouth, I lifted her from the floor and pulled her into my lap. Her hips wiggled as she moved against me.

"Paige, sweetheart, you'd better stop moving your hips like that."

"Or what?" she asked, her lips moving to my neck and dropping kisses there as her hips still moved, driving me crazy.

"Or maybe I'll stop being so nice and I'll start taking advantage of you," I whispered against her lips.

"Maybe I want you to take advantage of me." She pulled back, leveling a serious gaze on me, and I met her eyes.

"Is that what you want? You're ready to do this?" I asked as I desperately tried to keep my real brain in control.

"Are you?"

And that was the million-dollar question. Was I ready to have sex with her? Every molecule in my body wanted to get lost in her, but I knew my head would be royally screwed up if I allowed that to happen and then had to let her go. I was never good at the whole one-night-stand thing, and I definitely wasn't the love-'em-and-leave-'em type. Being physical with her meant getting attached, and I couldn't afford to do that with someone like Paige Lockwood.

"Not yet," I admitted, and I swear I heard my dick cry out in protest.

Paige smiled. "Okay then. No more dry humping," she said with a laugh before scooting off my lap.

"Aw, man. I didn't say that," I said with a whine.

She leaned down, giving me another mind-blowing kiss before saying, "I'm going to head to bed in the house. I'll see you in the morning." Her lips brushed against mine. "Don't forget to start researching. Maybe we can make a list of everything you need to do just to see what sounds good to you, or where the schools might be. We can do that tomorrow, if you want."

"Would that make you feel better about my future?"

"Don't make fun of me. But yes, it would. I want to help, and I know this is the only way you'll let me."

I'll be damned if she wasn't right about that.

"Okay, babe. Tomorrow we'll start researching my shit."

"Yay!" She clapped her hands with excitement and I grabbed her by the waist, pulling her back down on me so I could lose myself in her lips.

"I changed my mind," I mumbled between kisses, and she moved her mouth away from mine.

"About what?"

"I want you."

I needed to get out of my own head for once and live in the moment. If I let Paige go without really knowing her inside and out, she would be one more thing I'd regret. This amazing girl materialized like magic into my life, and I was acting like a damn chick about it.

"Are you sure?" she said, her voice sounding so damn sweet, I wanted to taste it. "We don't have to."

But I wasn't sure. Not entirely, but my body convinced me otherwise. "As sure as I'll ever be. You?"

"I was just waiting on you."

"So sweet."

Without another word, I swept her up into my arms and walked us to my bedroom, my lips pressed against hers the whole time. The truth was, I was nervous. It had been a long time since my dick had seen any action, and even longer since my brain had wanted it to. My dick always wanted to get laid, but the smarter parts of me tended to win out. Thank God.

After laying her gently on top of my bed, I knelt on the bed and took a deep breath. Knowing what she was about to give me excited me in every way possible. Why would I ever deny myself this kind of connection with her?

Her hands found their way to the hem of my shirt, then she pulled it over my head and sighed a little as she stared at me.

Leaning back on my calves, I reached for her top with both hands and gently tugged while she shimmied out of it. Seeing her like this made my pulse race. I'd already seen her in a bikini, but a man knows the difference between a bathing suit and a bra. Seeing one usually means you're getting lucky, and the other just means "Look, but don't touch."

"You are so beautiful, Paige." I leaned down to kiss her neck, then skimmed my lips down her chest to drop another kiss in that sweet space between her breasts.

"So are you," she said with another sigh, and I laughed.

"Really? Beautiful?"

"Hot, sexy, beautiful. Whatever."

When she smiled up at me, I melted in her gaze. She trusted me; I could see it in her eyes. What we were about to do required trust on both our parts, and she was giving hers to me. Completely. I could see it as clearly as I could see her breathing beneath me.

I took my time exploring her body, removing the rest of our clothing bit by bit before I made love to her. Tasting every inch of her exposed skin, I found a new piece of heaven, right here with Paige. When I entered her, she cried out, and I almost lost it right then and there at the passion in her voice.

Slowly I moved in and out of her, not wanting it to end too soon, and that took almost all my self-control. Out of practice in this arena, I refused to let her down, but it took everything I had to hold myself back. Her body molded to mine as if she'd been made for me, her softness fitting perfectly with my firmness, and the closeness and warmth of her took my breath away.

"I'm not gonna last much longer, babe," I whispered against her neck as our bodies moved in sync.

She said nothing, but dug her fingers into my back and pulled my hips toward her. I brushed my fingertips along the side of her face, stroking gently until she opened her eyes. Emotions overwhelmed me as she kept her eyes open to watch me move within her. She lifted her head and her lips met mine as our connected bodies moved together in an easy rhythm.

Her breaths came in little pants, and a moment later her back arched as her eyes widened with surprise. I thrilled at the knowledge she was coming and watched, mesmerized, as her eyes opened and closed while she absorbed the wave that moved through her until it was no more. I lost myself to it as well, my body rocking with spasms until they subsided, and then I rested my forehead on hers as my heart galloped within me.

Rolling onto my back, I pulled her with me and kissed the top of her head. "That was amazing," I huffed out, my breathing still ragged.

"That was incredible. I've never felt anything like that before."

Her admission made relief filter through me. Making love to Paige had felt better than I ever remembered it being before, and I wasn't sure if it was just me or not.

"Stay with me tonight," I whispered as I tightened my arm around her.

"For a little while," she said in a sleepy voice. "I don't want to be disrespectful to your mom."

I fell asleep with her in my arms, but when I woke up, I was alone.

It's Time

PAIGE

A HARD KNOCK at the door startled me from sleep. The knocking continued, harder and harder until I heard voices coming from outside the house, the sounds drifting clearly to me through the open window. Mrs. Montgomery shouted at whoever it was, sounding like she was trying to calm them down, but it was no use. The male voices grew more agitated as she pulled the door open.

"Where is she? Paige! I know she's in here. Paige, I see your car out front!"

Pulling the sheet up to my nose, I recognized the voice immediately as my insides shriveled up and died on the spot. Jayson was here, but how? Buster wouldn't stop barking and growling, yapping madly as I eavesdropped from the safety of my bed.

"Excuse me, young man, but you can't just barge into my house and start screaming like you own the place." Mrs. Montgomery's voice was strong and, if I wasn't mistaken, very pissed off. "You get out of my house, and we can address whatever it is you want like adults."

"I don't think so, ma'am. You have something I need."

I cringed, knowing that I was the "something" he referred to. Jayson would never let me stay. And I wasn't ready to leave.

"Didn't your mama teach you any manners?" Mrs. Montgomery sounded as though she was seething, and I wanted to run out there and hug her.

The sound of the screen door slamming made me jump. "What's going on in here? Who the hell are you, and what are you doing in my mama's house?"

Tatum.

His voice alone caused my breathing to even out, even though my heart wouldn't stop pounding out beats like crazy. Tatum would protect me. He would keep me safe.

"Oh, this is just priceless." Jayson's laugh sounded sinister. "Come out, Paige. I know you're here, and I can see now why you didn't want to come home."

Half-surprised that Jayson hadn't tried to sign Tatum to his agency already—since he never missed the opportunity to represent a pretty face—I crept out of bed and quickly pulled on a sweatshirt and jeans. My hand on the bedroom doorknob, I took a deep breath to steady myself and then stepped out into the living room.

"Calm down, Jayson. I'm right here."

Tatum rushed to my side, blocking my view of Jayson with his body before pinning me with worried eyes. "Tell me what to do. What do you want me to do?"

He sounded confused and desperate, and I wanted to take him in my arms and forget about the world. Although, that was what I'd been doing for the past three weeks. I was surprised I'd been able to stay away that long.

"There's nothing you can do," I said sadly.

The second Jayson arrived, my escape was all over. Everything I'd built in my time here was swept away in an instant. Out with the brave new-and-improved Paige, and in with the old scared-to-let-anyone-down Paige.

It was like being in an abusive relationship where freedom only came from being away from your abuser. Separated by a few states seemed like a good start. My soul had soared when I'd cut off ties with everyone who controlled me in LA, but it crashed to the ground in spectacular fashion as soon as Jayson's voice broke the sanctity of the peaceful space I'd found for myself.

"I brought you a present, Paige." Jayson eyed me. "Although I have to admit that I didn't realize you wouldn't need it."

Confused, I frowned at him. Whatever Jayson referred to was completely lost on me until I heard the knock on the screen door. My cheating rat bastard of an ex-boyfriend stood outside, his face forlorn and his hair mussed in what I was sure was a calculated way.

Tatum tensed beside me, and I gave his hand a reassuring squeeze. He squeezed back, but didn't release the pressure. I couldn't believe that Jayson had brought Colin all the way out here. It was one thing for my agent to come and play hardball, but it was downright dirty to bring Colin with him.

"You never answered my calls," Colin said from behind the screen. "Or my texts or e-mails."

I straightened my back and sucked in a breath. "I didn't want to talk to you."

Emotion tinged my words, and Colin's face softened as he stepped through the screen door uninvited, clearly mistaking the meaning of my tone. Tatum must have misunderstood too because he dropped my hand and stepped away from me.

Surprised, I glanced at Tatum, wanting to tell him that he had it all wrong. I didn't want Colin; my tone only reflected my surprise at seeing him here, nothing else.

"Don't be like that, babe," Colin said in a cajoling voice.

"Don't call me babe, and don't tell me what to do. Why are you even here?" I said harshly.

"Because I miss you. I wanted to see you. We belong together, Paige."

When Colin took a step toward me, I edged back. I fumbled for Tatum's hand and linked my fingers with his. "I don't want you. And we don't belong together. You're delusional."

"Don't say that." Colin practically growled at me, and Tatum sucked in a deep breath.

The air crackled in the emotionally charged room as

Tatum stood a little taller and flexed his muscles as he boomed at Colin, "Your ears busted or something, man?"

Colin shifted his weight from foot to foot as Tatum leaned forward slightly and bit out, "Did you hear the lady or not?"

"I heard her," Colin said, sounding more like a punk kid trying to talk back to his parents. "But we have history. And what—you think she's going to stay here forever with you? What are you, a farmer?" He laughed, and Jayson followed suit.

From the corner of my eye, I could see Mrs. Montgomery's hands ball into fists at her side, and I felt my own anger rise.

"You're a good-looking guy, I'll give you that." Jayson smirked at Tatum, then said smugly, "But there's no way that this thing you two have going on would ever last in California. I'm sure it was a nice little fling, but it's over now. Do you need me to write you a check to make you feel better?"

"Jayson!" I shouted as Tatum once again tensed beside me. I knew Jayson's words were embarrassing him, and it killed me. This was the type of game they played in Hollywood, but Tatum wasn't from there. He'd never had to deal with this kind of thing before.

"Don't listen to them," I whispered at him. "They're just trying to get inside your head. Please don't let them. They don't know me at all. You know me. Don't forget that."

Jayson wiped the smile off his face and softened his tone, obviously changing tactics. "I'm sure you're a reasonable guy. You can certainly understand that Paige has been off the radar for weeks now and, well, that's not good for business or her reputation."

It was my turn to be shocked as I flinched at his words, wondering how much of what he was saying was true.

"She left town during a pretty chaotic time, as I'm sure you both know." Jayson glanced between Tatum and his mom. "And the rumor mill won't stop churning out the stories. Paige, did you know that you're in rehab? That's why no one's seen you. You've been in rehab for depression over what happened with Colin."

My stomach churned. That couldn't possibly be true, or Quinn would have told me. Wouldn't she?

"I don't believe you," I said, and crossed my arms over my chest as I narrowed my eyes at my agent and my ex.

Jayson pulled out his phone and swiped at the screen before turning it to me. A tabloid headline read:

Paige Lockwood Attempts Suicide Over Colin's Mistresses. Details Inside!

"Oh my God! Why didn't you put a stop to this?" I asked as the horror of it all came crashing down around me. I sucked in a quick breath, my head shaking as tears filled my eyes. "Because bad publicity is still publicity, right? And as long as people are talking about you, you're still relevant. It doesn't matter what they're saying as long as they're saying something. You taught me that."

Jayson's features settled into what looked like pity and disapproval. "Honestly, Paige, Corryn's working on putting out that fire, releasing statements nonstop, but they're very hard to corroborate when no one can find you or talk to you. Everyone believes these stories because no one's seen you for weeks. This little stunt you pulled backfired. Big time."

What had I done? What the hell had I just done to my career?

Tatum dropped my hand and turned to me. "Go talk to them. Figure this out."

I nodded. "Okay. I'll be right back." I leaned up on my tiptoes and planted a kiss on his mouth. His lips barely moved to kiss me back.

"Let's talk outside." I motioned to both Colin and Jayson.

My heart broke a little as I walked away from Tatum and out the front door. When Colin held the screen door open for me, I edged away from him, not wanting to chance touching him in any way.

"You gotta come home, Paige. It's bad," Colin said, sounding sincere as he reached for my hand.

I pulled away quickly. "Don't. Don't touch me."

"Sorry." He bowed his head as Jayson reached for my arm and pulled me aside.

"Pack your things, we're leaving right now. There's no time to waste, and you've already wasted plenty."

"I don't want to go," I said, practically whining. It was pathetic.

"I'm sure you don't. He's a pretty distraction. But, Paige, you want to talk about career suicide? That's what is happening to yours right now, and you don't even know it's happening. You've spent the last month out here in Bumfuck,

Egypt, doing who knows what while your reputation is being flushed down the toilet."

"I'm sure you're trying really hard to stop it all. You're probably calling in the tips," I shouted, and Jayson's face reddened.

"Like I told you inside, Paige, no one believes that you're not in rehab because no one can find you! Listen to me!" he yelled, and I noticed Tatum heading for the door before his mom stopped him. "You've been off the radar for weeks, and they're asking everyone who's close to you where you are. They're all saying the same thing."

"Which is what?"

"That they don't know! And you and I both know that's code for 'She's in rehab,'" Jayson shouted, his hands emphatically slashing the air around him.

"So when I get back, I'll put out a statement or something. I'll tell them all that I wasn't in rehab, that I just—"

Jayson cut me off. "That you just what? Spent the last month in some small-time, off-the-map town? They won't believe that either."

"I don't care what they believe. It's the truth!" Completely frustrated, I turned to pace back and forth on the wood porch.

"You've been in this business long enough to know that reporters don't want the truth, Paige. They want what sells."

"Then we'll give them something else to talk about instead. This is your area, think of something!" I shouted, emotions running wild through my body. There had to be something I could do to stop all the lies.

"Fine. But first things first, you have to come home." Jayson pointed toward the house. "Go get your things."

Knew It Wouldn't Last

TATUM

THE SECOND COLIN appeared on our doorstep, I wanted to burst through the screen and rip his head off. Paige looked horrified, and I had to fight my instincts to protect her.

Instead, I stood there silently and let her deal with this, since it was way out of my league. A helpless feeling consumed me while she talked to both Colin and her agent out of my earshot. I looked over at my mother, who was absentmindedly stirring her latest batch of tea.

"Mama?" I said, breaking her concentration.

"Yeah, honey?"

"What should I do?"

Before she could answer me, Paige walked back up the porch and inside the house, her face red and her eyes glistening. "They need me to go."

Pain ricocheted through my chest. "When?"

"Now," she said, and without another word turned to walk down the hallway toward her bedroom.

I inhaled a choppy breath that stabbed its entire way down. Turning away from her, I shouted for Buster and headed outside. I needed air. I needed space.

Buster barked and ran for Jayson and Colin, who stood whispering to each other next to a Mercedes. My anger only grew as I yelled for Buster to come to me and leave the two dickheads alone. Traitorous dog. The least he could do was bite their ankles.

Paige is leaving me.

I knew this day would come, but I foolishly thought it would be on our terms. How the hell I could ever think that, I wasn't sure, probably because I didn't know any better. I hadn't thought much about her actually leaving, and how it would happen. I'd been so caught up in her simply being here with me.

Pain filled my chest and the simplest task, like breathing, became something I needed to remind myself to keep doing. My heartbeat echoed in my ears as my entire body tensed at what needed to be done. I'd lived through much worse than losing Paige Lockwood, but damn, if it didn't feel like this was worse. Realistically I knew it wasn't, but try telling that to my heart. And here I thought I had no heart left after my dad died and Brina left me.

Way to prove me wrong, heart. Now go screw yourself; you've done enough damage.

Paige walked back into the hallway, her things clearly packed and ready to go. She turned to look at me, her face twisted in some sort of pleading look that I couldn't read for certain. Maybe she wanted me to save her and make them leave?

I didn't know, so I stiffened my back, sucked in a breath, and knew this was going to hurt like hell. "Just go, Paige. We both knew this wasn't a forever thing."

"I know that, but..." She stumbled on her words as her voice broke, and nearly broke me with it.

She knew that?

I hardened my heart, then bit out, "It's been fun."

"It's been fun?" Her face twisted as tears pooled in her eyes, and something inside me snapped.

"You're a good time," I said as coldly as I could.

"Is this a joke right now? It's not funny."

"No joke. I'm telling you to go. You should have never been here in the first place."

"You don't mean that."

When she took a step toward me, I pulled back, knowing that if I let her touch me I'd be done for. I'd never let her leave if her fingers even grazed my skin. Ever.

"I do," I lied.

"I know what you're doing," she whispered as tears spilled over her lashes, each one killing me a little more than the last. "You're just acting tough, but you don't mean it. You don't, you can't."

Her words stabbed at me, but I had to make her leave and

go back to where she belonged. Paige had never intended to stay in this town, and if for some crazy reason she convinced herself that she wanted to, she'd eventually resent me for it.

I couldn't live with that. I had to make her think I wanted her gone, had to push her away. It was for her own good, and mine as well.

"I mean it, Paige. I want you to leave. You've been here long enough. Go back where the people actually miss you and care that you're gone."

She gasped as if I'd slapped her, and the sound nearly caused my knees to buckle. I was too good at being a dick, too well versed in being mean to her.

"I don't believe you," she whispered. "I know you feel what I feel." Her eyes pleaded with me as she lifted a trembling hand to her heart.

"I don't feel anything." The words practically burned my tongue as I spit them out, my lies choking me from within.

"I know that's not true." She sucked in a gulp of air, and I wanted so badly to be her oxygen. "But I'll go," she added with a nod, then pushed back her shoulders with determination.

I watched as she hesitated before turning away from me and walking toward her car. Colin grabbed Paige's things from her, his hand brushing against hers, and placed them in the trunk. My blood boiled as I witnessed the simple gesture. He ushered her to the driver's door and opened it for her.

She slid into the front seat of her BMW and started the engine. Colin tried to get into the passenger side, but fumbled with the door. I wanted to cheer Paige on when I realized she'd locked it and refused to let him in. That was my girl.

My girl. And I was letting her go. Hell, *making* her go was more accurate.

She's not my anything. Not anymore. Only an idiot would think she ever was.

Paige turned to me one last time, her eyes locking with mine before she dropped a pair of black sunglasses over them. The car's tires spun as she pulled out and headed down the drive.

I followed behind, Buster tagging along with me, until she got to the main road and turned down it. When the taillights of her BMW faded out of view, I fell to my knees, the gravel from the road piercing the denim in my already ripped jeans.

How long does a man have to stay on his knees until a woman knows—innately knows—that he's on them waiting for her?

Probably forever. And I deserved nothing less.

So I stood there like an asshole and watched her go, doing nothing. I never tried to stop her, begged her to stay, asked for more time, or anything. Instead I pushed her out the door and forced her to leave.

I'm a coward.

Right now I should be chasing her car, begging her to never go anywhere without me.

Maybe she'll turn around?

Maybe she'll come back?

I smacked the side of my head, pissed off at myself for

being such a dick to her. My defense mechanism kicked into the gear the minute I saw Colin here. He was lucky I didn't beat that smug grin right off his face. Instead I handed her over to him like she was a prize at the fair that he didn't deserve to win. But I gave her up anyway.

Take her. You can have her. I don't want her anymore.

Only an idiot would do something as stupid as that.

Only a fool watches the girl he cares about drive away and does nothing about it.

Only me.

I must have kneeled in the road for hours. At least, it seemed like hours. Staring at the empty gravel road, watching the dust from her car settle after she was long gone, I wished I could take back every single harsh word I'd spoken and bring her back to me. But it was too late for that. She was gone.

After sucking in one last long breath, I turned away from the deserted road and noticed Buster waiting for me, his head resting on his paws. "C'mere boy," I whispered and he whined, sidling up to my side with his tail between his legs.

Slowly we walked together toward my mom's house, just my dog and me, heads low, no tail wagging in sight.

"She's gone?" Mama's strained voice sliced through me as the screen door closed at my back.

I nodded, feeling responsible for both of our losses— again—as Mama turned away without another word and walked down the hall. The door to her room closed softly, and I moped to the back barn to wallow in solitude.

Buster didn't follow me there. Even my own dog didn't want to be around me after what I'd done, and he was right.

I didn't want to be around me either.

Long Drive Home

PAIGE

I LOST TRACK of how many states I'd cried tears in. I wasn't stupid when it came to Tatum and why he acted the way he did. In my gut, I knew that he didn't mean any of the harsh words that spilled out of his mouth, but my mind wouldn't stop replaying them, as if to try to convince me otherwise.

He didn't want me. He told me to leave. The anguish of it all repeated, making sure I didn't forget a single word of it.

"You're a good time," he'd said to me in an icy voice.

"No joke. I'm telling you to go. You should have never been here in the first place."

Tears continued to spill down my cheeks each time his hateful tone echoed inside my mind. My entire body ached in a way I didn't recognize.

The pain with Colin had been so very different from this.

I'd thought I loved Colin, but now I wasn't sure what exactly it was that I felt for him. Tatum made my relationship with Colin seem like such a joke; juvenile, at best.

Realizing that I was heading back to my reality, following the two men in my life that I currently liked the least, I reached for my cell phone tucked inside my purse and pulled it out. Glancing at it quickly, I turned it on for the first time in ages. It came to life, synched with my car, and started beeping out message alerts for what felt like five minutes straight.

Ignoring them all, I told my car to dial Quinn.

"What's up, babe?"

"Don't you ever work?" I teased through my tears.

"I'm actually in my trailer, brat, so start talking before I get called back on set," she warned, and I lost it.

I sobbed for a moment, and after Quinn asked me three times what was wrong, she stayed silent until I stopped sounding like a wounded animal.

"Jayson and Colin came here," I stuttered.

"Shut up. Oh my God, how'd they find you?"

"I have no idea."

"Where are you?"

"Driving."

"Driving where? Back home?"

"Yeah."

"What about Tatum? Is he with you?"

"He told me to leave." I sucked in a shaky breath as more tears fell. I wanted to say more about him, but I couldn't.

"He told you to leave?" When I couldn't respond, she

finally added, "I'm sorry, Paige. Where's Colin now?"

"In Jayson's car," I spat out. "I wouldn't let him ride with me."

"Good girl," she murmured. "How long until you're back?"

"I'm not sure. Probably another couple of days."

"I can't believe Jayson drove out there and brought Colin with him. That's just a low blow."

"They flew." I didn't know why I felt like even the most minute details were important, but for some reason I wanted Quinn to have all the facts. "But then they rented a car to make sure I'd go back with them. It's awful the way they showed up, demanding I leave. And I did it, Quinn. I just packed up my stuff and followed them like the good little obedient girl that I am."

"No," she snapped at me, her voice turning harsh. "Do not do that to yourself. Please don't act like getting away didn't change you, Paige, because I heard it in your voice. That trip was a good thing. Don't diminish it. And you had to eventually come back, anyway. It's not like you could stay gone forever."

She was right. I would have had to come back to LA soon enough, so I allowed a smidgeon of that particular guilt to evaporate, even if I didn't entirely agree with it. I felt like I was being bossed around, and I allowed it.

"Call me as soon as you get in, and I'll come right over," she insisted.

"I will." I almost hung up before I whispered, "Quinn?"

"Yeah, babe."

"Why didn't you tell me what the tabloids were saying about me?"

My car speakers blared out a raspy crackle as she breathed into her cell phone. "It only just started happening, I swear. And I figured it would all die down, but so far, your being away has only kept the talk going. I was going to tell you about it the next time you called me, but honestly—"

She paused for a long enough time that I thought our call dropped. "Quinn?"

"Sorry. It's just that part of me didn't want to tell you about it because you needed to be away from all this bullshit. You were having such a good time being free that I didn't want to make you feel like you had to come back to your chains. I didn't want to be the reason you came home before you were ready."

Her words soaked into me, traveled through my body, and settled square in my heart. "You're a good friend, Quinn."

"The best," she added with a small laugh.

"You are."

"You understand, though, right? You aren't mad at me?" she asked, her voice small.

"I do understand. I'm not mad. Thank you for always looking out for me."

"I love you. I'll see you when you get home. Hurry up. I miss you."

"Miss you too. 'Bye."

I disconnected the call before she said anything else and continued following the Mercedes in front of me.

AFTER LONG DAYS of monotonous driving, my apartment building was finally in view. Over time, the hurt I'd felt about Tatum's reaction had been replaced by anger. It was the only way I could deal with everything my body and mind were currently attempting to process. As long as I was mad, I wasn't sad or reeling in the loss.

Jayson and Colin still led the way, and I found myself annoyed even more by their heavy-handed behavior. I didn't need a freaking escort into my own home.

As I pulled into the entrance, I was suddenly surrounded by hordes of people rushing to my car from every direction. I had almost forgotten what it was like to be accosted at every turn. *Almost.*

Being in Hanford had been such a relief in every way. I didn't realize how stressed I had become by simply choosing this career. It's amazing the things that you'll live with and stop noticing because they become a part of you—like the weight of certain anxieties and burdens. You simply carry it all on your shoulders and forget it's there because you eventually become used to the extra weight.

Cameras flashed all around me, blinding me even in the daylight. Reporters shouted questions so loudly, I couldn't tune them out. It was worse than when I'd escaped to Quinn and Ryson's house, so much worse.

No longer were the questions about Colin and his stupid cheating ways, but about my apparent inability to handle it all. Because why else would I have been gone for so long?

"Paige, did you really try to kill yourself?"

"How was rehab? What were you in for, sweetie?"

"We heard Colin found you and saved you. Are you two back together?"

"Do you have a drinking problem? Drug overdose?"

"Colin's here! Did Colin bring you home from rehab? Is this a new start for you two?"

I stepped out of my car at the same time Colin exited Jayson's. If I thought the flashes were blinding before, they were nothing in comparison to the flurry that started then. The press loved a good drama, and that was what my relationship with Colin had become since the news of his cheating broke.

Colin wrapped his arm around my lower back. When I tried to wiggle out of his grasp, his fingers dug deeper into my side.

"Get off me," I hissed at him, knowing that this was the ultimate publicity stunt for him. What better way for him to save his own hide than to be seen with me? If Paige Lockwood could forgive Colin, then why couldn't the rest of the world?

"Stop being so difficult, Paige," he said through clenched teeth. "Let me help you inside." He smiled brightly at the cameras before kissing the side of my head.

The moment his lips touched me, I recoiled and fought off the urge to puke all over my shoes. The paparazzi continued to shout, cameras continued to flash, and I no longer cared about any of it. I pressed my palms against Colin and shoved him away from me so hard he almost fell to the ground. I wished he would have.

"Stay away from me," I yelled without considering the implications. "I don't want you here!" I rushed into the lobby of my building and into a waiting elevator, in which Sam held the doors. It was nice to see a familiar, friendly face.

"They've been here for days, Miss Lockwood. It's like they knew you were on your way back. They won't leave," Sam said, and his concern for me was touching.

I considered his words for only a moment before saying, "I'm sorry."

"It's not true, right? All the things they're saying?"

"No, Sam, it's not true," I said with a tired sigh. I was exhausted, and I'd only just returned.

A wide smile transformed his face. "I knew it. None of it sounded like you at all."

Thankful to finally have someone on my side, I said, "Sam, please make sure that no one lets Colin or Jayson up to my apartment without verbal permission from me first. Okay? It's important."

I no longer trusted Jayson. I had only considered the notion before I left town, but was now convinced that he didn't have my best interests at heart.

"No one will come up," he said with a nod. "Except Miss Quinn and your family?"

"Perfect. No one except them. Thank you."

"Anything for you." He leaned around me and pressed the

proper floor on button panel before slipping out of the elevator and leaving me alone.

As the doors closed, Tatum's face appeared in my mind's eye and I winced. Would I never see him again? Even the thought of that broke my heart. But right now I needed to focus and figure out my future, and not worry about the guy who sent me packing.

What the hell had I done to my career and reputation by leaving?

Just a Fling

TATUM

I HADN'T ACCOMPLISHED a damn thing since I pushed Paige out of town. My computer at the shop had been bookmarked up the ass with celebrity gossip sites and entertainment channels.

I was a man obsessed. Every time I saw a photo of Paige and Colin together, like the one splashed on every website of him walking her into her apartment building, his hand on her waist, I wanted to throw this piece-of-shit computer across the room and watch it shatter the same way my heart had.

As much as I wanted to believe they weren't back together, there was no denying the pictures I saw. Even the one where it looked like she was shoving him away, but the photo was followed by a headline that made even me question exactly what I was seeing, and I had just spent weeks with the girl.

I needed to rein it in. Paige stopped being my business the minute I allowed her to drive away without me.

Knuckles rapped against the door frame of the shop's office, forcing me to find some sense of inner calm. I leaned back in the squeaky swivel chair, and my eyes fell upon Celeste's sad expression.

"What do you want? Come to rub it all in my face?" I ask snidely, knowing that Celeste wasn't at all the cause of my ire and didn't deserve it, but I'd been an unbearable bastard since Paige exited my life.

"Don't be mean to me," she snapped, and shame washed over me.

"I'm sorry."

Pulling up the guest chair closer to me, she sat down uninvited. "I know you're hurting, Tatum, that's why I came. I know who ratted out Paige's location, and I couldn't keep that information from you. Not once I knew for sure."

I leaned forward, my arms pressing down on top of my old man's desk. "Who?"

Her eyes closed briefly before she opened them again. "One guess," she said, her head nodding along with my changing expression.

"Brina." My throat constricted with the single word as fire started to flow through my veins. "Why would she do that?"

"Because she's a jealous bitch, Tatum. There's no other reason for her awful behavior other than if you weren't going to be with her, then you weren't going to be with anyone. Especially not someone famous. Brina can't handle it. She can't handle the fact that you want nothing to do with her. She can't handle the fact that a famous Hollywood actress wants something to do with you, so she got rid of her. She found out Paige's agent's name and she called him. Told him exactly where Paige was."

"I wondered how the hell he found her," I said, my voice almost failing me.

"I had my suspicions and once I caught her in a lie, she couldn't keep her information straight, she let it all out. Not only did she call Jayson, she was the one who suggested he bring Colin along. She told him it might help. That Paige missed him."

My head spun as my insides churned. "Haven't I been through enough hell in my life without the people who are supposed to care about me working to screw it all up? What the hell!"

"Hell hath no fury like a woman scorned." Celeste's eyes met mine.

"I didn't scorn her, she scorned me!" I shouted and then fought back a laugh at how ridiculous this conversation had become.

"I'm just saying," Celeste said with a shrug, "women can be cruel. And Brina doesn't like losing."

"She lost a long time ago. None of this makes any sense." I battled with my growing fury, thanking God I wasn't a woman, but couldn't help but wonder why some of them were so screwed up.

Celeste frowned. "I'm done with her. I can't be friends with someone like that anymore. I've overlooked a lot of things over the years, but this is something I can't get past."

I shook my head, unable to form a response because, really, what was there for me to say? I'd given up on Brina the day she gave up on me.

"I just wanted you to know what was going on, Tatum. And I needed you to know what she'd done."

I assumed she was done and would get up to leave, but she stayed seated, staring at me. "What?" I asked her, shrugging my shoulders.

Celeste tilted her head as she studied me. "What the heck are you gonna do about Paige? You're not just going to let her go without a fight, are you? That's not the stand-up guy I know."

I dropped my head into my hands, feeling worse than ever. "I don't think it was anything more than just a fling. She was in a bad place and needed to get away, and she happened to find me in the process."

"That's crap and you know it." She narrowed her eyes at me as a scowl appeared. "Or maybe you don't know it. But I saw the way she looked at you, and I saw the way you looked at her. That was no fling. And if you're too stupid to realize it, I'm sitting here telling you. That way you have no one to blame but yourself if you don't go after her."

"I can't just pick up and leave!" I snapped before forcing myself to calm down. "I have a business to run. This shop is our livelihood and I can't abandon it, or my mom."

Reaching across the desk, Celeste tapped my arm and said, "Tatum, you are so much more than this small town. I don't think your mama would want you to stay here at the cost of your own happiness. You've been doing that ever since your daddy died."

I knew she was right, having already discussed this with Paige on more than one occasion. I remembered the other night where I promised her that we could start looking toward my future. That was before I shoved her out of my house, when every day felt like a promise just because she was a part of it. Now my days felt like a sort of punishment. A well-deserved one, at that.

"Have you even talked to her since she left?"

Her question burned a hole in my gut, and I shuddered at my own cowardice. "No."

"Don't you think you should at least apologize?" Celeste's eyes bored through me, her disappointment as clear as the sun on a cloudless day.

"I should do a lot of things, Celeste. Thanks for the pep talk," I said sarcastically, sensing myself starting to shut down.

She shook her head. "It's like I don't even know who you are anymore. And it's sad."

"Why are you on my ass?" I shouted. "Why do you care so much about what I do?"

She inhaled a deep breath before saying, "Because you have no idea how happy you looked these past few weeks. It was like we had the old Tatum back. And I want that for you."

Her words stung. "What do you think I should do?" I asked.

"I think that for starters, it's time you had a frank conversation with your mama. Like yesterday," she said pointedly before getting up and walking toward the door.

"It's not that easy," I called out to her.

Celeste stopped in the doorway and turned to pin me with a serious look. "The best things in life aren't always easy, Tatum. But they're worth fighting for. I'm scared to death you'll never get over this thing with Paige if you stay here and give up." And just like that, she walked out, leaving me in the office alone with my thoughts and her words echoing in my mind.

She was right, which thoroughly pissed me off. I wanted to toss something after her or punch something, but I buried my head in my hands instead. I'd really screwed things up with Paige. Even if I did get my shit together and work on my future, how could I do that and still include her in it?

Paige probably didn't even want me at this point; she probably hated my guts. But Celeste was right—losing Paige would ruin me if I let it. A girl like that was worth fighting for, and it was time I took a turn in the ring.

The Land of Spectacular Lies

PAIGE

"HI, MOM," I said into my cell phone as I settled onto the couch. I'd slept most of the day away, my mind filled with dreams of a place that suddenly felt achingly far away.

"Hi, honey. How was your night? Did you sleep okay?" she asked, although I half wondered if she already knew the answer.

"Once I finally fell asleep, yeah. Actually, I just woke up not too long ago," I said, glancing over at the wall clock that read 4:42.

"Well, that's good. You're probably mentally exhausted. Do you want me to come over?"

Seeing my mom sounded so appealing, but I needed more time. "I do want to see you, Mom, but not just yet. I need to figure some things out first. You've seen all the reports about rehab and stuff?" I squeezed my eyes shut with the ridiculous notion.

She sighed. "There are some paparazzi camped outside the house. They're relentless. I lost it and yelled at one of them the other day, but they wouldn't believe me."

"What happened? What did you say?" Curious, I leaned forward and rested my elbows on my knees.

"They were asking me all these horrible questions about your battle with drugs and alcohol and suicide. I told them that you simply needed a break, but when they asked me where you were, I couldn't answer, and so I think I made it all worse. I'm sorry, honey. I was only trying to help."

She sounded exhausted too. It was one thing for the stories to affect me and my day-to-day life, but when they affected my family, it stung. I hated the way they got dragged into anything that had to do with me. If I lost sleep over anything, it was things like that.

"Mom, you didn't make anything worse. Don't worry about it. You know they're going to say whatever they want to make money. Just don't talk to them anymore. They aren't worth your energy." I tried to believe my own words, but it was easier to give advice than it was to take it.

"Paige, I'll come over anytime you need me to. Just let me know, okay? I'm dying to see you. Your sister is too," she added, sounding happier at the notion.

"That sounds really nice," I said, meaning it more than she knew. The thought of being with my family was incredibly comforting. "I'll see you both soon. I miss you."

We said our good-byes, and I hung up the phone. Reaching for my laptop, I started scrolling through all the false reports and pure guesses being reported as fact as to my whereabouts. I stopped reading the articles after I realized it wasn't doing me any good. There were only so many lies you could attempt to absorb about yourself before you wanted to run outside and show them all the true meaning of crazy.

Because I hadn't been seen for weeks, rehab was a natural assumption. Although I didn't entirely blame the press for that, I completely blamed them for their horrific reasoning for it. The tabloids reported that I couldn't handle Colin's infidelity and that I was too embarrassed to show my face in public. They claimed that I'd tried to overdose on pills, and one even quoted me as saying I wanted to "make the pain go away forever."

The most frustrating part for me was that in all the years of being famous, I'd never once made a spectacle of myself. I'd never handled myself badly or acted like a girl who couldn't live without her boyfriend. So it pissed me off for everyone to be so quick to believe I was suddenly pathetic, weak, and self-destructive.

Was there no loyalty anymore? Had nothing I'd done counted for anything? Apparently not when it came to selling magazines or online ad space.

A swift knock at my door startled me, causing my breath to quicken. Since the lobby hadn't called up to inform me that I had a guest, I knew it had to be Quinn.

"Come in," I shouted from my comfy spot on the sofa. I

glanced behind me to see my best friend burst through the door and run in my direction.

"My God, I've missed you!" She plopped herself into my lap and wrapped her arms around me, her blond ponytail swishing from side to side.

Squeezing her back, I choked out, "I missed you too. Now get off me."

She glanced at my laptop screen before reaching over to slam it shut. "Don't read it. It's all total horseshit pulled out of thin air."

"Pretty hurtful horseshit," I muttered.

Her mouth dropped open. "Paige Agatha Lockwood, did you just swear? Why, I never!" she said in a thick Southern accent.

"I did, but I didn't enjoy it," I said with a pout.

"You enjoyed it a little," she teased, and when I vehemently shook my head in disagreement, she hopped up and said, "I'm grabbing a water. You need anything?"

"I'm good." I raised my already full water glass in her direction.

"We're going to talk about all the press and stuff in a minute, but first I'm dying to hear about Tatum and all the red he made you feel," she shouted from the kitchen as if she were a thousand feet away.

When Quinn mentioned Tatum, my heart seized. I flashed back to the conversation where I told Quinn that Tatum made me feel in color, just like a Taylor Swift song.

"A little louder," I called out. "I don't think the people on the street heard you."

"I said," she yelled even louder, then laughed at herself as she walked back into the living room. "Sorry, I've been an angry wife all day on set, so there's been a lot of raised voices."

"Can we not talk about Tatum?" Thinking about our last night together—his lips all over my skin, his strong body on top of mine—I couldn't handle those feelings right now in addition to everything else. I was certain that if a body could short-circuit and spark out, mine would in this instant.

Quinn plopped onto the other end of the sofa and sipped at her water, eyeing me over the rim of the glass. "But I've never heard you talk about someone the way you talked about him. I know you said he made you leave, but you have to know that's some stupid machismo boy bullshit," she deduced with little effort.

"It absolutely was. I know it was, but it doesn't change anything."

"Meaning?" she asked, her brow furrowed.

"Meaning, I'm not interested in a guy who needs to have a defense mechanism when it comes to me when things get tough. I can't be pushed away like that. He tried to make me feel like I didn't matter, like what we did didn't matter. I would have never done that to him. I could have never treated him that way." I sat up a little straighter, my inner decisiveness shocking even me as the words spilled from my lips.

"*What you did*," she repeated. "Paige Nightingale Lockwood, did you sleep with him?" Quinn's voice rose an octave as her jaw dropped open again.

I shut my eyes for a moment and willed the burning feeling that swirled in my stomach to subside. Nodding was the only answer I could give her.

"Well, I'm proud of you. I sort of love that Colin isn't the last guy you've been with."

"Me too," I said with a weak smile.

"But I am sorry that Tatum treated you that way," she added, the pain in her eyes reflecting my own. "That had to be really hurtful."

"It was. Even though I know he didn't mean it, doesn't mean I have to accept it or put up with it. I'm mad at him. I deserve better than that."

I let the anger fill me; it was easier to deal with than the pain of his loss. The sadness made me feel less alive, but the anger burned with a fire that reminded me how alive I still was.

Quinn stared at me in silence, and I wondered what exactly she was thinking before she spoke up. "You're right. You do. You absolutely do." She reached across the couch and squeezed my hand before letting it go. "So, no more red?"

"No more red. At least, not right now."

"That sucks. I liked the whole color thing."

I giggled. "We can still use it for you. Quinn, what color has Ryson made you feel today?"

"I haven't seen him since this morning, so…*green*," she said, drawing out the word.

"And with that answer, we're done playing this game." I

rolled my eyes and looked away from my best friend's grinning face.

"All right then, let's talk about the press. Instead of you wading through that shit online, why don't you ask me any questions you have? I'll fill you in on what's been said about you in your absence."

I sucked in a quick breath. That I could handle. "That sounds good. Okay."

"Whenever you're ready," she said, then took a long gulp of her water. "But are you really over Tatum? I mean, just like that?"

I huffed out a small laugh. "God, no. But I can't focus on him right now. I've got to do damage control on my life and my career. Help me do that first. Please?"

"I get it," Quinn said before she filled me in on the fact that the rehab rumors had only recently started to take life. The length of time I'd been out of the public eye just happened to correspond with a normal rehab stint by someone who was serious about kicking an addiction or getting mentally healthy. There really wasn't much that I didn't already know, except that Colin kept aligning his name with mine.

"He says you're fine," Quinn said, her lips curling as if she'd tasted something bad. "He speaks on your behalf any chance he gets, and tells the world that he's in constant contact with you."

"What did I ever see in him?" I narrowed my eyes and groaned at the idea of him being so conniving and gross.

"You never saw this side of him. We've been through this

already. But, Paige, you need to put Colin and everyone else in their place. You need to stand up for yourself and address where you've been."

"But they'll want to know where *exactly* I was." I pushed the memories of the field party, the swimming hole, and our last night together from my mind. "And I can't do that to that town. They were so great to me, keeping my secret for as long as they did. I can't have the press overrun the place and ruin it. It would take them all of two seconds to find out about Tatum and his mother, and harass them both half to death."

Quinn tapped a finger against her lips. "You're right. Maybe you can just allude to where you were. Just say you were in a town they've never heard of. Something. You have to do something."

"I'll see what Corryn and Jayson think I should do," I said, so used to depending on them for every little detail of my professional life.

"Oh, screw both of them! They don't care about you. And if you don't know that by now, then maybe you should check into an institution."

I pushed back into the couch, wishing that it would swallow me whole as the weight of her words hit me like a baseball bat to the chest.

"Did you learn nothing by being away?" Quinn insisted, then raised her voice. "Seriously?"

I flinched. "Don't yell at me." If Quinn didn't back off a little, I was afraid I'd have another meltdown of a different kind. I was doing extremely well in my attempts to hold it together, but her pushing me so hard wasn't helping.

"I'm sorry, but come on. You were a changed person while you were gone. You were stronger and free and brave. I need you to be that person here. You need you to be fearless here too, Paige, or you'll never survive this."

Quinn was right. I had finally developed a backbone while I was away, and I couldn't pretend that strength wasn't still somewhere inside me, even though it felt buried since returning home. I wasn't only a different person because I had been out of Los Angeles; I had dug deep and found the courage that existed within me. It had apparently been dormant all my life because I'd never needed it before. And I definitely needed it now.

"I hate when you're right," I said with a sigh.

Holding back a smile, she said, "You must hate me a lot then."

"You know what sucks the most?"

"What?"

"It's that I felt the difference while I was gone. Lighter, you know? Less burdened. But the second I got back here I could literally sense that feeling leaving my body. The heaviness returned with every breath I took and settled on my shoulders, pressing me down. It was the most depressing feeling," I said with a shudder.

"Shit, Paige, I'm sorry. I know I'm too hard on you sometimes, it's just that I hate the people you have working for you. They aren't on your side at all." She set her water glass on the coffee table, then spun back to face me. "Tell you what.

Call them right now. See what they say. Give them a chance to prove me wrong."

Quinn's agency had a built-in publicity department, so she didn't have to hire someone separately. It was times like this that I wished I had a well-oiled machine working for me too.

I reached for my phone and dialed Corryn's number first. She was my publicist, after all, and this was her department.

When the call connected, Corryn's voice rang out. "Paige! Finally!"

"Hi, Corryn. I just wanted to check in and find out how you think I should handle this mess." I eyed Quinn, who leaned her head toward mine as she tried to hear Corryn's response.

"Now that you're back in town, the rumor mill will most likely die down. I mean, at some point it will. It will probably get worse before it gets better. But you should use this to your advantage. Strike while the iron's hot, and people will talk about you in ways they never have before. You know what we always say, bad publicity is still publicity."

I hated when she said that; it didn't make any sense. What the hell was she even talking about?

I growled with frustration, feeling myself coming unglued. "Don't say that! I hate when you and Jayson say that about bad publicity. This is my life, my career. I've worked hard to not have any bad publicity—*ever*—and I'm not going to start now. Figure out how I can fix this, Corryn. That's what I pay you for!" I pressed the END button and slammed down my phone, releasing a quick huff of indignation.

"My hero." Quinn raised her hand in the air for a high five.

"Holy cow, that was terrifying and exhilarating," I admitted with a small smile. "I'm not sure she deserved that."

"Oh, she deserved that, all right. It's been a long time coming."

"Now what?" I asked my best friend, hoping her advice would be worth taking.

Quinn leaned against the cushions and stared at me for a moment before speaking, obviously collecting her thoughts. "I think that there's a time to stay quiet and a time to stand up for yourself. For example, when Colin cheated and the press went crazy, you stayed quiet. Which was fine because it wasn't your issue to address publicly. You didn't do anything wrong, and there really was nothing you needed to say. You know what I mean?" She looked at me as I nodded along with her assessment.

"But this is a direct attack on your character and on you. So I think staying quiet is a mistake. If it were me, I'd want to defend myself. I wouldn't want anyone thinking those things about me, especially when they aren't anywhere close to the truth. I think you need to figure out what you want to say, but you should absolutely talk about this. But do it how you want. Post a blog on your website, an open letter to your fans, a post on social media, something."

The more she talked, the more animated she became. Her eyes lit up as she said, "Yeah, you be the one in complete control. You tell the public what you want to, how you want to, and only what you want to share in your words. We can guess at what everyone's questions will be, and we can figure out how to answer them without spilling any secrets about Tatum or Hanford. You can do this," she insisted, then added, "and I'll help you."

Quinn's idea had merit, and as I rolled it around in my head, I found myself perking up. "I like this plan. This feels right. I think I'll ask my mom what she thinks too. You know, just to get a second opinion."

"You need a new agent, Paige," Quinn noted abruptly.

Nodding, I added her suggestion to the growing mental list of things I needed to accomplish since getting back. "I know."

"And a new publicist as well."

"Probably."

"And please tell me you'll put Colin in his place. Or let me do it. Violently," she said darkly as she cracked her knuckles.

Laughing, I said, "I'll do my best."

"One thing at a time, I guess."

Quinn tried to reassure me, but I knew these things needed to happen now or I'd never do them. If I didn't act now, my will for so much change would fade. Days would turn into weeks, and I'd grow complacent and accepting again— two things I never wanted to be again when it came to my career and my life.

"There is something I'm sort of dying to do right now. And it's a bit crazy, but—"

"I'm in," Quinn said before even hearing my idea, and I laughed. "What is it?"

"I want to cut my hair."

Her head tilted to the side as she assessed my current style. "Are we talking like new long layers, or chop it all?"

I grinned. "Chop it all off."

"Like a pixie cut?" Her eyes widened in horror, and I cringed.

"Not that short, no. I'm thinking maybe shoulder length with layers."

Quinn jumped up and tugged at my hand. "Oh my God. Let's go right now before you change your mind."

It might seem stupid to someone not in the entertainment industry, but when so many things in your life felt like they weren't within your control, you fought to change the things that were. I'd wanted to cut my hair for years, but the long length was always tied into studio contracts and movie roles I'd signed on to play, even though it never made any sense to me with the invention of hair extensions and clip-ins.

I wasn't currently committed to a project, so I was free to do whatever I wanted with my own hair. And I wanted something new, something daring, something bold. Honestly, losing any inches off my long locks was a pretty bold move for me.

And I couldn't wait.

Get the Girl

TATUM

HEEDING CELESTE'S ADVICE, I closed the shop early and headed for home. I needed to have a heart-to-heart with my mother and if I didn't do it now, I might chicken out completely.

When did you turn into such a pussy, Montgomery?

I took my time walking home, trying to sort out my mind and my heart. It wasn't clarity that I needed on the two issues that were nothing but clear to me—my future and Paige—it was permission. Realizing how much I needed my mother to be okay with my plans, I walked home with new resolve.

When I stepped through the door, the smell of fresh-baked bread hit me immediately, and my stomach rumbled as my mom greeted me.

"You're home early," she said, wiping the flour from her

hands on a towel.

Not sure if I was ready for this, I forced a smile. "I wanted to talk to you about something."

Her expression turned curious as she waved a hand toward the kitchen table. I moved to sit as she placed a plate of the fresh, hot bread in the center, butter melting off the top. Removing her apron, she tossed it on the counter before joining me at the table.

"What's going on? Is everything okay?"

Sucking in a long breath to steady my nerves, I realized I had no idea where to begin. "It's just...I miss her, Mama." Suddenly at a loss for words, I dropped my gaze and focused on a knot in the wood table.

"So, what are you going to do about it?" she asked.

It wasn't the response I expected. I thought she'd agree with me or say something similar, but that was it. When she didn't, my gaze immediately darted up to meet hers. "What am I supposed to do?"

"Tatum, I've sat here and watched you give up everything you ever wanted in life. And I'll admit that when you first stayed home after your daddy died, I was grateful. I'd lost so much and I couldn't stand losing you too." She glanced away for a second and wiped at her eyes. Pinning her gaze on me again, her face flushed as she said, "But that was me being selfish. I always figured you'd eventually leave, but you didn't. And every year that passed, I allowed you to stay."

"You didn't make me stay," I interrupted, but she waved me off.

"I didn't help you leave, either. I didn't encourage you to move on and follow your own dreams, did I? I simply allowed you to put your life on hold and stay here. What kind of mother does that?"

I reached across the table and took her warm hand in mine. "Don't you dare do that. You didn't force me to do anything I wasn't willing to do. I've never once regretted coming back home, Mama. I want you to know that."

"But I regret keeping you here for so long," she said with a sigh.

"You don't live my life for me. I made these choices," I said, refusing to let her take all the blame for my still being here.

"I'm trying to tell you that I should have done things differently, Tatum, and I'm sorry. I'm so sorry." Her eyes filled with tears, and I pushed out of my chair and pulled her to her feet.

Hugging her, I whispered against her hair, "Don't be sorry. Just tell me what to do."

She sniffed, wiped her tears away, then pushed at my chest and sat back down at the table. Her expression stern, she said, "You don't give up. You don't quit. You go get that girl."

"But I screwed up. I told her to leave. I was mean to her." I winced as I said the words.

She nodded. "That you did, and that you were. But you're not above apologizing, are you, son?"

"No, ma'am," I admitted, because it was the truth.

"Then you go there and you find her. And you apologize

to her. Don't stop apologizing or trying to fix things until she takes you back. You hear me?"

"I hear you," I answered, my voice unsure.

"Unless that's not what you want? Unless you don't want her to forgive you?" she asked as I leaned back into the chair.

"Of course I want her to forgive me. I want to be with her," I admitted. "But I'm not sure how. We're so different; our lives are so different."

A thousand questions filled my mind. Paige forgiving me and wanting to give us a try meant that I'd be living there, or she'd be here, and there was no way in hell I'd allow Paige to give up her career and move here. Not that she ever would.

"That's something the two of you will figure out. But, Tatum, you'll hate yourself if you don't at least give this a try. I may not know much, but that much I know for sure."

Her lips curled into a sad smile, and I knew she was right. Losing Paige without a fight was something I'd most likely never get over.

I hung my head and let out a sigh. "She probably hates me."

Mama laid a hand on my shoulder. "She most certainly does not hate you. But I bet you hurt her heart, so she'll be leery about trusting you with it again. That's on you to be the man I know you are to fix it."

"What if it's not enough?" I asked, worried that nothing I did would make Paige forgive me. What if I couldn't make her see how stupid I was to let her go? Or worse, what if she didn't care anymore now that we were apart and she was living her life?

"Whatever you're telling yourself right now in your head, Tatum, doesn't matter. I know you have doubts. I know you're scared, whether you admit it or not, but I have to tell you that I haven't seen you that happy in years. Maybe ever."

I nodded; as usual, she was absolutely right. I had never been as happy with anyone as I was with Paige.

"What will we do with the shop? Who will run it while I'm gone?" I started going down the checklist that had formed in my mind.

She waved a hand at me, dismissing my concerns. "I'll take care of that. You know that someone will step up to help out. Let me worry about those things. I'm tired of you putting your life on pause. I can't have you doing it anymore."

"But—"

"But nothing. I don't want to hear another word about it," she said as I opened my mouth to argue, and she raised a warning finger at me. "I mean it. Not another word."

I smiled, but responded anyway. "What will you do while I'm gone?" Leaving the only town I'd truly ever known was hard, but leaving my mom for any length of time since my dad died was a thousand times harder.

My mother gave me a brave smile. "Don't worry about me. I'll be fine. I'm a grown woman. And honestly, I've always wanted to see California. Maybe you'll settle down out there and I'll come visit," she suggested, and her face lit up in a way I'd never seen before.

"I'm just going out there to see Paige and try to fix this.

That doesn't mean I'm never coming back here," I said, my voice stern.

"We'll see about that," she said with a grin as a knock on the screen door startled us.

I turned around to see Brina on the porch, clearly dressed to impress and wearing way too much makeup. I groaned, but didn't move from the table to greet her as my mom cast a glance my way and I shook my head at her.

Mama narrowed her eyes at me in disapproval before pushing out of her chair and giving my ex a friendly smile. "Brina. How lovely to see you," she said as she stepped toward the door.

"Hi, Emily. I was wondering if I could talk to Tatum for a minute." Brina tilted her head so that she could see me past my mom's shoulder.

"What do you want, Brina?" I spat out. I didn't want her here. I didn't want Brina anywhere near me after everything she'd done.

My mom walked over to me and whispered, "Maybe she came to apologize. At least give her the chance to do that."

Without a word, I walked toward the screen door, pushed it open, and stepped out on to the porch.

"Can we walk?" Brina asked.

Waving my hand, I signaled she should lead the way before falling in step beside her.

"So, Paige is gone, huh?" Brina said nonchalantly.

Really? Is that how she's going to play this?

I stopped and glared at her. "You know damn well she's

gone. You're the one who called her agent and told him where to find her."

Her expression changed to shock before quickly turning to anger. "Celeste," she practically growled.

"What about her? As far as I can tell, Celeste is the most decent person I know here. You, on the other hand—"

Brina jabbed a finger into my chest as her cheeks flamed. "I what? Huh, Tatum? So I got rid of her. You were never going to get back together with me as long as she was still around, so I did what I had to do. Any girl would have done the same thing."

I saw red. Everything that spewed from this delusional woman's mouth only fueled my quickly building temper. "Brina, listen to me and listen well. We are never getting back together. You and me? That shit's old news."

Putting on a practiced pout, Brina said, "Are you trying to tell me you don't still love me? Because I don't believe you."

Tempted to pull my hair out strand by strand, I leaned toward her, my mouth mere inches from hers as if I were leaning in for a kiss, but I felt nothing but anger. "I don't love you, haven't loved you for years. We're done. We've been done. The only reason you're acting like this is because it's the first time you've seen someone else want me. And not just any someone, but Paige."

"Oh, please, like that's going anywhere. She's gone now, and we can—" She reached out and touched her fingers to my cheek, but I jerked back as if it burned.

"Don't touch me."

"Why are you being like this?"

Frustrated at how clueless she was, I spat out, "Are you on drugs? No, seriously, are you on something that makes it impossible for you to live in reality? Have you heard a single word I've said?"

Scuffing at the dirt with her boots, she said, "I heard you. I just don't believe you." She tilted her head flirtatiously and pulled out the smile that used to do me in every time.

Disgusted, I shook my head. "I don't know what else to say to you. I don't want you. I don't love you. And I think you're a bad person," I added with a shrug.

Apparently that shot hit its mark. Brina narrowed her eyes at me as she hooked her hands on her hips. "Oh, right, I'm a bad person because I got rid of my competition. Because I made sure the one person who didn't belong here in this town left. She wasn't going to stay anyway, Tatum. God, I did you a favor!"

"The fact that that's how you justify your behavior speaks volumes about your character, Brina. I don't know what I ever saw in you." I raked my gaze up and down her body and knew immediately what I'd seen in her as a kid. Unfortunately for her, that wasn't enough for me anymore.

"Stop saying that!" Her eyes filled with unshed tears as she looked up at me.

That old trick used to work with me, but not anymore. "I won't. I don't want you."

"What do you want then? You want *her*?" she spat out.

My breath hitched as I looked Brina straight in the eyes.

"Hell yes, I want her. And I was actually on my way to go get her before you interrupted. So I need to go."

I turned away from Brina's shocked expression and walked back toward my mom's house a short distance away.

"It will never work!" she shouted at me as I walked away. "You'll be back here in a week, begging me to take you back."

I did my best to ignore her words because they mirrored my worst fears.

"Don't hold your breath, sweetheart. You'll die. Guaranteed," I shouted over my shoulder as I pulled open the screen door with new resolve.

I'd prove them all wrong. Especially myself.

Find Somebody New

PAIGE

I'D SPENT THE last few days laying low in my apartment, except for the single afternoon and evening I'd spent at my parents' house. Despite the paparazzi camping out on the street, it was really nice to be home and enjoy the comfort of my supportive family.

My mom had agreed with Quinn about the open letter to my fans on my website, and my sister thought it was the perfect thing to do to reach them directly. She said that they would love reading something like that from the person they admired, so I'd spent half the day writing and rewriting it so it would be perfect. It would be a personal message from me, in my own words, that I could continue to add to if necessary. Or I could just let it stand on its own and be done with the whole situation.

It felt good to take control of my life, to be in charge of my reputation in the public eye. I sat on my bed with my legs crossed, typing away at the laptop on my lap as my mom walked into my room and sat down next to me.

"Have you heard from him?" she asked.

My fingers froze on the keys as I sucked in a breath. At least she was thoughtful enough not to mention his name.

"No." I turned to her and blinked away the tears that threatened, but that was harder to do considering who I was talking to. Confiding in your mom about things made it that much more emotional. You could be vulnerable with your family in ways you couldn't with others.

"I'm sorry, honey. I can't imagine what that boy's going through with you gone," she said as she pulled me close and kissed the top of my head.

"What do you mean?"

"I just think that you were probably like a tornado of the best kind, coming into his life and ruffling him all up, and then leaving just as quick as you touched down. He probably doesn't know what the heck to do with himself."

"Are you defending him? He pretty much shoved me out the door and into Colin's arms. It was embarrassing," I admitted.

"I know, honey. But he's a man. And they tend to make a lot of mistakes," she said with a light laugh that only irritated me.

"I don't want to talk about Tatum right now. I need to focus on fixing my career and everything I've worked so hard to build professionally. Then I'll deal with my heart."

Mom nodded. "Fair enough. So in that regard, I don't think you should tell Jayson or Corryn about the letter," she warned, and I agreed.

"Honestly, I wasn't planning on it."

"Good. I'm not sure how I feel about those two anymore." She frowned, her concern causing wrinkles to form around her eyes and mouth.

"Well, if they know I'm planning on posting this, they'll try to book me on every entertainment show and website to talk about it. Anything to garner extra attention," I said, unable to hide my sarcasm.

No way would I let that happen; I wanted to keep Tatum and his town to myself. There were things I was willing to share, but Tatum wasn't one of them.

"And I'm not sure they're the best people to have in my corner." With a sigh, I added, "I honestly don't know if they ever were."

Mom gave me a sad look. "I'm so sorry, honey. I feel like I should have taken better care of you, watched out for you more. When your career took off, you had to grow up so fast." She wrapped one arm around me and squeezed.

Hugging her back, I said, "Mom, you didn't do anything wrong. I believe that my team should grow with me and want the best for me, but I'm just now realizing that they don't. We were both duped when it came to Jayson. He's good at his job. You didn't know he was like this any more than I did."

"When'd you get so smart, huh?" she asked with a smile.

I grinned back at her. "Probably at birth. I come from good stock, after all."

My phone vibrated, and I glanced down to see MADISON MYERS flashing on my caller ID.

Scrunching my face in apology, I said, "I need to take this. It's Madison Myers. She's an agent." I pushed up from my bed and closed the door after Mom slipped out. "Hello?"

"Paige, it's Madison Myers," she breathed out, her voice instantly soothing me.

"Hey, Madison, how are you?"

She laughed. "I'm fine. It's you I'm worried about."

I shuddered. "Oh. The tabloids, you mean? It's not true." My shoulders slumped forward as I realized that everyone who ever knew me in this town probably believed what was being reported about me.

"Oh, please. I know it's not true," she said, her confidence in me breaking me out of my funk.

"You do?"

"Of course I do. I don't believe any of that crap, especially not about you. What a joke. I was just calling to make sure that you were okay and to see if you needed anything."

"Seriously?"

"Yes, seriously. Why? Paige, are you all right? Jayson and your people are handling this for you, aren't they? I mean, I know Jayson's a complete dickwad, but he wouldn't hang you out to dry like this."

I remembered when Madison used to work for Jayson as his assistant. That was before she told him off and walked out of the job. She eventually landed her own agent role at the Warren Taylor Agency with the help of her super-hot singer boyfriend, Walker Rhodes.

"Paige? Hello?"

"Sorry, I'm here. No. No, he's not helping. Madison, do you think I could come see you?" I glanced around my bedroom for my shoes and purse.

"Of course. You want to come to the office, or do you want me to come over? Or would you rather we meet somewhere?"

"I'll come to you. I'm at my parents' house, so it might take me a few minutes to get there."

"Okay. You coming now?"

"If that's all right."

"Of course it's all right. I'll see you soon."

I pressed the END button and pushed my feet into a pair of sandals, slipped my sunglasses onto my head, and headed out of my bedroom. My mom sat in the kitchen drinking what was most likely tea from a steaming mug.

"Leaving already?"

"I'm going to go see Madison and talk to her about everything that's going on." I leaned down and gave my mom a quick squeeze.

"You trust her?"

I nodded. "I do, actually. A lot."

"That's good. Call me after. I want to hear all about it."

"I will. Thanks, Mom. I love you," I said with a smile as I walked toward the front door.

"Love you too."

The paparazzi that had camped outside followed me again all the way to the Warren Taylor offices, but stopped short of entering the underground parking. This wasn't front-page news, but my visiting an agency that didn't currently represent me would make headlines. I speculated about the news reaching Jayson before I ever talked to him.

The elevator doors opened, and I walked through a set of glass doors and into the spacious lobby area.

"Miss Lockwood." A young receptionist greeted me by name as I entered. "Miss Myers is expecting you. If you'll follow me." She unplugged her headset from her phone and led me around a white column where the offices opened up.

As I walked down the long hallway, I experienced a nostalgia from a time I wasn't a part of. Old black-and-white head shots of celebrities from days past lined the walls, evoking eras that felt more like eons ago than decades. I couldn't believe how many stars had been associated with this company, and pride filled me at my merely being in their presence, even if it was only in photographs. As we walked, I scanned the walls that seemed to be divided by era, the photographs eventually transitioning from black and white to color as they became more recent.

Waving a hand toward an open door, she smiled. "Right in there," she said before walking away.

I stepped through the doorway into an outer office, where an assistant looked up from her computer screen. "Hi, Miss Lockwood—"

"Please. Call me Paige."

She smiled and nodded before peeking through the open doorway behind her into what I assumed was Madison's office. "Paige Lockwood is here to see you, Miss Myers."

"Ooh, send her in." Madison's voice rose in pitch, and I laughed softly to myself.

I turned to her assistant and thanked her before entering the office. The door closed behind me, and I glanced back before turning around to see Madison walking toward me. She engulfed me in a friendly hug, and I almost broke down right then and there at her genuine and unexpected affection.

"It's so good to see you," she said. "And I love your hair. It looks great!" She smiled as she reached out to touch a shoulder-length strand.

"Thanks. It's good to see you too. Nice office." I looked past her desk and through the floor-to-ceiling windows at the busy street below. The paint was white but with the faintest hint of blue that had a calming effect.

"Isn't it ridiculous in here? I feel so out of place half the time with my one whopping client and all." She waved a hand toward the space on her wall dedicated to Walker Rhodes. Walker wasn't only the hottest singing-sensation-turned-actor in the United States; he was also her boyfriend.

"I bet he loves all the one-on-one attention." I smiled at his framed head shot on her wall.

"Oh yes, he's quite a handful, that one. I'll probably ditch him soon," she lied with a playful grin.

"I would," I teased her. "You know how those celebrities

can be. And forget even trying to date them."

We both laughed before Madison's expression grew serious. "Paige, what's going on? Why are there all these false reports about where you've been, and why is no one putting a stop to them? I find it hard to believe that you were in rehab, had an abortion, or tried to kill yourself."

"Well, at least one person knows the truth."

She sucked in a quick breath. "Look, usually I might suggest you ride this out, wait until a bigger story comes along and takes the spotlight off of you. But for now I don't see that happening, and as long as you continue to ignore it and not say anything about it, you're only fueling the fire."

"What am I supposed to say? That I left town and drove until my car got a flat, and I fell in love with some guy and didn't want to come back?"

Madison fell back into her chair. "Is that what happened?"

"Pretty much."

"Sounds like a book I read recently," she said with a smile.

"Sounds like a cliché. My God, my life is such a cliché." I rolled my eyes at the ceiling, thinking about how often I'd thought that about myself lately.

"That's how clichés get made. Because they're true," she said sagely.

My mind made up, I plopped down into her guest chair and announced, "Madison, I want to hire you to represent me."

She instantly sat up and pushed her shoulders back. "Really?"

"Yes. I'm going to fire Jayson, but only if you say you'll take me on."

"I have to check with my bosses, but I bet they'll be thrilled. Are you sure you want me? I'm still really new and learning a lot."

"Madison, I trust you. And I firmly believe that you'll have my career and what's best for me at heart. Walker said you're good when it comes to things like that."

Her cheeks flushed as I mentioned her boyfriend talking about her. "He said that? When did you talk to him?"

"I called him on the drive over here to ask how things were here for you, and if you loved what you were doing. He said you were the best thing to ever happen to his career, and that he'd still feel that way even if he wasn't in love with you."

She fanned herself as if all this information was far too much. "He's lying. He definitely thinks I'm more amazing because I give him sex."

"Probably," I said with a smirk. "But I still want you to be my agent, and you don't have to give me sex like you do him." We both broke out into laughter at that, and when the giggles died, I gave her a serious look and said, "If you say no, I don't know what I'll do."

Pushing away from her desk, she rose to her feet. "I'll be right back. Don't move."

I smiled and checked my e-mails and text messages while I waited for her to return. It had been almost a week since I left Tatum, and still no word from him. I had half expected an apology, or at least some sort of communication from him.

How could he be perfectly fine without me when I had to work hard to hold it together without him?

Madison walked back into the office with a giant smile and an older gray-haired gentleman in tow. "Paige, this is my boss, Gerald Taylor. Mr. Taylor, this is Paige Lockwood."

I extended my hand and he gripped it tightly, surprising me as I said, "It's nice to meet you."

"You too. You're kind of a big deal, you know, young lady," he said teasingly, and I blushed. "Madison says you'd like to come on board, and I wanted to be the first to welcome you to our agency. You're in good hands with Miss Myers."

"Thank you so much. I'm really excited to have her on my team."

After his personal welcome, Gerald Taylor excused himself, leaving me alone with Madison.

Catching her eye, I smiled and said, "Guess I'd better go fire Jayson."

She grinned back at me. "And then I can e-mail you the contracts to sign. This is going to be awesome, Paige."

"I seriously feel a thousand pounds lighter already. Oh, I wanted to ask you something."

"As your new agent, or as a friend?" she asked before sitting back down at her oversized desk.

"Agent," I answered.

"Shoot."

"I was thinking about writing an open letter to my fans about what really happened and posting it exclusively on my website. People will still have questions, and the media will most likely still want interviews with me, but I wanted to tell my story in a way that I could control it."

Madison nodded. "I think that's a great idea, honestly. I love it. Send me the final draft before you post it?"

"Absolutely. Oh, and one more thing." I paused as she lifted her eyebrows at me, signaling for me to continue. "I want to fire Corryn as well. She's my manager, and I believe she has my best interests at heart about as much as Jayson does. Do you think I'd be okay with only an agent for now?"

I could practically see the wheels turning in Madison's head as she mulled it over. A moment passed before she said carefully, "That's entirely up to you. But if you're looking to head in a new direction for a while, I don't see what your manager would handle that I couldn't. I mean, in the grand scheme of things it's a manager's job to look out for you and plan your future, your roles, where you're headed, and what you want to do going forward. But those are all things that I'm interested in as well when it comes to my clients." Gazing at me with hope in her eyes, she said, "I'd like to think that until I'm proved wrong, I could sort of bridge that gap and play both roles."

Comfort immediately filled me, and I smiled. "I think it's worth a shot. Thank you, Madison. For everything. Give Walker a kiss for me," I said with a wink as I stood up to leave.

I chuckled under my breath, happy that things were finally falling into place, and proud of myself for being the one to make them happen.

"Will do. And, Paige?" she called after me.

I paused at the doorway and turned to face her.

"One day I want to hear all about this broken-down town and this guy, okay?"

I gave her another smile, trying to hide the sadness that filled me at the realization that my time with Tatum now only existed in memories.

"Okay." Unable to resist glancing down at my phone again, I noticed that he still hadn't called or texted.

That was fine. I'd be fine.

I had to be.

BACK IN THE solitude of my too-quiet apartment, I picked up my phone and dialed Jayson's number.

"Paige, why were you at Warren Taylor's?" he yelled instead of answering with a normal greeting. "What the hell is going on?"

"I'm about to tell you," I said evenly, forcing myself to stay strong.

He groaned. "What is it?"

"You're fired."

"Excuse me?" he shrieked.

"I'm pretty sure you heard me," I said firmly, my inner confidence growing and building upon itself. "My lawyer has sent you an e-mail asking to terminate our business relationship effective immediately."

He breathed harshly into the phone line, and knowing what was coming, I pulled it from my ear.

"I made you what you are, Paige! Good luck getting any work in this town again! You think that Madison, my *assistant*," he added snidely, "can do anything for you? What a fucking joke! You're both a pair of idiots. Idiots who will be out of work by the time next pilot season rolls around," he screamed before hanging up.

Instead of feeling nervous or worried with his threats, I instantly felt relieved. My shoulders lightened as the load I subconsciously carried lessened.

Dialing Corryn while I was still brimming with confidence, I listened as the phone beeped each time it rang, signaling that she was on the other line. When her voice mail clicked on, I left a message.

"Hi, Corryn, this is Paige. As of today, I will no longer be requiring your services. You should have an e-mail detailing our termination clause in your in-box from my lawyer. Thank you for your time and help over the years. I wish you the best." And with that, I ended the call and danced in my living room, freedom filling me from the inside out.

After my five-second dance party, I pulled open my laptop to read over the draft of my open letter one last time before sending it to Madison for review. I attached it to a quick e-mail telling her that I was officially on the market for a new agent, and asking if she knew anyone who wanted to represent me.

I giggled, amazed at my ability to be and feel silly with all the chaos that constantly hounded me. In a way I felt like a new person, with my new short hairstyle that I chose for myself, and my professional chains cut free.

Dear Fans, [Madison, I hate calling them fans—it seems too snobby and rude. How else can I address them that makes them feel more appreciated?]

There has been a lot of speculation about where I've been the past few weeks. Since returning to town, I've been bombarded with accusations and unkind words, brutal reminders of the reality of this business that I otherwise normally love. I'll admit that part of me wanted to say nothing and hope it would all go away on its own. But the rest of me really wanted to set the record straight.

You have no idea how hard it is to read such utter lies about yourself printed everywhere for everyone to read. Worse than the made-up stories is the fact that people believe them...a lot of people. And that's why I'm here, writing this letter to you now. I needed to talk to you the way friends do, and I wanted to be the one to do it—not a publicist or an agent or manager, but me.

It's not an exciting story, to be honest. The truth is that I needed to get away in the wake of everything that was going on around me. I'm human, just like you, and sometimes I want to escape from my problems and disappear for a while. And frankly, that's exactly what I tried to do (in the form of leaving town, that is, not in the form of rehab, drug overdose, alcohol binges, or any other of the made-up excuses). I realize that being a twenty-one-year-old actress is nothing to complain about, and believe me when I tell you that I'm not complaining. But please understand that choosing this life means that I miss out on so many of the amazing things that you all get to do and experience every single day.

I know, I know—you're probably rolling your eyes and calling me crazy right now because you're supposed to be the ones envying my life, not the other way around. But to be honest, sometimes I crave normalcy with every fiber of my being. A normalcy that I never seem to get. A normalcy that I've decided to fight for because this is my life and I want to be the one in charge of it. :)

In the midst of the destruction of my relationship with Colin, I did exactly what I said above. I escaped. My heart landed in a tiny town I'd never heard of before, but I'll never forget. Part of me is still there, and I think it always will be. Because in this tiny town in the South, I got to be Paige Lockwood, normal twenty-one-year-old girl, instead of Paige Lockwood, Hollywood actress.

I spent my nights drinking sweet tea and watching the sun set with an adorable black Lab at my side. I now own the most beautiful pair of authentic cowgirl boots I've ever seen (thank you, Emily). I got to experience my very first bonfire field party with giant trucks, hay bales, and some really good-natured people. Have you ever swam in a swimming hole complete with the obligatory rope swing before? Well, I never had, not before a few weeks ago. Heck, I didn't even know that kind of thing really existed outside of the movies. And I loved every minute that I was away because for the first time in a long time, I was just like everyone else. I felt normal.

Being away was exactly what I needed. And no, not because I hated myself after what Colin did, or because I couldn't get over him (I am SO over him, for the record). I'm not pregnant. I most certainly did not try to kill myself, and why anyone would even make light of something so serious is beyond me. Suicide isn't a joke. I don't find it funny, and I don't think that the press should be able to throw that type of accusation around whenever it suits them (but that's a discussion for another time).

There are so many things that each of us take for granted in our lives. I don't believe we do it on purpose; we just get used to the things we have, the things that surround us on a daily basis, that we stop seeing how unique they truly are. Sometimes the most beautiful things in our world stop being so pretty because we see them all the time. But that's on us to change our perspective and start really seeing again.

My eyes have been reopened. I can see clearly now exactly what it is that I want and need in my life to feel a little more like you and to be more relatable.

I'm sorry that I disappeared without a trace and made some of you worry. Please forgive me for causing you any distress, as that was never my intention. And please understand that escaping the chaos that surrounded me for a little while was exactly what I needed to do for me, but I won't do it again. At least, not without letting you know. I promise.

I hope that you understand and that you'll continue to follow me on my journey. It's been the most incredible seven years, and I wouldn't change a thing. But it's time to expand my horizons a little. I'm not quitting acting—so please don't think that—I'm just finding my balance, my happy place in this world.

It's a space that exists in each of us that only we truly know what fuels it. I hope you have yours. And I hope you'll stick around to watch me find mine. I love you all so much!

Sincerely and with respect,
Paige

My cell phone rang within minutes with my new agent's

name on the caller ID. "Is it okay?" I asked instead of saying hello.

"It's perfect. I wouldn't change a thing," Madison said, making me really smile for the first time in what felt like months. "Did you get the e-mail with the contracts?"

"I did. They should already be headed back to you right after my lawyer looks them over."

"Perfect."

"Any idea on a word change for fans?" I asked before I forgot, caught up in the excitement over posting that online.

"Oh! Yes. I was thinking friends."

I released a short breath as I smiled to myself. "Oh jeez, of course! The answer was so simple, it was hard to find. I love it. Thank you."

"One last thing. You can either hit publish on that now, or you can wait until I get all the websites updated with your new agent contact information. It's up to you," Madison said, all business, and I liked it.

"How long will that take?"

"About fifteen minutes."

I laughed. "Oh! I thought you were going to say like two days or something. Text me when you're done with the update. I'll make sure my website contact information is updated as well before I post it."

"I'm excited, Paige!"

"Me too," I said before hanging up.

And I was. This would be the first time I was truly standing up for myself, speaking my piece in a way that no one could take away from me—not the press, not Colin, not Jayson, not anyone who wanted to bring me down with lies, accusations, or false words. There would be no reading it wrong or getting the wrong idea, no misinformation, because it would have come straight from me.

I sucked in a long breath before I exhaled it slowly, a smile on my face as I waited for the signal to press POST.

When my phone dinged, I glanced down and saw the message from Madison that simply said, "GO FOR IT."

So I did.

Who Cheated First

PAIGE

MY PHONE HAD been ringing off the hook since the letter went live on my website. Madison informed me that we crashed the server multiple times, and that screenshots of the letter were currently going viral on all media outlets and social media sites.

Feeling quite happy with myself, I silenced my phone for the night. For the first time since getting back to LA, I fell into a deep, dreamless sleep.

Reaching my hands over my head in the morning as I stretched, I instinctively reached for my cell sitting on my nightstand and turned the volume up, noticing the insane amount of missed calls, text messages, and e-mails. My phone hadn't blown up like that since the news of Colin cheating had broken.

I wrongly assumed that overload of messages were from the press wanting further comment about my open letter, but as I opened up the Internet browser on my cell, my breath caught in my throat as headlines with my name caught my eye.

Paige Cheated First! And We Have the Proof!
Colin Heartbroken Over a Cheating Paige!
Paige Gets Cozy with this Southern Hunk!

My heart dropped as I scanned the photos that accompanied the lies, all pulled from various social media accounts. One was of Tatum and me at the field party, sitting in the back of his truck, and the other was of us kissing inside the bar. And I'd just mentioned the field party and the trucks in my letter the night before.

Dropping my head into my hands, I wondered when this nightmare was going to end. When had I become a target for constant scandal? Refocusing, I clicked on one of the headlines and scanned the contents of the article, noticing the mentions of "reliable sources" that meant absolutely nothing when it came to sensational journalism these days.

How could I have forgotten that I told everyone from Hanford they could start posting the pictures once I left town? Rubbing my eyes with the palm of my hands, I was suddenly scared for the sweet town. The press, not to mention the world, would soon know everything about my time away and the people who were a part of it. The one thing I had longed to keep quiet would soon become an absolute circus. I could never stand to show my face there again if I ruined their peace and quiet. How would I forgive myself?

Glancing back at the pictures, I couldn't ignore the way my stomach flipped when I looked at Tatum's face next to mine. And the photo of us kissing in the bar almost made me come apart completely. Everything I felt for him seemed so transparent, so glaringly obvious in that picture. I missed him. But as quickly as that emotion entered my body, I dismissed it, forcing myself to remember that he hadn't so much as called since I'd been back.

I jumped out of bed and dialed Madison's number as I walked into the bathroom and reached for a washcloth. She was quickly becoming someone I trusted, and I realized that I always had to some extent. Calling her was almost second nature, and we'd only just become business partners the day before.

"Paige," she answered.

"My God." I didn't know what else to say; I was at a loss.

"It's okay. We'll deal with this. Do you want to release a statement?"

I balled my hand into a fist a few times before responding. "But I just released a huge statement on my website. We just posted that last night, and now this?"

"I know you're frustrated. Why don't we see how the day plays out, and then we can figure out what we want to do, if anything."

I was tired. Tired of this constant defense of myself, my actions, my thoughts, my movements. It was something I'd never dealt with before, so I wasn't necessarily good at it. The letter to my friends had drained me, and I'd already said everything I wanted to. I didn't want to talk anymore, suddenly feeling like all my honest words from last night were negated by a few pictures and lying headlines.

"Okay, Madison. Let's just sit on it if we can. I'm tired."

"I know you are. This will be okay. But can I ask you something?"

"Of course."

"If that's the guy from the broken-down town, I wouldn't have wanted to leave either."

A small smile tugged at my lips. "I know, right?" I said halfheartedly.

"I'll be in touch," she said.

Tossing my cell aside, I fought off the urge to dive back into bed and hide out under the covers. Instead I padded into the kitchen after brushing my teeth and started my coffeemaker. I rifled through the cupboard, then pulled out a box of cereal and started munching on it straight out of the box.

I reached for my laptop, then hopped up on my countertop and placed it on my lap as I waited for my coffee. It seemed like every outlet had picked up the pictures of Tatum and me and were running them nonstop. They printed articles saying how I cheated on Colin first, and that's why he did what he did. Suddenly, I was the bad guy and Colin was the victim. It sickened me.

When I came across a post from Colin that said, "Now everyone knows what I was dealing with," I almost threw my laptop across the room. The utter betrayal enraged me, forcing to wonder again how any one person could be so malicious toward a person they claimed to have loved.

All of this was beyond ridiculous. My shock started to wear off as anger replaced it. I decided that I liked feeling angry; it was empowering. Not that I enjoyed the things that were happening to me, but being angry was a heck of a lot better than being confused, hurt, and overwhelmed. Those emotions didn't constitute action like anger did. It fueled it.

After showering and getting dressed, I grabbed my things, fully intending to head over to Quinn's house. This time I wasn't going over there to cry, but to talk and form some kind of a game plan.

As I stepped out of the elevator and into the lobby, I was shocked by Tatum's familiar blue eyes looking back at me from the concierge desk. Sam was speaking to him softly, but I couldn't make out the words.

I stopped in my tracks and pinched myself to make sure I was awake. Tatum noticed me do it and smiled as he moved to close the space between us.

"Miss Lockwood, this is okay, right?" Sam asked, his expression pained as he nodded his head in Tatum's direction.

I nodded. "Yes, this is okay. For now," I added quickly. "Thank you, Sam."

Sam directed his attention toward his ringing telephone as Tatum took another tentative step toward me.

"Are you really here?" I asked through my shock as all the righteous anger whooshed out of me. My first instinct was that I wanted to protect Tatum from the paparazzi waiting outside, knowing that he would absolutely hate the way they would attack him, if they hadn't already. I needed to warn him about the pictures. Did he already know?

"I'm so sorry, Paige." He cautiously stepped toward me, clearly unsure of my reaction. "I'm so sorry I let you go. I'm sorry I haven't been there for you, or tried to call."

I bowed my head and squeezed my eyes shut as words all but failed me.

"Am I too late? Is it too late?" he pleaded as I lifted my head to look at him.

"Too late for what?" I asked, willing myself not to cry. *He's here. My God, what does that mean that he's here?*

"For you. For us. Did I wait too long before coming here to apologize and tell you what a fool I was? And how sorry I am and that I don't want to live without you?"

My body reacted favorably to his words, but my mind held out. I shifted on my feet, my internal parts at odds with one another.

I looked into his eyes. "I can't trust you anymore. I want to, but I don't."

The hurt my words brought to his eyes pained me, but it did little to curb my sudden resolve. I had given Tatum my trust completely, and he'd tossed it right back at me. He hurt me when he discarded me like last night's garbage.

His eyebrows pulled together as he clenched his jaw. "I know you don't. But I'll do whatever it takes to earn your trust back, Paige. I was an idiot. I didn't mean any of it, you have to know that. I was so damned hurt, I couldn't stop myself."

"I know why you did it, but I don't like that you did. This business I'm in," I waved a hand at the throngs of press taking pictures from outside the windows, "it's not easy, and I'm scared you'll run when it gets ugly. And as you can see, it does get ugly."

He took a step toward me, reaching out to grab my arms as he pulled me close. "I won't run. I promise. I. Won't. Run," he gritted out, emphasizing each word.

"I don't—" I pressed my lips together as I summoned more strength. "I don't believe you."

As the blood drained from his face and he loosened his grip on me, my stomach turned and rolled. It was hard to be this close to Tatum and not give in.

"I thought you might say that," he said as he glanced down at the floor and swiped at his eyes.

It hurt to see him like this. My heart wanted to leap into his arms and tell him we'd work it all out and things would be fine, but my head refused to allow that. My mind continued to remind me that he pushed me away, told me to leave, handed me to Colin without a second glance.

Defense mechanism or not, that was something I didn't need in my life. With all the inner strength I'd recently found, I needed the man in my life to be just as strong as me, if not stronger.

"Do you have any feelings for me at all?" he asked so softly, I almost didn't hear him.

"This has nothing to do with how I feel about you." I reached for his chin and tilted it up so he could look at me and recognize that I was hurting too. "Of course I have feelings for you. But you didn't handle things well when Jayson and Colin showed up."

He opened his mouth to interrupt, but I placed a finger on his lips to silence him. God, they were soft.

"I know why you did it. I know you didn't mean the things you said. But dating me is hard, Tatum. It's not easy being in the spotlight, or being with me, or around this lifestyle. There are things that happen constantly that I can't control. I just don't think it's something you want to be involved in, but I don't fault you for that. I just—" I stopped as the rest of my thoughts and words failed me.

"I screwed up, Paige. I know that. I knew the second you drove away that I'd never be the same again. I want to be with you." He grabbed my hand, his thumb skating across my knuckles. "I know you don't think I'm worth it, but I'll show you that I am. I'll prove it to you. I want you. I want this," he said as he waved his other hand between us. "I want there to be an *us*, Paige. I get that you're nervous, but I'm not going anywhere this time. I'm so in love with you."

"What?" I coughed out.

He loves me? My heart jump-started inside my chest, battering against the cage I kept it in.

"You didn't hear me the first time?" he said with a smirk. "I'm in love with you, Paige. I love you. I'll never forgive myself if you don't forgive me, but I know you need proof. Don't give up on me." His lips grazed the top of my hand as he let it go and turned to walk away.

"I thought you said you weren't going anywhere?" I called out at his back, and he stopped.

"Oh, I'm not. Not permanently. But I have something to do first." He moved toward the glass doors before turning back to me. "By the way, I really like your hair."

I smiled as I absentmindedly reached for the short ends, pulling at them as Tatum walked outside, where the paparazzi all but attacked him. Watching him for a minute, I wondered how he would handle himself in all the chaos that surrounded him. I half expected him to lose his cool or do something rash, but he didn't. Tatum was the picture of calm.

Which made me wonder how the heck he was doing it, and what the heck I was going to do about *him*.

Forget going to Quinn's. I needed my mom.

Stand Up for My Girl

TATUM

I WOULD HAVE never imagined that Paige could look any hotter than when she was with me, but she did. Holy hell, she did. Her shoulder-length hair seemed to suit her way more than the long hair ever did. Maybe it was the new her? More self-assured, confident, and sexy as hell.

I ran outside, telling Paige that I had something to do. But what the hell I was trying to accomplish, even I didn't know. My instincts had told me to confront the paparazzi, tell them everything they wanted to know, but now that I was outside and surrounded by them, it seemed like a completely foolish idea. There were too many of them, and I was convinced they'd twist my words.

"Why are you leaving, Tatum? Did Paige kick you out?"

"Did you two break up?"

"How long were you guys cheating before Colin found out? Does he know you're in town?"

"How does it feel to be a home wrecker?"

"So Paige cheated first, huh? Never would have thought that America's Sweetheart was really a dirty girl. Is that why you like her?"

"How'd you two meet?"

"How long has Paige been keeping you a secret, Tatum Montgomery?"

Holy hell. How Paige dealt with this kind of shit on a daily basis was beyond me. I wanted to pull my arm back and clock most of these assholes in the face for the things they were saying, the insinuations about her that they made, the lies they propagated.

Every one of these pricks knew who I was; they knew my first and last name. It was unnerving, to say the least. The whole scene made me feel like I was living in an alternate universe, but I was determined to stay cool, both for Paige's sake and my own. She needed to know she could trust me to handle this kind of thing, and I needed to learn how to do exactly that.

My mom had warned me when I stepped off the airplane about the pictures in the press. I knew no one from Hanford meant to cause any harm, but it still happened. And now I needed to fix it. Sometimes I wish life came with a manual—I could sure as shit use one now.

Paige didn't deserve to have her life in constant upheaval like this. She needed someone to defend her honor, and I wanted that someone to be me. I meant every word I said to her just then, and I wasn't even pissed when she didn't tell me she loved me back. I knew she did, even if she had herself convinced that she didn't. I'd show her how wrong she was.

While Hollywood and this ridiculous scene might not be my most favorite thing in the world, I'd realized that Paige is. And she was worth all the bullshit I'd go through just to be with her. Unfortunately, I made her feel like she wasn't worth it. My actions and words made her to feel like I didn't think she was worth the trouble. But she was wrong, so very wrong, and I planned to prove just that.

With the paparazzi screaming in my ear, I watched as half of them ran to their cars when Paige slipped out the doors behind me and jumped into her car, sunglasses covering her eyes. Her head turned in my direction, and she gave me a little smile before making a quick right out of her complex. I stood there dumbfounded, feeling like a fish out of water as cars peeled out of the parking lot to follow her. My stomach churned at the sight, and I felt helpless as I realized she was being relentlessly chased.

Damn it, why aren't superpowers real?

Scanning the single photographer left, I turned toward the guy, who looked to be about my age. I took a step in his direction, and his dark, beady eyes watched my every move as his fingers tightened their grip on his camera.

"So, why are you still here?" I asked, trying to keep my tone calm when my insides were anything but. "Why didn't you chase Paige like all the others?"

He pulled a baseball cap from his back pocket and tugged it over his jet-black hair, his tanned face suddenly shaded as he nodded at me. "One of the other guys on my crew followed her, so I stayed here with you. Maybe you'll tell me all about the cheating and give me an exclusive?"

I narrowed my eyes and swallowed the growl that wanted to escape at his accusations. "There was no cheating," I said, my response clipped.

"So, why are you here, Tatum?"

"I came here for her," I admitted before snapping my lips shut.

"Then why'd she leave without you?"

Good question. No, great question.

"Do you know where she was going?" I asked, wondering how much guys like this knew about her.

He shrugged. "Probably to Quinn Johnson's house, but she could be going anywhere. To see her agents, or her parents in the valley. Who knows, really?"

"Thanks," I said before walking away.

"Hey, wait!" he shouted, and I stopped. "Will you give me a quote? Tell me something? Anything?"

I sucked in a lungful of air before responding, "No." Then I turned back toward Paige's apartment building, and the guy from the concierge desk held the door open for me as I walked back inside the lobby.

"She left. You know she left, right?" the man asked, his accent so thick he was hard to understand.

I nodded. "I wanted to talk to you. I can't trust that kind

of guy out there." I lifted my chin in the direction of the lone paparazzi. "But I figured that you, I could trust."

He smiled and extended his hand. "I'm Samuel Montoya, but everyone calls me Sam."

"Nice to meet you, Sam. I'm Tatum Montgomery." Our hands met, and he gripped mine tighter than I had anticipated.

"I know who you are. Read all about you this morning."

"Right. So, about that—" I started, but Sam's expression turned serious and his eyes grew wide.

"Mr. Montgomery?" he interrupted, and I dipped my head toward him, thinking he was about to divulge some secret. "Mr. McGuire is pulling up."

"Mr. McGuire? You mean Colin? He's here?"

He nodded. "Yes, sir. That is most certainly his car."

I turned around to see a sporty black Porsche pull up outside with blacked-out windows, black rims, and all-black wheels. *What a douche.* The door opened and Colin climbed out. Bracing myself, I hadn't expected to see him again so soon. Or ever, for that matter.

Watching as he held up one finger toward the valet to signal that he would be right back, he entered the lobby where I stood with Sam. He pulled off his sunglasses before squinting at me, as if trying to place exactly how he knew me. I could tell exactly when he connected the dots, because his expression turned smug.

"Oh, you've got to be shitting me. What the hell are you doing here, country boy? Come all the way to LA to face the music?"

Instinctively, I straightened my spine and pulled back my shoulders, reminding Colin just how much taller and bigger I was than him. "Face the music? What the hell are you even talking about? The real question is what you're doing here. I'm pretty sure Paige doesn't want to see you."

"And how would you know that? I'm pretty sure she doesn't want to see you either, or you wouldn't be sitting in the lobby right now. Am I right?"

Touché.

"Miss Lockwood gave me strict instructions. She does not want to see you, Mr. Colin," Sam said from behind his desk, and I tried to hide the smart-aleck grin that spread across my face.

Colin looked me straight in the eye. "It's good that you're here. Now people will really believe the rumors about you and her. They would have had a hard time buying it before, but not now. Thanks for helping my cause, buddy. I'll make sure the paparazzi know you're in town and how heartbroken I am that Paige left me for you." He started dialing on his cell phone before putting it to his ear, and I growled as Sam reached out to steady me.

"How has everyone not seen through your act yet?"

Colin sneered before looking me up and down. "Because they don't want to believe the bad. They want to love me. Just like your girlfriend does." He snickered as he pulled his black sunglasses over his eyes.

I clenched my fist and pulled out of Sam's grip to storm over to Colin.

"What did you say?" I practically spat in his face.

"You know you can't erase the history I have with Paige. You're nothing, country boy. And as soon as you're gone, I'll be the one fucking her every night just like before. She is a good lay, don't you agree?"

Everything around me blurred except for Colin and his shit-eating grin. I pulled my arm back and swung, the sound of my knuckles meeting his jaw echoing in the otherwise empty lobby. Colin's head practically spun around on his shoulders as he reached up and cupped his face.

"Say another word like that about Paige and I'll hit you again." I glared at him as he tried to smile, but grunted with the pain instead.

"Thanks for that. You're real good at giving me ammunition, country boy," Colin said before he turned and ran out of the building like the little coward he really was.

Turning toward Sam, the reality of what I'd just done hit me like a tsunami wave as I looked down at my already bruising hand.

"Shit, Sam. Did I just completely screw it all up? Did I ruin everything?"

Sam shrugged. "I've wanted to do that for a long time now."

His unexpected response made me chuckle. "Hit Colin?"

"Yes, sir."

"So, now what? How long until that's reported?"

I hadn't necessarily thought everything through, what my being here might do to Paige's hard-earned reputation; I hadn't even considered it. All I knew was that I needed to make things right with Paige, and I was only screwing it up more.

"I'd say it's probably already live." He pointed across the street where Colin stood talking to the lone paparazzi guy I had spoken to earlier, holding his cheek and swaying back and forth.

"Paige is going to kill me." My cell phone vibrated in my pocket, and I pulled it from my pants, seeing my mom's name.

"Ma?"

"I've been following the gossip sites since you left. They're saying awful things, things that polite people don't say, Tatum." Her voice cracked, and I knew her heart hurt for both myself and for the girl she'd grown to care about.

"I haven't seen anything since I got here, but I appreciate the heads-up…again. And just so you'll know…it's going to get a little worse."

"What have you done, son?"

"I might have hit Colin."

She laughed into the phone, my mom actually laughed, which eased my anxiety a bit. "Good. I'm sure he deserved it. Now, have you seen her?"

"Briefly." I all but sighed as the lobby telephone rang in the background, and Sam moved to answer it.

"She's mad, isn't she?" my mom asked.

"She is."

"You don't come back here until you've made things right. You hear me?"

"Yes, Mama," I said with a smile, not wanting to let her down.

"'Bye, son. I love you," she said, then ended the call before I could say my own good-bye.

"Tatum?"

I turned to find Sam holding the phone receiver out toward me.

"It's Miss Quinn."

"Quinn?" I asked before remembering that Paige's best friend was named Quinn. "She's calling for me?"

He nodded, and I reached over to accept the phone he offered me.

"Hello?"

"Oh, good," a woman's voice said. "You really are in town. Don't move, I'm coming to get you." Then she hung up.

A little numb with surprise, I handed the phone back to Sam. "She's bossy."

Sam laughed. "That she is, sir. But it suits her."

I glanced outside where Colin had stood and noticed he was no longer there. Breathing out a sigh of relief, I braced myself for what was to come.

QUINN ARRIVED SHORTLY after hanging up in my ear.

I blew out an exasperated breath as she exited her

ridiculously overpriced car, her blond hair blowing in the breeze. Being a young actress in Hollywood sure had its perks. The paparazzi that had gathered again attempted to swarm and attack her, but she maneuvered through them with ease, appearing completely unaffected by their presence. It was as if they didn't even exist to her as she refused to acknowledge them or even look their way.

Bursting through the double doors like a hurricane, she raised her sunglasses and narrowed her eyes at me. "Tatum?"

"Quinn?"

"Hi, Sam," she said before giving the man a hug, and I watched as the older man practically turned to goo in her arms.

"How'd you know I was here?" I asked as she faced me and placed a hand on her hip.

"I get any media alerts about Paige sent to my phone. And I was already close by, so I figured why not come here and see what you're all about."

"All right then," I said, my tone hesitant.

She narrowed her eyes on me. "You hit Colin." It wasn't a question.

I shrugged. "Allegedly."

She grabbed my hand and inspected my knuckles. "Allegedly, my ass. Sam, I'm stealing him for a bit. Make sure his car stays here, and don't tell Paige I have him. Promise?"

Sam frowned before slowly nodding his head.

"Say you promise, Sam. You can't tell Paige."

"I promise," he reluctantly agreed, his gaze pinging between the two of us.

I shrugged at his unasked question. I had no idea what Quinn was up to any more than he did.

"Unless she kidnaps and murders me," I told Sam with a grin. "Then definitely tell Paige, okay?"

"You're too cute to murder." Quinn gave me a slight smile. "Now hurry, before she gets back from wherever she went." She turned toward the door and started walking.

"Where are we going?" I asked as I followed in her wake. The woman was like a force of nature.

"To my place."

Quinn drove like a crazed lunatic, swerving in and out of traffic as the paparazzi trailed behind us. How celebrities lived this way seemed utterly insane to me. When you viewed a chase like this onscreen, it didn't seem entirely real, as if it were a movie. But actually being chased like this felt pretty damn real. And it was terrifying.

"This is crazy," I said as I glanced back at the cars following dangerously close behind us.

"Don't look at them. Ugh, Tatum, open the glove compartment." She pointed, and I did as she asked. "There's a pair of sunglasses in there. Put them on."

"Damn. You really are bossy."

"Nice to meet you too." She glanced over and smiled, then turned her gaze back to the road.

I stared out at the ocean scenery whipping past us as Quinn drove. It was beautiful. Mesmerized by the waves crashing against the shore, I immediately saw the appeal of living here, especially if you got to see this view every day.

"I'm mad at you," she announced, but I had figured as much.

"I know."

"Do you even want to know why?"

"I'm pretty sure I already do," I said, figuring it had to do with the way I left Paige.

"Then how come you're in LA?"

Her tone wasn't entirely friendly, but I assumed it could be much, much worse. Something told me that Quinn was many things, but stupid wasn't one of them.

"I'm sure you can figure that out," I teased gently, hoping to lighten the mood and sway her toward my side, even if just a little.

"Well, it's about time you showed up. I mean, seriously, how long were you planning on going without talking to her? Not even a single text? Who does that?"

I burst out laughing. "Bossy and direct. I don't have any excuse other than the fact that I'm a complete idiot."

"We can both agree on that. Hold on," she warned before turning the wheel sharply to the right. We cruised through a residential neighborhood and pulled up to a house unlike anything I'd ever seen before in my life.

The large iron gates swung open as she pulled her car inside, then ground to a halt before shutting with a groan when she pressed a button on her rearview mirror.

"This is your house?" I asked.

"Mine and Ryson's," she said offhandedly, as if I should know who she referred to.

I followed her inside as reporters gathered outside the gate, shouting our names as cameras click away.

"Babe, that you?" a guy's voice shouted from somewhere deeper in the house.

"No. It's a robber," Quinn called out with a giggle as I followed behind her, unsure where we were headed.

"Do you have him?"

I stumbled to a halt as Ryson rounded the corner, his face instantly familiar, and I wanted to smack myself for not realizing who Quinn had been referring to. Immediately, I sized him up, unsure of what was about to happen. He stood about an inch or so taller than me, but we had a similar build. If he threw the first punch, I was fairly certain I'd be able to get the next one in.

He extended his hand toward me and I automatically reached for it; a gentleman never shies away from a handshake, no matter what.

I sucked in a deep breath as we both squeezed hard enough to break the other's fingers if we truly wanted, which made us both break out into a fit of laughter as we pulled apart. I stood there, shaking out my already swollen hand as Ryson glanced at it, noticing the bruising around the knuckles.

"You need ice," he said with a chuckle.

"What the hell are you two laughing at?" Quinn stomped her foot, and we both straightened up.

"I'm Ryson. It's nice to meet you, man. It's about time you got your Southern ass out here." He cocked a grin at me as he pulled open the freezer and tossed me an ice pack. "Beer?"

"Definitely. After the way this one drives." I jerked my thumb in Quinn's direction, and she snarled at me.

"Tell me about it," he joked. "We don't let her out of the house much." When she smacked his head in response, he shot back, "Woman! Don't hit me."

"Don't call me a bad driver. You know how hard it is to drive on PCH with those assholes trailing me like hunters," she said with a little pout, and he leaned down to kiss the top of her nose.

I shifted my weight, feeling a little uncomfortable at the PDA since we'd all just met.

Ryson pulled two bottles of beer from the fridge and popped the tops, handing me one.

I took a swig and swallowed it hard. "Thanks."

"No problem. What happened to your hand?"

"Colin."

"Did you hit him?" he asked, and I nodded. "I've always wanted to hit him. I'm so jealous." He smacked me on the back, and I almost choked on my beer. "What'd he do?"

"Said something shitty about Paige."

Quinn sneered. "I hate him so much."

"Did you tell him why you kidnapped him?" Ryson brought the conversation back on track.

"I haven't told him yet." Quinn tried to glare at me, but I could tell she was already warming up to me. I was convinced that her boyfriend accepting me so easily might have something to do with it.

"Told me what?" I asked, downing another gulp.

"It's a brilliant idea, actually. Hear her out before you say no, okay?" Ryson's tone had turned serious, which worried me. "Let's go sit down first, though."

I followed them through the kitchen, loving how the natural light filtered in from every angle. A glimpse outside at their backyard and view nearly took my breath away. It was spectacular, the kind of thing that dreams were made of, and I was convinced only existed in LA for the rich and famous.

When we reached the dining room, Quinn and Ryson sat down next to each other, so I picked a seat across from them. It felt like a business meeting, not that I'd ever really been in one before.

"First of all, I need to ask you a couple of questions," Quinn said, her hands folded on top of the table.

I shrugged my shoulders in response and waited, so she went on.

"I heard how Paige talked about you while she was in Hanford. She likes you, really likes you."

My insides warmed with that revelation, even if I had already hoped for it to be true. "Good, because I'm in love with her and I want to be with her. That's why I'm here."

Quinn's eyebrows practically shot up to her hairline. "You're in love with her? Well, that will help things. And we already know how you feel about Colin, which is another point for you."

The mere mention of that douche's name soured my mood. "I want to kick the living shit out of that guy. He's lucky I only hit him once."

"I call dibs on the next Colin beat down," Ryson said seriously as he turned toward Quinn and jerked his head my way. "I like this guy."

"Me too. Maybe," Quinn said to him before glaring back at me. "You really hurt her. She's my best friend and you hurt her. Worse than jerk-off Colin did, I think."

"I know," I admitted honestly because I knew it was the truth. Something inside me knew that things with Paige and me were vastly different than they had been with her and Colin.

"So, what do you plan on doing about it?"

I shook my head. "I don't know."

She slammed her hands on top of the table, making me jump. "Did you really come out here without any sort of plan at all? Nothing? Just thought you'd show up and be all hot looking," she waved a hand in my general direction, "and she'd take you back?"

"So, your girlfriend thinks I'm hot?" I directed the question toward a now-smirking Ryson.

"Apparently."

"Will you two stop the bromance already," Quinn said with a frown. "Your plan?"

"I didn't come here with a plan at first. I just wanted to apologize and get her to give me another chance."

"How'd that work out for you?" she asked, cocking her head to one side.

"Not great," I admitted. "I know that I need a gesture, something that will prove to Paige that I can handle being here for her and that I won't run. I know what she's afraid of, and I deserve it. But I need to prove her wrong. I need to show her that this lifestyle doesn't scare me, and that I'd go through all of it to be with her."

"So you do have a plan, you just don't know how to execute it. Fortunately for you, I do." She rubbed her hands together as Ryson raised his eyebrows and took another sip of beer.

Quinn outlined the details of her idea, excitedly going through each point one by one.

When she finished, I looked over at Ryson, feeling a brotherly bond with him already. "You think this is a good idea?"

"I do, actually. It's sort of brilliant, if you're up for it."

"I think I could pull it off." Taking another swig of beer, I added, "I hope."

"You can do it," he reassured me as I internally freaked out. This was something completely out of my comfort zone, but I was willing to do it.

"And you think it will work?"

"Hell yes, it'll work. Paige is a romantic at heart, and she'd never expect this from you. She knows that this will be a totally uncharacteristic thing for you to do, so she'll fucking melt over it," he added.

I nodded in agreement, praying this would be enough, then directed my gaze toward Quinn. "Why are you helping me?"

Her expression finally softened. "Because I love my best

friend, and I know she wants to be with you, even if she doesn't. She's going through a lot of stuff right now, and she's trying so hard to be strong in every aspect. I'm really proud of her, but this thing with you...I think she would regret it eventually if she let you walk away."

I met her eyes and sighed. "I know that feeling all too well."

Forgiveness

PAIGE

AFTER SEEING TATUM, I'd driven straight to my parents' house. I was dying to tell my mom how he'd shown up unannounced, then ask for her advice.

My heart hurt and my head was confused. I didn't know what the right thing to do was when it came to Tatum. I wanted to take him back into my life the second I saw him, but I knew I needed to stand up for myself when it came to him. It was hard as hell, but I had managed to survive it. Barely.

"I wish you hadn't sent him away," Mom said, practically pouting in her disappointment.

"Mom!"

She shrugged. "I'm just saying that it would have been nice to meet him."

"You're supposed to be on my side," I complained as she

wrapped her arms around me.

"Oh, honey, I am on your side. You can't blame me for wanting to meet him."

I let out a dramatic sigh and rolled my eyes. "Fine. I don't blame you for wanting to meet Tatum, but I want you to tell me that I did the right thing."

My phone started to ring with Quinn's ringtone and I reached for it, my mom currently saved by my best friend.

"Hello?"

"Turn on Channel Seven right now."

"What?" Nerves coursed through my body as what I assumed was more bad news about me being spread. "I can't take any more bad press, Quinn."

"Paige Lagertha Lockwood, turn on Channel Seven this instant before I hunt you down and hurt you!" she screamed into the phone before hanging up on me.

"Apparently we need to turn on Channel Seven," I told Mom before looking around the living room for the remote. Pressing the power button, I switched the cable box to the right channel and felt the color drain my face immediately.

"Oh good Lord, is that him?" my mom asked as I all but fell back onto the couch.

Tatum looked stupid hot in his charcoal-gray suit as he sat across from Wendy Wong, a well-known entertainment reporter with golden skin and long dark hair.

"What is he doing?" I breathed out to no one in particular, knowing how uncomfortable he had to be.

I clicked the volume button up on the remote until I could

hear him loud and clear, the drawl in his voice pinching my heart. I recognized the candles adorning the wall behind him, along with the other artwork that barely showed in the television frame. He was at Quinn's house. Reaching for one of the couch pillows, I pulled it to my stomach and squeezed it against me.

WENDY: Would you care to clear up the rumors about you and Paige cheating long before Colin ever did?

TATUM: I didn't even meet Paige until after she and Colin had broken up. *He* cheated on her, and not the other way around. Paige isn't the type of person to do that, and I think you all know that. Colin, on the other hand, every time I see him, he gives me a new reason to dislike him.

WENDY: Is that why you hit him?

What? Tatum hit Colin? When had they even seen each other?

My mom turned to look at me, her mind clearly filled with the same questions as mine.

TATUM: I hit him because he said something horrible about Paige. He said things a guy should never say about a girl.

WENDY: So you admit to assaulting him, which is what Colin is claiming.

TATUM: No, I admit to punching him. Once. In the jaw.

WENDY: Would you do it again?

TATUM: If he talked like that about Paige, then yes, I

would. I don't understand why y'all always take his side.

WENDY: We don't take Colin's side.

TATUM: It sure seems that way.

WENDY: Well, I'm sorry we've given you that impression. Colin tends to speak out a lot.

TATUM: That's because he's a liar and he's conniving. He gets pleasure out of throwing innocent people under the bus to save his own skin, and the only way he can do that is if he's constantly in your face. Colin is the type of guy who only cares about himself, and he doesn't care who he hurts in the process.

WENDY: Are you referring to Paige or yourself?

TATUM: (Laughs) Colin doesn't hurt me. But I don't like him hurting Paige or anyone else with the stories he tells. Especially when he gets caught doing something wrong. He can't own up to it. Instead, he makes up a story and hides behind it.

WENDY: One of the girls from that original video spoke out earlier today and basically echoed your exact sentiments. But you know what? Let's move on. How did you meet Paige?

TATUM: She got a flat tire when she was driving through my town. I run the only mechanic shop there, so it was on me to help her.

WENDY: And this was where?

Tatum fidgeted in his seat, the discomfort in his eyes growing, and I wondered what on earth he'd gotten himself into. For me.

TATUM: In Louisiana.

WENDY: And now you're here in Los Angeles. Why exactly?

TATUM: Well, ma'am, I wanted to set the record straight because how y'all do things out here isn't how we do them back home. And when a man loves a woman, he defends her honor. He stands up for what's right, and that's what I wanted to do here today.

WENDY: So you and Paige are in love?

TATUM: I'm in love with her. I'm not sure how she feels about me at this point.

WENDY: And why do you say that?

TATUM: Because I messed up, Wendy. I'm a man, and I make mistakes. I didn't handle things well, and that's why I'm here with you today. I want her to know how sorry I am.

My heart skipped a beat at his very public declaration. Of course, he'd made that very statement to me a few hours ago in the lobby of my apartment building, but this was on national television for the whole country to see and hear. Including everyone back in his hometown.

WENDY: What did you do, exactly? There weren't other women, were there?

TATUM: No, absolutely not. It's nothing like that. Let's just say that when things got difficult, I pushed her away.

WENDY: I'm sure it can't be easy for someone like you to date a world-famous celebrity. You seem so normal, Tatum.

TATUM: (Laughs) I am. And no, it's not easy. But Paige is worth it. And that's where I messed up, Wendy. I let her walk away from me. Things got scary, and I got uncomfortable and I let her go. But I was wrong. Because Paige Lockwood isn't the kind of girl you push out of your life; she's the kind of girl you run toward. The kind you fight for and pray like hell she'll take you back after you've been an idiot of epic proportion.

WENDY: Wow. I hope all the guys across the country are taking notes tonight because this is how you do it. That's one heck of an apology. I hope Paige accepts it.

"Mom, I have to go," I said as tears streamed down my face.

"Yes, you do. Go accept that boy's apology. And then bring him over here for dinner!" she shouted after me as I ran to my car.

AFTER PULLING TO a screeching stop into Quinn's driveway, I all but sprinted inside the front doors. The camera crews had already packed up and gone, but I could hear the sound of Tatum and Ryson's voices filling the air as I rushed through the house.

"Tatum!" I shouted as the sound of a chair scooting across the tile floor hit my ears.

"Paige!"

We both rounded corners at the same time and stopped at opposite sides of the kitchen.

"I'm so sorry," he said, then took a tentative step toward me.

I bolted toward him and surprised him by jumping into his waiting arms. Wrapping my legs around his waist, I squeezed him as tightly as I could.

"I can't believe you went on TV," I said softly against his neck.

He shivered, and I smiled to myself as his grip on me tightened. He pulled his head back, his eyes meeting mine.

"I did it for you. And Quinn helped. A lot."

"Yeah, I did," she shouted from somewhere in the dining room.

Tatum rested his forehead against mine, a smile on his lips. "I love you, Paige."

"I love you too," I admitted for the first time as my previously cracked heart clicked into place, making me feel whole.

"I'm so damn sorry for how I reacted. I can't promise you that I'll never act like a dumbass ever again, but I can promise that I'll try. I meant every word I said tonight. You're worth it. I should have fought for you, and I'm so sorry I didn't."

"Shut up. God, just shut up already."

I crushed my mouth against his, all my feelings pouring out as I reacquainted myself with his mouth. I kissed him for all the days we'd been apart, as well as all the nights I'd dreamed of him, wishing we were still together.

As I unwrapped my legs from around his hips, he lowered me gently to the floor, his hands never breaking contact with my body, our mouths still connected.

"Jeez, get a room already," Ryson pretended to complain as he walked past us.

We pulled apart, smiles on both our faces. "Maybe we can christen the Jungle room since you're a boy and Quinn never lets me stay in there?" I asked loud enough for Quinn to hear, and she groaned.

"Damn it, Paige, what is it with you and that room?"

"Can't we go home instead?" Tatum looked down at me, looking happier and more relaxed than I'd ever seen him.

"Home? Like my home?"

"Yes, Paige. Your home. Our home. Whatever. Let's go home," he insisted, and who was I to argue.

Epilogue

PAIGE

Six months later…

TATUM MOVED IN that night after the interview. Actually, he just never left. My family met him soon after. They not only forgave him for hurting me, but practically gave their blessing for our future wedding and kids, something Tatum and I hadn't even talked about yet. It had been a little awkward, but secretly I craved their approval and was thrilled at how much they seemed to love and accept him.

Aside from flying back home once to pack a single bag of his things, Tatum refused to be away from me. It was during that trip home that his mom finally told him that his dad had left a life insurance policy for them. She'd put aside half the money for Tatum when the time was right, and when she presented him with a check for almost two hundred thousand dollars, he refused to take it. That was, until his mom reminded him that she had the other half and would not be hurting for money if he left her on her own.

Our moving in together might have seemed crazy to some, too soon to others, but it felt right to us. It still does. We both knew that if he moved all the way out here and I forced him to rent his own place purely out of principle, it would be a complete waste. Rental property in Los Angeles was overpriced and ridiculously expensive. And that was something I didn't feel right about doing—wasting his family's money when it wasn't necessary. Plus, waking up in his arms each morning was the highlight of my day.

I got accepted into UCLA and started attending classes in the fall. It was a difficult adjustment, way harder than I'd anticipated, and I'm not sure how long I'll keep attending. The students in my classes did a lot of staring at first, but no one really talked to me, so I ended up feeling very out of place and alone. People talked *about* me, but never included me in the conversation. It was as if they were too afraid to approach me, but weren't afraid to stare at me and make things awkward.

Tatum promised me that it would eventually die down, and he kept encouraging me to give them more time. I didn't believe him, but he was right.

Despite what Jayson said, my career didn't falter. I still did the occasional audition when the part was too good to pass up, not wanting to put my career completely on hold while I went to school. Plus, I'd be lying if I said I didn't miss acting at all. I missed it more than I ever thought I would, so with Madison's help, we attempted to find a balance until I figured it all out. So far, so good.

Hiring Madison has been the best career decision I've made so far. Working with her is like a dream come true. Having her and Walker as good friends has been an added bonus, and when we all get together with Quinn and Ryson, it's always a loud and fun time.

It's been exciting to make normal friends and talk about normal, everyday things with people. But Tatum was also right all those months ago—my life will never truly be normal. Despite that, this experience that I've fought so hard for has been thrilling. Even the homework doesn't bother me, much to the chagrin of my new friends who constantly call me crazy.

Hell, maybe I was, and maybe I am. I don't care, though; I like the new me. Being crazy has its perks.

TATUM

AFTER MY INTERVIEW, it didn't take long for the press to find out exactly where I'd been born and raised. They bombarded Hanford with camera crews and reporters, taking over my tiny town. Paige had freaked out, feeling responsible for ruining the place, but the truth was that she helped give it new life. My mom's bed and breakfast was filled to capacity on most weekends now, thanks to the busloads of tourists that Paige's visit had inspired. Everyone wanted to sleep where Paige Lockwood had slept. Even the swimming hole had become a tourist attraction for families and couples.

My dad's garage did more business in the last six months then we'd done in the last six years. Whenever I started to feel guilty about not being there to run the place, my mom reminded me that they were doing just fine and that I wasn't missed.

I knew she was lying about the last part because she's been out here to visit me and Paige three times already since I moved. As much as I love living here with my girl, I love it even more when my mom comes to visit. She claims that once she retires, she's moving here. Nothing would make me happier than having both my girls in one place.

Yeah, I know, I'm a total mama's boy. I don't even care.

I've been working with Walker Rhodes at his studio. I never intended to let Paige pull any strings for me, but when her agent, Madison, set up a dinner at their Malibu house to welcome me to town, well, Walker and I bonded instantly the same way that Ryson and I had.

Creative people tended to gravitate toward one another, I soon realized. After several beers, Walker convinced me to play a couple of songs I'd written about Paige for him. He got on the phone with someone the instant I finished, and when he hung up, he shook my hand.

"We have a deal," he said with a smile.

"A deal?" I asked, not sure what the hell he was talking about.

"I want those songs. Both of them. I'll buy them, but I want you to produce them with me. Come up with a few more to show me next time we get together. You're really talented, man, and your sound is fresh. LA needs someone like you, but I want you first," he said with a laugh.

"Are you shitting me right now?" I couldn't believe that it was happening this easily and quickly. But then I remembered that nothing in my life had really come easily to me. I had sacrificed my own dreams for years. When you're so used to failing, success feels foreign. I suppose when things are meant to be, they fall into place effortlessly. This was the best I'd felt about life and my future since high school. And high school felt like a thousand years ago.

"Dead serious," Walker said. "I want the songs. You help me produce. You'll get writing credit on the album, which means you'll make money on each sale of the songs you write for me that we release. I'm so excited, man. I want to go in the studio now and record this, but Madison will kill me if we don't get back out there." He patted my shoulder.

"Thank you so much. I really appreciate it." I didn't know what else to say.

"I know you do. I like helping out good people, and Paige is good people. I can tell you are too. Welcome to LA, man."

We walked out of his home studio and back to where our girls sat on the balcony overlooking the Pacific Ocean. I'd only seen houses like this in the movies, and now I was having dinner in one.

How was this my life? I glanced down at my short-haired

brunette beauty and smiled, wondering how on earth I had ever gotten so lucky, and promised myself that I'd never let her go, no matter what life threw at us. I would never walk away, push her aside, or leave her ever again. I planned on marrying that girl someday.

But probably not before Ryson and Quinn tie the knot.

Coming Soon

Coming next in The Celebrity Series:

Losing Stars – Quinn and Ryson's story.

About the Author

Jenn Sterling is a Southern California native who loves writing stories from the heart. Every story she tells has pieces of her truth in it, as well as her life experience. She has her bachelor's degree in Radio/TV/Film and has worked in the entertainment industry the majority of her life.

Jenn loves hearing from her readers and can be found online at:

Blog & Website:
www.j-sterling.com

Twitter:
www.twitter.com/RealJSterling

Facebook:
www.facebook.com/TheRealJSterling

Instagram:

www.instagram.com/RealJSterling

If you enjoyed this book, please consider writing a spoiler-free review on the site from which you purchased it. And thank you so much for helping me spread the word about my books, and for allowing me to continue telling the stories I love to tell. I appreciate you.

Also by J. Sterling

In Dreams

Chance Encounters

10 Years Later - A Second Chance Romance

THE GAME SERIES:

The Perfect Game

The Game Changer

The Sweetest Game

THE CELEBRITY SERIES:

Seeing Stars- Madison & Walker

Breaking Stars- Paige & Tatum

Losing Stars- Quinn & Ryson (Coming Soon)

HEARTLESS - A SERIAL ROMANCE

Episode #1

Episode #2

Episode #3

Heartless, The Box Set

Episodes 1- 3

Please join my mailing list to get updates on new and upcoming releases, deals, bonus content, personal appearances, and other fun news!

http://tinyurl.com/ku7grpb

CPSIA information can be obtained
at www.ICGtesting.com
Printed in the USA
LVHW112228011220
673182LV00035B/214